©Yu-nagi

THE HOLY GRAIL OF ERIS

Randolph Ulster

A lieutenant commander in the Royal Security Force. Also known as His Excellency the Grim Reaper.

Pamela Francis

A baron's daughter. Doesn't like Constance, tries to steal her fiancé.

Cecilia Adelbide

The crown princess. Made Scarlett jealous and was nearly poisoned ten years ago.

©Yu-nagi

Scarlett Castiel

The duke's beautiful daughter
beheaded ten years ago. Her ghost
appears before Constance.

Constance
(Possessed by Scarlett)

Constance Grail

The plain, unremarkable
daughter of a viscount. Gets roped
into helping Scarlett exact revenge
on her enemies.

Characters

"...What do you mean by that?"

Who is this girl? Pamela Francis's spine froze as Constance Grail gave her an unfathomable grin.

"A thief? Ha! Just which one of us is the thief here?"

©Yu-nagi

"I saved you, and I won't take no for an answer!"

Contents

Prologue 1

Chapter 1 — The Incident at the Grand Merillian 9

Chapter 2 — The Wickedest Woman and an Ordinary Girl 41

Intermission — Emilia Godwin 79

Chapter 3 — What Does It Mean to Be Sincere? 85

Intermission — Teresa Jennings 119

Chapter 4 — Answers and Beginnings 125

Intermission — Shoshanna 157

Chapter 5 — The Silent Ladies' Tea Party 161

Chapter 6 — Rooster's Crow at Dawn 199

Exclusive Short Story
A Hand to Hold 243

The Holy Grail of Eris

author Kujira Tokiwa
illustration Yu-nagi

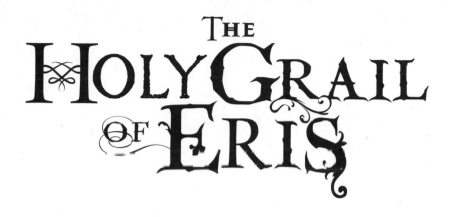

THE HOLY GRAIL OF ERIS

1

KUJIRA TOKIWA

ILLUSTRATION BY YU-NAGI

YEN ON

New York

THE HOLY GRAIL OF ERIS

1

KUJIRA TOKIWA

Translation by Winifred Bird
Cover art by Yu-nagi

Eris NO SEIHAI Vol. 1
Copyright © 2019 Kujira Tokiwa
Illustrations copyright © 2019 Yu-nagi. All rights reserved.
Original Japanese edition published in 2019 by SB Creative Corp.

This English edition is published by arrangement with SB Creative Corp., Tokyo
in care of TUTTLE-MORI AGENCY, INC., Tokyo.

English translation © 2022 by Yen Press, LLC

Yen On
150 West 30th Street, 19th Floor
New York, NY 10001

Visit us at yenpress.com • facebook.com/yenpress • twitter.com/yenpress •
yenpress.tumblr.com • instagram.com/yenpress

First Yen On Edition: April 2022

Yen On is an imprint of Yen Press, LLC.
The Yen On name and logo are trademarks of Yen Press, LLC.

Library of Congress Cataloging-in-Publication Data
Names: Tokiwa, Kujira, author. | Yu-nagi, illustrator. | Bird, Winifred, translator.
Title: The holy grail of Eris / Kujira Tokiwa ; illustration by Yu-nagi ; translation by Winifred Bird.
Other titles: Eris no seihai. English
Description: First Yen On edition. | New York, NY : Yen On, 2022.
Identifiers: LCCN 2021060246 | ISBN 9781975339579 (v. 1 ; trade paperback) |
ISBN 9781975339593 (v. 2 ; trade paperback) | ISBN 9781975339616 (v. 3 ; trade paperback)
Subjects: LCGFT: Light novels.
Classification: LCC PZ7.1.T6223 Ho 2022 | DDC [Fic]—dc23
LC record available at https://lccn.loc.gov/2021060246

ISBNs: 978-1-9753-3957-9 (paperback)
978-1-9753-3958-6 (ebook)

10 9 8 7 6 5 4 3 2 1

WOR

Printed in the United States of America

Cling, clang, the bell chimed.

Connie had misbehaved that day. She had gone to see the "ex-e-cu-tion" against her father's orders. She'd explicitly been told not to go, but she snuck out of the mansion and made her way to Saint Mark's Square. To make matters worse, she'd taken Kate with her.

The leafy plaza usually served as the perfect playground for Connie and Kate. They would play tag or hide-and-seek and sometimes sneak into the town hall and make mischief there, too, but the good-natured workers never scolded them. That's why Connie thought it would be fine—because nothing scary ever happened in this place.

But on that day, Saint Mark's Square was different.

To start with, the crowd! It seemed every person in the capital had turned out for the event. The only other times she had seen such a gathering were at Christmas and the Astrology Festival. But the gleam in the eyes of these people was different from at a normal event. There was something horrible about the excitement in those eyes.

That awful gleam must mean an "execution" was something bad. Connie remembered what her father had said: *"It's cruel and inhumane."* He'd looked unusually stern when he said it. But six-year-old Connie hadn't understood what he meant.

Cling, clang, the bell chimed.

Swept along by the jostling crowd, Connie was soon separated from Kate. The instant she realized what had happened, the blood drained from her face. After all, the plaza felt strange that day. Suddenly anxious, she pushed through the sea of people, screaming her friend's name, but her calls were drowned out by the even greater frenzy of the crowd.

What do I do? What do I do? She pushed farther and farther forward, calling out, "Kate!"

Suddenly, she found herself at the front of the crowd. There, at the center of the plaza, stood a platform she had never seen before. Had it been put up for the "execution"? It distracted her for a second, but then she shook her head. No—Kate came first. Where could she be?

Aside from the strange platform, the plaza itself looked the same. On the left was the statue of the hero Amadeus, founding father of the kingdom, and on the right was the statue of Saint Anastasia. Off to the side, looking down on everything, was Saint Mark's Bell Tower.

Just as Connie was about to turn around and continue looking for Kate, the crowd exploded with shouts. The gate leading to Moldavite Palace had been unlocked to admit a horse-drawn wagon into the square.

A young woman wearing a black hood emerged from the wagon, together with several men. The men varied in age from young to old, but all were dressed formally. In contrast, the woman was dressed in a hideously plain gray dress that was fraying at the edges.

No sooner had this group appeared than the cries of the crowd grew more heated, changing to jeers and angry shouts. Strange words that Connie had never heard before flew around her.

She found herself unable to move, her legs frozen by the oddness of her surroundings. The young woman who was the target of all the terrible hatred, however, seemed not to care at all. She stared straight ahead without a glance at the uproar around her.

The formally dressed men led the young woman toward the platform at the center of the plaza. Which is to say, they were walking straight toward Connie. The young woman drew closer. Connie noticed that a wooden block was fastened around her wrists.

The crowd's excitement seemed to have reached a peak. Some people were pointing at the young woman and screaming, while others clapped and leered.

Cling, clang, the bell chimed.

Connie hadn't noticed the thick black clouds rolling in over the plaza. Raindrops began to stain the ground.

One of the men gave some kind of command, and the young woman listlessly shook her head. The motion caused her hood to slip off, and her shiny black hair spilled out. Finally, she turned her face toward Connie.

Connie gasped.

She was the most beautiful creature Connie had ever seen. Her skin was white as snow, and her lips were like ripe red fruit. And her eyes—her eyes sparkled like caged amethyst stars.

The phrase *divine beauty* must have been invented just for her. Connie couldn't have been the only one thinking that, because the noisy heckling vanished into silence.

Each and every person in the plaza was gazing at the young woman as if bewitched. She did not flinch under their rude stares. To the contrary, she looked slowly around like she was making note of each of their faces. Connie could see them flinching under her gaze.

The young woman narrowed her eyes and snorted.

"Curse you," she said slowly.

Although she hadn't spoken at all loudly, her voice rang over the plaza.

"May every last one of you be damned!"

Connie could have heard a pin drop. Next to her, someone gulped. Of

©Yu-nagi

course, curses weren't real, but the young woman's particular confidence had shaken them.

"Wh-whore!" someone shouted suddenly. The voice was shaking slightly. Still, the insult brought the rest of the crowd back to their senses, and people started jeering again.

"Harlot!" "Devil woman!" "Murderer!"

Connie trembled in fear. At the tender age of six, she had never before witnessed human malice. She glanced around in terror, unsure what to do. Her eyes met the eyes of the young woman.

The pair of jewellike irises pulled her in. They blinked, maybe because their owner was surprised to see such a young child there, and then suddenly, she smiled. Yes—smiled!

Connie widened her eyes. Her heart began to pound. What was happening? What was this? Had she seen something she shouldn't have? This, this—

The young woman grinned with what looked like satisfaction, then whispered something.

For better or worse, Connie didn't catch her words.

The rain began to pour, pricking Connie's skin. The wind howled. Black clouds swirled overhead. The executioner commanded the woman to get down on her knees and raised his sword above his head. That very second, a loud boom shook the ground. There was a flash of light. The world in front of Connie went white. She couldn't see a thing. As she shaded her eyes and squinted, something warm splashed her cheek. The smell of rusted iron choked her.

By the time color returned to the world, everything was over. The man with the sword was holding up *something* round and dripping with red liquid. Cheers ripped through the crowd.

"See! She's gotten what she had coming!" "Serves the whore right!" "She's dead!" "She's dead!" "She's deaaaaaad!"

Connie stood rooted to the ground. She couldn't even scream. She couldn't believe what she had just seen.

Someone whistled, and the crowd exploded in excitement. The shouting spread across the masses like a contagion. The circle of celebration widened—but it did not last long.

"Look out! Fire!" someone yelled suddenly.

They were pointing to the town hall, which was in flames. "It's been hit by lightning!" someone else shouted. The flames crackled loudly. The crowd was silent for a moment, then erupted in chaos and screams. People pushed one another aside and collided in their mad rush to escape. Angry shouts came from all directions.

"Out of my way!" someone yelled, knocking Connie to the ground. The hard earth slammed into her chest, knocking the wind out of her. *It hurts. It hurts, and I'm scared. Someone—someone help me!*

Every inch of her little body throbbed with pain. Unable to stand, she looked up and saw someone else who had fallen. It was a woman with black hair. Connie started to reach out her hand, then snatched it back. It was *missing*.

Her body is missing.

The instant Connie realized what she was looking at lying there on the ground, she screamed. Her father's words flitted across her mind. *"It's cruel and inhumane."*

She squeezed her eyes shut. Above her, blown by the violent wind, Saint Mark's Bell was ringing as if it had gone crazy. *Cling, clang, cling, clang.*

Wait, no—!

Constance Grail's mouth was agape, both hands pressed against her cheeks. Inside her head, she was screaming.

It was dusk in the garden. A couple was embracing in front of her. Of course, people are free to love whomever they want, and a little cuddling could hardly be called an offense to public morals.

There was just one small problem.

The man was her fiancé.

※

It all began several months earlier, because, like all viscounts from this family, the eleventh viscount was *sincere*.

The great Percival Grail, hero of the Ten Years' War with the neighboring kingdom of Faris and first Grail viscount, had once been asked the secret to victory, and his answer had become the Grail family motto: "Thou shalt be sincere." Needless to say, Percival Ethel Grail, Constance's father and the current master of the house, was no exception. If anything, he had taken those words too much to heart.

For instance, he was so sincere that when a friend came to him crying and begging for his help, he agreed to be the guarantor for a suspicious loan and ended up responsible for loads of debt.

Incidentally, the friend promptly vanished, and there hadn't been as much as a rumor of his whereabouts since.

To underline the point, the Grail family had not two, not three, but one single motto: sincerity. That, plus simplicity and thrift. They viewed luxury as an outrage and immediately redistributed to the commoners any profit they made off their land. Thanks to this detestable tradition that the family had been meticulously implementing since the days of Percival Grail the First, they had no savings whatsoever.

"In other words…"

Finishing up his explanation of the *situation*, Percival Ethel turned to his daughter with a solemn expression. Connie gulped.

"I-in other words…?"

"I don't have any money to pay."

The fate of the Grail family was hanging by a thread.

It appeared they were in dire need of cash.

It was Damian Bronson, a businessman who had befriended the Grails on his frequent visits to their home, who heard the rumors and extended a helping hand.

"It seems you're in quite a difficult situation," he'd said.

Damian was the third generation to helm the Bronson family business and had been granted the title of baronet.

He, however, was not a nobleman.

Although baronets were treated better than commoners, they could socialize only in limited circles. The Bronson Company was a well-respected old firm headquartered on Anastasia Street in the capital, with several branches in the provinces. Business was stable. Too stable, in fact—it never branched out in novel directions. Which was exactly why the company needed new connections.

"You're so utterly trusting, sir," Damian went on. "I believe you need someone by your side who can help you keep an eye on your interests. As it happens, I have a son…"

Neil Bronson, his seventeen-year-old progeny.

And so, very soon, an engagement was arranged.

"Are you sure you don't mind?" Connie's father asked her repeatedly, but she wasn't particularly dissatisfied with the arrangement. The family was up to its ears in debt, and as the oldest child, she felt the opportunity was the best she could hope for.

Her looks weren't exactly striking, but Connie was still a nobleman's daughter. Of course, she had dreamed of marrying for love. Very much so, in fact. The book about how Crown Prince Enrique and Crown Princess Cecilia fell in love despite their mismatched social status was practically her bible. But none of that mattered in comparison to the survival of her family.

Plus, it wasn't as if everyone in the world could marry for love. That was especially true for a plain, meek, withdrawn girl like her.

Neil Bronson was tall, handsome, and gentlemanly. Connie thought it would be just fine for a person like him to become her husband. She truly did.

That is, until she heard he was head over heels for another woman.

"Pamela Francis?"

"Yes. Apparently, Neil Bronson is simply mad for her. I heard someone saw them kissing off in the shadows. But isn't he *your* fiancé?"

She'd learned this exactly one week before the incident, from a young lady she knew.

"Neil and Pamela…"

Pamela Francis was an extremely attractive young lady. She was always surrounded by admirers, and handsome men were unfailingly among the crowd.

The amazing thing about Pamela was that even though she wasn't unusually beautiful to start with, she knew just how to make herself look prettier than everyone else. Her soft platinum-blond hair was always skillfully braided, and she got her evening gowns at the Moonlight Fairy, the high-end dressmaker whose creations were the envy of every nobleman's daughter.

"I hear Pamela goes through men as quickly as you and I change partners at a ball."

That was a terrifying thing to imagine. Connie trembled at the thought. How could a mousy viscount's daughter possibly compete?

Plus, even though they were only barons, the Francis family had made a fortune far greater than the Grails could ever hope for. They traded in ore mined in the kingdom. Pamela would probably make an ideal daughter-in-law for the Bronson Company. They would get the noble connections they longed for, and they might even get the rights to the ore. That was far better than marrying into the family of a poor nobleman whose only saving grace was sincerity.

Connie looked up at the sky. If she hadn't, her eyes might have spilled over and disgraced her.

She couldn't talk to her father about it. That was out of the question. After all, the engagement had already been finalized. Just the other day, she and Neil had gone to the church with their parents to make their oaths. Now they were marking time until the wedding while they made the engagement public. Most likely, the announcement had already reached the whole kingdom. The very idea of accusing Neil of infidelity *now* was unthinkable.

Of course, if Connie raised an objection, the engagement could probably be broken off. But if that happened, her family wouldn't be able to pay off their debts. And if the situation became public, her thoroughly sincere father would no doubt drag his dusty old rifle out from the back of the closet and throw down a white glove at Neil's feet.

In other words, either Neil or her father would end up dead.

Somebody save me…

She was only sixteen, but her life was at a dead end.

※

Ultimately, no one answered Constance Grail's plea for help, and she ended up witnessing a most shocking scene—but let us begin an hour or two earlier.

"Congratulations on your engagement, Miss Grail."

"Thank you very much."

"I must say—marriage is like being thrown into a nicely maintained dungeon. Welcome to our pigpen, newborn piglet. Make yourself at home."

"Um... Thank you?"

The person who delivered this less-than-celebratory congratulations was the somewhat difficult countess Emanuel.

"I heard you got engaged, Constance!"

"Yes, it's true."

"Oh, how lovely! I know we're not the closest of friends, but I do hope you'll invite me to the wedding!"

"Uh, um, yes, of course."

"How wonderful! By the way, I've been wanting some of that silk the Bronson Company is selling only in the capital."

"...Um, I'll make sure it's in your wedding favors..."

Baroness Borden was her usual calculating self.

"I heard the news, Connie! But that Neil Bronson you're engaged to, isn't he the one everyone says is running around with Pamela? You simply must tell me all the details!"

"I'd like to know them myself."

The sassy, insensitive Mylene, a viscount's daughter like Connie, adored gossip.

A week had passed since Connie first heard the rumor. Her engagement was the talk of the town, but she hadn't been brave enough to confirm whether or not the rumor was true.

Around that time, she was invited to a ball at the Grand Merillian, on the grounds of Moldavite Palace.

The host, Viscount Dominic Hamsworth, was in high spirits as he theatrically offered up his gratitude to the Moirai, the three Fates. In addition to being the head of a noble family, the viscount was a priest, which was unusual.

He was the youngest of five children and, ever since childhood, had spent all his time at church. But shortly after he reached adulthood, an epidemic had swept through the kingdom, killing his parents and all his siblings. For this reason, he had taken over as viscount even though he was already a priest.

The church's teachings on the virtues of poverty must not have suited him, because as soon as he became viscount, he took up a life of dissipation. Rumor had it the only reason he hadn't been stripped of his priest's robes was because he donated *cartloads* of cash to the church.

The Hamsworths were unusually wealthy, thanks to their lush lands.

If they weren't, they would never have been able to host a ball at the Grand Merillian.

There were two detached buildings in the sprawling gardens surrounding Moldavite Palace, where the king and queen lived.

One was the Elbaite Villa, residence of the crown prince and princess. It had been built recently—simple but outfitted with all the latest conveniences.

The other was the Grand Merillian, a lavish pleasure palace built in the prosperous reign of King Michelinus. Today it was a tourist attraction, and during the social season, any noble family with a history going back at least three generations was permitted to rent the grand hall to throw balls. That said, the rental fee was through the roof and came with reams of restrictions, which meant any sensible nobles who lived in townhouses would never consider it.

Incidentally, the grand hall at the Grand Merillian was the stage upon which His Highness Enrique had condemned Scarlett Castiel—the notorious sinner—for her crimes.

Since that was also the moment when he'd broken off his engagement to Scarlett and announced his engagement to Crown Princess Cecilia, who at the time was still a viscount's daughter, the hall had become one of the capital's hubs for starry-eyed romantics.

The hall sparkled with candlelight refracted from its magnificent chandeliers. Guests had gathered to dance in the center of the room, matching their lively steps to the musicians' melodies. Refreshments were set out in the four corners of the room, and those who weren't dancing—Connie included—stood around with drinks in hand, chatting elegantly.

"Congratulations, Constance."

"Thank you very much."

An endless stream of acquaintances came to congratulate her, mostly because her engagement had just been publicly announced. Answering them all with a smile was no easy job. Since she was fairly certain that she'd greeted everyone she knew personally, she figured taking a brief moment to herself would be forgivable. Neil had disappeared from the table where she'd spotted him playing cards with his gentleman friends, so she assumed he must be off taking a break somewhere, too.

She slipped out of the grand hall and into the conservatory. The glassed-in room with white wooden window frames was overflowing with unusual southern flowers and exotic plants. Even the ceiling was made of glass, and she could see the stars twinkling brightly overhead. Some of the windows must have been open, because a cool breeze tickled her flushed skin.

People might laugh and call her a fool, but the truth was, she still trusted Neil.

After all, they'd already exchanged their oaths at church and publicly announced the engagement. If he really loved Pamela, wouldn't he have done something before all of that happened?

Plus, Neil was acting completely normal. He was kind to Connie. Just today, he'd told her that her dress looked nice on her. And she hadn't heard about Pamela directly from him. Wouldn't it be a bit *insincere* of her to believe the rumors over him?

He'd come to fetch her for the ball in his carriage and escorted her in when they got there. The rumors must be a simple misunderstanding. Either that or completely unfounded nonsense. Definitely. That had to be it.

When she thought about it in those terms, she felt a little better. She might even be able to dance a Viennese waltz in triple time.

Thinking she would shut the open window before heading back to the grand hall, she began to search for the source of the breeze. That was when she realized it wasn't a window at all but instead a door to the garden that had been left slightly ajar. When she got close, she could see two figures near the shadowy bushes beyond the glass. Who could they be? She squinted—and then screamed. In her mind.

Wait, no—!

The couple embracing before her eyes were two people Connie knew well. The precise two people she least wanted to see together right now.

Neil Bronson and Pamela Francis.

Pamela was the one who noticed Connie standing there gaping at them. She must have sensed Connie's eyes on her because she suddenly looked up at her from her position in Neil's arms. They were on the palace grounds, and an even row of lamps illuminated them. Connie could see very clearly how flushed her rosy cheeks were. Their eyes met. They definitely met. But for some reason, despite being caught in the act of infidelity, Pamela gazed coolly back at Connie. The corners of her lips curled up provocatively.

Then she wrapped her arm around Neil's neck and slowly brought her lips to his face.

There's simply no way.

Connie was in the passage leading from the conservatory to the grand hall, propped up by one arm against an opulently decorated marble pillar, her head drooping.

Now that I've seen them, what in the world do they want me to do?

If this were a popular romance novel, the standard reaction would be to scream, *How dare you!* at the offending woman and slap her on both cheeks, or else bear down on the unfaithful man with a knife in hand, declaring, *I'll murder you and die myself...!* but both those options seemed a little advanced for a rookie like Connie.

She was fairly sure Neil didn't know she'd witnessed him cheating on her.

"I wish I could pretend I never saw it...," she muttered to herself.

After all, theirs wasn't a romantic marriage to start with. His family wanted connections to the world of nobles, and her family wanted to pay off their debts. She should have known from the start that love had no part in it.

"My heart did flutter a bit, I'll admit. I mean, he's so handsome! And so kind. But it was only a little splash of excitement—only a few tiny drops. I couldn't care less about something like this. In fact, I'm not hurt at all..."

The conditions of the marriage being what they were, she didn't want to make an unnecessary fuss. Nevertheless.

"It might not be sincere of me to stay quiet about what I know..."

Thou shalt be sincere—that was the family motto.

She wanted to pretend she'd never seen Neil cheating on her, but in order to build the foundation for a sincere relationship with Neil as her life partner, she felt like she had to gather up her courage and confront him.

Plus, he was the one at fault. It was hard to imagine he would break off the engagement from his side. Only the *infamous* Scarlett would deserve something like that.

Scarlett Castiel, wicked woman without equal. She had gone from merely harassing her opponent in love—the viscount's daughter Cecilia Luze—to plotting her assassination. Everybody knew the story of how she had lost her fiancé, the prince, and ended up being executed for her cruel actions.

That story was entirely different from Connie's.

"...I'm ready."

She would start by confronting Neil. They'd talk and decide together what to do. Yes, that was best.

Having determined that was the sincerest path and resolved to take it, she looked up. Then she screamed. "Eek!"

A girl was standing in front of her.

Probably because Connie was so deep in thought, she hadn't even noticed her approach. She appeared to be about the same age as Connie. She wasn't looking at her, but instead in the direction of the music and laughter coming from the hall. Her expression looked vaguely wistful.

"Um..."

Connie was about to ask if something was wrong, but instead she gasped. The girl was incredibly beautiful.

She had glossy black hair and skin as white and translucent as unblemished snow. The dress encasing white skin was a fiery scarlet.

And her eyes—her jewellike eyes were like unblemished amethysts. In this land, purple eyes were associated with royalty, as many members of the royal family had them. Connie ran through the current roster of royalty, but she couldn't come up with anyone this girl's age. The only other people with purple or even purplish eyes were from families with royalty in their lineage. Which meant this girl was of quite high birth.

Thinking back on the revelers in the grand hall, Connie realized that none was higher than a marquis. The Hamsworths might be filthy rich, but they were still viscounts. Other than at the huge balls held by the royal family, higher- and lower-ranking nobles didn't mingle with each other much. Most of the guests tonight were either viscounts or barons. The eccentric, confident countess Emanuel was the only person of her rank present.

But a certain number of high nobles actually preferred the evening parties of the lower ranks. Sometimes these high-ranking nobles would sneak into such balls incognito.

Connie guessed that the girl with the amethyst eyes must belong to that category.

"Um… I'm Constance Grail. I don't mean to be rude, but do you feel all right? Shall I call someone?" she asked, stepping forward. Suddenly, though, she flushed and looked away.

The neck of the girl's scarlet dress was cut low to reveal a large swath of her pillowy breasts.

She was the same age as Connie; how did she ooze such indescribable allure? Fashionable dresses these days usually had high necklines meant to emphasize the chastity of their wearers. In that sense, the design was a bit outdated, yet it didn't look at all unsophisticated. In fact, it suited this girl with her gorgeous, willful face perfectly. It didn't strike Connie as the least bit vulgar—just overwhelmingly beautiful.

If this girl showed up in the grand hall and smiled even once, Connie was sure fashion trends would change instantly.

"…It looks so fun, doesn't it?"

The sound of her voice snapped Connie out of her trance. The girl was still gazing into the grand hall.

"Won't you go in?"

The question had seemed logical to Connie, but the girl looked puzzled and tilted her head.

"Would that be all right?"

Now Connie was the one who felt confused. "Of course it would be," she said. There was no reason for it not to be.

She gestured toward the hall, and the girl stepped unsteadily forward. She looked like she might totter right over.

She walked across the line dividing the corridor from the grand hall, then suddenly froze.

"…I was able to go in!"

Of course she was. But she sounded so surprised about the fact that Connie began to feel suspicious. Before she'd thought the girl had had a

©Yu-nagi

few too many drinks, but now she wondered if she'd taken some kind of illegal hallucinogen.

The girl let out a peal of clear, tinkling laughter.

"—And I've got you to thank, girl."

When she turned to Connie, she was smiling from ear to ear.

Before Connie could recover from that brilliant smile, the girl had skipped lightly into the grand hall, vanishing from sight.

Once she was gone, Connie grumbled, "Girl...?"

The girl in the scarlet dress had sounded just like a queen. She must be some high-ranking noble attending the ball incognito after all.

Connie went back into the grand hall, snatched some tarts off a platter, and crammed them into her mouth. She was stress eating. Neil was still nowhere to be seen. Neither was Pamela. Before Connie knew it, the platter was empty. She moved on without pause to the next one.

As she was chomping on a mouthful of candied violets, she heard a voice timidly congratulating her. She turned around to see the baron's daughter, Brenda Harris, standing behind her. Startled, Connie gulped down the violets.

Brenda belonged to Pamela Francis's clique. She was timid, anxious, and constantly appraising Pamela's mood.

Having finished the standard congratulations, Brenda hurriedly turned on her heel, obviously relieved to get away. Why had she come over in the first place, then? Was she a genuinely conscientious person? As Connie indifferently watched her walk off, she let out a soft "oh!"

"Brenda, your hair ornament is about to fall out." Brenda stiffened, but Connie ignored that and walked up to her, pointing to the back of her head. "Your hair's coming loose, too. You wouldn't want the ornament to fall out, would you?"

"Oh, n-no."

"Why don't we just take it out altogether?"

"Yes, I suppose," Brenda whispered with tragic determination. Was she really so afraid of her hair looking messy?

"Do you mind if I help you?" Connie asked.

Brenda's shoulders trembled. This was unexpected. It wasn't as if Connie planned to steal her hair ornament. After a pause, Brenda nodded fearfully. With a few quick movements, Connie rearranged Brenda's chestnut hair.

"See? Now it looks pretty even without the ornament," she said encouragingly. Brenda looked as if she was going to cry, while Connie was getting more confused by the second. As she was trying to decide what to do next, Brenda opened her mouth and managed to say something.

"Oh, um, I—I left my bag on the second floor. I'll just run and get it, b-but would you mind holding on to my ornament until I get back?"

"Yes, of course. With pleasure," she agreed, since she had a small clutch with her anyway.

The delicate ornament Brenda handed her was decorated with a flower pattern in gold leaf and rows of white pearls. She wrapped it in a handkerchief so it wouldn't break, then slipped it into her bag. Brenda climbed the stairs without a backward glance. What was that about?

All those tarts and cakes had left a sweet taste in Connie's mouth, so she took a cup of tea from a nearby waiter. Sensing someone's gaze on her, she glanced up. It was Wayne Hasting, a small young man she'd seen several times at other balls. He seemed to have been watching her exchange with Brenda. She knew him as a noble of similarly low rank, but they weren't friendly enough to chat. She nodded at him, and he nodded back.

The lively, cheerful music had given way to a slower song, and men and women were dancing in a large circle.

Brenda still hadn't come back. When Connie looked absently up the spiral staircase, she spotted Pamela Francis walking jauntily down it. Neil was next to her and behind them was Brenda, looking down.

"Constance Grail!" Pamela cried, loud enough for the whole hall to hear. "What an outrageous thing to do!"

Everyone turned toward her, wondering what had happened. Pamela curled her lips with great satisfaction.

"I know your family has fallen on hard times, but don't you think this is going a bit far? Honestly, I question your character."

The eyes of the crowd turned toward Connie.

"Wh-what are you talking about?"

The strange situation made her voice sound high and excited.

"Oh, you intend to play the fool? That won't work. You know you stole Brenda's hair ornament."

She stole Brenda's hair ornament?

Connie had no idea what Pamela was talking about, but she did recognize the cruel intent in her voice. Connie's heart pounded.

"Brenda told me what happened. You said her ornament was falling out and offered to fix it for her, but then a few minutes later, she noticed it was missing. What do you have to say about that, Constance Grail?"

"What do I have to say?"

"It was made with pure gold and the rarest of teardrop pearls from the Yera Sea—just the kind of thing someone in need of money would kill for. Oh, yes, I understand exactly how you must have felt. After all, I've heard about the pitiful situation your family has gotten yourselves into."

"B-but Brenda asked me—"

"She asked you? Oh, of course, you claim you didn't steal it."

Connie wanted to explain herself, but Pamela talked so fast, she hardly even had time to answer.

"Yes, but—"

"Then show me your bag."

"What...?"

"If you didn't steal it, then you shouldn't mind showing me your bag, should you?"

Connie winced. Brenda's hair ornament was in her clutch. Her panic probably showed on her face. Neil had been looking suspicious, but now his eyes widened.

"Constance, I can't believe it."

"It's not true!" Connie screamed. But someone was already wrenching the bag from her hands. It wasn't true! Pamela dumped the contents onto a table. Connie heard something hard clatter on its surface.

"Dear me!" someone exclaimed.

"Look here, Constance Grail," Pamela said. "You said you didn't steal it, so what's this? Explain yourself immediately."

The golden ornament was peeking from the handkerchief she'd wrapped it in. Neil stared at it in silence. The people around them began to whisper.

But it wasn't true! Connie hadn't stolen anything! She felt something hot rising in her throat. She clenched her fists, holding it down.

"...Brenda asked me to hold it for her."

That was the truth. Connie had no reason to feel guilty.

But Pamela was cruel, and she pressed Connie mercilessly.

"She *asked* you to? As far as I can see, this ornament isn't especially bulky or fragile. But you say she asked you to hold it? Brenda did? Even though you don't know each other very well? That's an awfully strange story."

Connie could hear mocking laughter in the crowd; they agreed with Pamela. They were suspicious. Suddenly, she was burning up.

"Brenda!" Connie shouted, unable to contain herself.

Brenda shivered in surprise.

"Please tell her the truth! You asked me to hold it, didn't you? You said you wanted me to keep it while you went to get your bag. Isn't that right, Brenda? ...Why won't you say anything? Brenda? You wouldn't...?"

With each of Connie's questions, Brenda curled further in on herself.

"Such pathetic little excuses."

Suddenly, a terrifyingly affectionate voice broke in.

"Poor Brenda. You're frightening her. It's all right, Brenda. You don't have to say anything... Now you see, Neil. This is the kind of girl she is."

Pamela clung vulnerably to his arm.

"You ought to raise an objection to the engagement right away. This is an irrefutable crime. If you marry her, you'll be putting the reputation of the Bronson Company on the line."

Neil looked back and forth between Connie and the hair ornament, clearly confused.

"But there's no proof…"

"Proof?" Pamela sneered. "Every person in this hall is a witness! And the priest Viscount Hamsworth is here, too. You might as well raise your complaint right away. Would somebody mind calling the viscount?"

"It's not true; I never stole anything!"

Pamela turned to Connie. "This is what the *sincere* Grails have to show? You're nothing but a petty thief!"

"But—"

Connie could hardly breathe from shock. She looked around, searching for someone who could help her. But all she found were cold, disdainful glares. Her eyes met those of Wayne Hasting, who was very pale. She was sure he'd seen what happened. She looked at him pleadingly, but he glanced away. From his expression, she could tell he was unwilling to get involved in something so troublesome.

The world swayed before Connie's eyes.

Somebody!

Somebody else must have seen what happened. She saw several people she recognized. But all of them only stared silently, deserting her.

Somebody help me!

A tear seeped from her eye. The back of her throat felt hot. It was strange. So strange. Nobody would help her. Nobody would help someone as insignificant as Connie.

"Fine."

Connie never expected to hear *that* voice in her ear.

"…What?"

It was a female voice, as light and clear as a tinkling bell. She'd heard it before. In fact, she'd heard it that very night.

"I'll help you."

The voice was pretty but also haughty and insolent. For some reason, Connie felt drawn to it.

"But in exchange…"

Constance Grail was unable to catch the rest of the sentence—because just then, something hit her, and she lost consciousness.

※

Who is this girl?

Pamela Francis's spine froze as Constance Grail gave her an unfathomable grin.

Until very recently, this plain little thing hadn't even registered in Pamela's consciousness. There wasn't one thing about her that stood out, and yet, she paraded around spewing meaningless drivel about *"sincerity."* Stupid girl.

She'd always hated the way this Grail got away with childish behavior that any other young lady would be ridiculed for. On top of that, she was engaged to *the* Neil Bronson. That tall, handsome young man with the charisma of an actor.

Why should Constance get everything good? After all, she was a *far inferior being* to Pamela when it came to both her looks and her family's wealth.

And so Pamela decided to crush her.

She'd summoned Brenda Harris just before the ball began.

"I c-c-couldn't do that."

When Brenda heard Pamela's plan, she shook her head weakly and scrunched up her face.

"Then you don't mind ending up like Maddy?" Pamela asked, narrowing her eyes. This time, Brenda shrieked.

Madison Scott had belonged to Pamela's clique until the previous year. Unlike gloomy Brenda, she was cheerful and fairly quick-witted, so she had been among Pamela's *favorites*. However, Pamela happened to overhear her saying something bad about her to a friend.

Ever since, poor Maddy had become Pamela's plaything. In the space of a few short months, she had fallen into a depression and was currently recuperating in the provinces.

Pamela walked up to the trembling Brenda and pulled with all her strength on the ornament in her hair. Her pretty updo unraveled. Pamela stared into Brenda's terrified eyes as she delivered her command.

"Now, Brenda, don't make me repeat myself. I'm not saying you have to force the situation. That's right—if Constance doesn't say anything about your unsightly hair, you can just come right back to me without doing a thing."

Brenda nodded repeatedly. No doubt she found a glimmer of hope in Pamela's words. But that was naive of her. Unfortunately for Brenda, she was dealing with Constance Grail.

Constance's looks might be plain, but Pamela knew she was a nauseatingly hypocritical do-gooder.

Or at least, she thought she knew.

"A thief?"

Pamela's plan was proceeding without a hitch. Brenda had left her hair ornament with Constance, and Pamela had accused Constance of stealing it right in the middle of the grand hall. Everyone was staring at the girl. Everyone was questioning her innocence. Shocked, Constance had lowered her head in exhaustion—but when she looked up again, something was different.

Pamela had no idea what the something was. But…

"Ha! Just which one of us is the thief here?"

Pamela hadn't known that angelic Constance Grail was capable of such a nasty smile.

"…What do you mean by that?"

The expression was horribly calm. Constance should have been the one under fire, but for some reason, Pamela felt like *she* was. She could hardly bear it.

But Constance just grinned like she didn't care and said loudly, "Didn't you know? The young man you were humping out in the bushes is my dear fiancé."

A buzz ran through the spectators at this vulgar accusation. Blood rushed to Pamela's face. How dare she! How dare she say that in front of a crowd!

"I did no such thing! Neil and I were just kissing! What a crude thing to say! You should be ashamed!"

"Pamela!"

Neil's panicked voice brought her back to her senses. Now she'd done it. She'd been trapped. By the likes of Constance Grail!

Constance smiled wickedly. "Dear me, I seem to have misspoken. You were only kissing—kissing someone else's fiancé. But wouldn't you call that the very definition of a thief?"

Their relationship was public knowledge, but a rumor was a different animal from an outright admission by one of the involved parties. And to admit it in such a shameful way! Tomorrow, everyone would probably be talking about how Pamela Francis was so foolish for letting her tongue slip. Her lips trembled in humiliation. But she hadn't lost yet. This was a draw. No—Constance had been wounded even worse than she had.

"That doesn't change the fact that you stole Brenda's hair ornament," she announced. But Constance just shrugged, so casually that Pamela wondered if she'd imagined her panic a few moments earlier. Constance scanned the room until her gaze rested on a certain person.

A certain young man.

"Excuse me, Mr.—*let me think for a moment*—oh yes, Hasting. Wayne Hasting!"

Pamela clicked her tongue at the familiar name. How unfortunate. That skinny boy was always so good at irritating Pamela.

A long time ago, she and her clique had picked on Wayne Hasting.

"You saw it happen, didn't you?"

"I—I…"

His freckled face turned appraisingly toward Pamela. Of course, she would never forgive him if he spoke. She narrowed her eyes. His shoulders convulsed, and he looked down. He did not finish his sentence.

Constance Grail was staring at him.

"Oh, it's fine if you don't want to talk about it. But be careful. Lots of other people know the truth."

She smiled gleefully and slowly surveyed the grand hall.

"You might not know this, but I have a very good memory. Viscountess Stan was there, and Baron Brower's daughter, and Knight Pelham, too. Oh, and I don't know *your* name, but you, in the lemon-colored dress. Yes, you. You saw it, too, didn't you? It's fine, though. It's just fine if none of you wants to speak up."

The people who had just been named were staring in wide-eyed shock. A second later, their expressions changed to mortification.

"After all, a shabby farce can be sorted out in no time if we look into it properly. But I simply hate wasting my mental energy."

Having said that much, Constance suddenly shifted her expression and tone.

"So I'll ask you one more time, Wayne Hasting. Please stop looking down at your feet. Remember your eye contact, dear."

This was no longer the ordinary, insignificant Constance standing before them. This was someone else—someone with a powerful presence. Pamela trembled as if her very heart were being gripped by a pair of talons. Wayne gasped softly.

"If your mother could see you acting in such an ungentlemanly way, Wayne, I'm certain she'd be crushed. Are you sure you don't have anything to say?"

He must be nearing his breaking point. Wayne Hasting lifted his head unsteadily. He looked like he was about to cry.

"Well done," Constance said, smiling with satisfaction. "Now, Wayne. I'd like for us to continue being friends in the future, wouldn't you?"

The truth was, Constance and Wayne were mere acquaintances. But Pamela bit her lip uneasily at these overconfident words.

"For instance, would you allow an innocent person to be falsely accused?"

The whole grand hall was silent now.

"And what would you think of someone who chose silence to protect themselves even while knowing the truth?"

She wove together her words as fluidly as a song.

"I'll tell you what I would think. I would think that person was going to hell, and so were all the other people who pretended they hadn't seen. Now, Wayne, think about it. When the truth becomes clear, which side will you be standing on? What will people say about you?"

Wayne was clearly shaken. His eyes darted around. He looked at Pamela again—

"Look at me, Wayne Hasting. I will not permit you to look away."

Wayne's face snapped back toward Constance. Her clothes and makeup were plain, but for some reason, she was radiating an undefinably powerful aura. The weak-kneed Wayne was probably going to crumble under the pressure at any moment. His face was paler than pale. Finally, he opened his trembling mouth.

"...I s-saw it."

Constance smiled. It was a thoroughly predatory smile.

"I s-saw it happen. You didn't steal the ornament, Miss Grail. You just fixed Brenda's hair for her. And Brenda said she wanted you to hold her hair ornament for her...!"

Useless boy! Pamela's eyes flashed with anger. If no one else was watching, she would have slapped him straight across his freckled face.

"I h-heard her, too."

Most annoyingly, the girl in the lemon-colored dress was now speaking up as well. Then more followed: "I saw it happen, too." "I heard them." "It's just like he said." "I saw her hand the ornament to Constance."

Now the suspicious looks were turned on Pamela. Her legs dissolved into jelly beneath the cutting stares. This wasn't supposed to happen. Not like this! Even Neil was frowning, his arms crossed over his chest.

"Is this true, Pamela?"

"N-no! I mean, I mean, Brenda—yes, Brenda must have lied to me!"

Her only option now was to blame it on Brenda. Pamela had simply been trying to help a friend in need, without knowing the truth. Wasn't that what had happened? Pamela looked at Brenda, and then—

"Poor Brenda. You're frightening her."

She'd heard those words before. She looked at Constance. Constance was smiling kindly at Brenda.

Her face was as plain and unremarkable as always. Nevertheless, somehow, she was very beautiful. Brenda was staring at Constance, enchanted.

"It's all right, Brenda. You don't have to say anything."

Constance was mimicking Pamela's earlier words perfectly.

Tears spilled from Brenda's eyes and rolled down her cheeks. Pamela bit her lip.

Her defeat was as clear as daylight.

"What in the world is going on over here?"

His round belly shaking, the evening's host, Viscount Hamsworth, descended the spiral staircase. At first, Pamela wondered what he was doing here, but then she remembered she was the one who had asked someone to fetch him.

"Nouveau riche pig."

Constance mumbled something, but unfortunately, Pamela couldn't make it out.

Right away, several people gathered around the viscount and seemed to be explaining the situation with great humor. The viscount widened his eyes theatrically at each twist in the plot, shrugged, and pretended to be in grief. When the story was complete, he turned to Constance, his eyebrows lowered in sympathy.

"What horror befalls you, Miss Grail."

Constance smiled coolly. Pamela had never seen her look so conde-scending before.

"Yes indeed. I was tempted to break my holy oath because of this hor-rible treatment. But before I become an apostate, I'd like to throw myself on the mercy of the goddesses. Would you favor me with your advice?"

"Do you mean you want to raise an objection to your engagement?"

"Would it be accepted?"

"The engagement has already been made public, so it will be difficult to do quickly. Your fiancé must have something to say for himself as well."

"Can you not give happiness to a poor lamb?"

"Me? Of course, I very much want to do that. Unfortunately, I oversee a different parish, and to start, it would not be easy to raise an objection in a place like this. Such things must be done at the correct place in the correct manner. As you know, the church is inviolable."

No doubt that was true. Even Pamela hadn't thought Neil would really be able to file his objection here and now. She had called the viscount only because she wanted to further shame Constance. Of course, she was running out of patience for Neil anyway and would have been happy if he did indeed raise an objection tomorrow.

A mere low-ranking noble had little sway over the church. Which was why Pamela could hardly believe the next words she heard.

"That's not my concern."

What did this girl just say?

"This misconduct took place at your ball. I demand you do something about it."

The words were spoken in the tone of someone accustomed to giving orders. But the person speaking them was Constance Grail. The crowd began to buzz once again.

"It shouldn't be difficult, especially for a person like you. Enough idle chitchat. Go now and annul this engagement, and be quick about it. If you don't—"

Her voice was by no means loud, and yet, it rang out clearly across the hall.

"—then I will do whatever I must to ensure His Highness hears a little rumor during Dominic Hamsworth's ball at the Grand Merillian. One about a young man and a young lady caught engaging in indecent acts in the gardens of our gracious royal family."

In that moment, Constance Grail held the grand hall in her palm. Bizarrely, even though Viscount Hamsworth had just been rudely insulted, his eyes were glittering, and he immediately issued an order to his chamberlain. It appeared that he was actually moving forward with dissolving the engagement.

Pamela desperately tried to think of a countermove. Whatever it took, she had to recover the situation. If she didn't, her place within society would be gone by morning.

Neil would probably be useless. However elegant, handsome, and smart he might be, he was no noble. Unable to keep up with the unfolding drama and unaware of what lay in wait, he simply stood there doing nothing.

"Ladies and gentlemen!"

Constance Grail—normally a wallflower unable to say a single clever thing around other people—was behaving like some sort of grand actress.

Didn't anyone else think it was strange?

"I apologize from the bottom of my heart for interrupting this lovely gathering. Please give your blessings to this young couple burning with illicit passion. The night has just begun. Enjoy yourselves."

You two.

Pamela felt as if those were the unspoken words directed straight at

her. The hair rose on her arms. She opened her mouth desperately. Her instincts were screaming that she was in dire danger. If she didn't do something fast, things would go very badly for her.

"Please wait a moment—"

Constance Grail was definitely the type to accept an apology. As expected, she glanced over at Pamela.

But that was all.

Having registered Pamela's words, she narrowed her eyes, then quickly looked away. This was not the attitude of a person in such a rage that they could not accept an apology. No, it was the expression of someone who had mistakenly looked at a disgusting little insect. And that was when the question occurred to Pamela.

Who is this woman?

She was not the Constance Grail Pamela knew.

"Oh my, I feel faint. You in the handsome peacock-blue vest—yes, you. Might I borrow your manly arms for just a moment? My heart hurts, and I'm afraid I can't walk on my own. I just need to go over there. Someone should be waiting for me outside."

Her face was plain, but the expression on it was undeniably alluring. It was hard to believe, but homely Constance Grail looked extremely attractive. Sure enough, the man she had called on smiled a little, then glanced condescendingly at Pamela.

"Of course, my lady."

She had lost. As a woman, Pamela had lost to Constance. She was so ashamed, her body was shaking.

"I must go. Please excuse me."

Her back held straight, Constance gracefully lifted the flowing hem of her dress. Then, with a smooth gesture, she lowered her head.

Her etiquette was so natural and flawless, even Pamela forgot her outrage for a moment and stared in awe.

No sooner had Constance left the hall than the musicians picked up their instruments and began to play. It was a lonely serenade signaling the end of the ball.

Pamela was undoubtedly in a fix. She sensed that everyone was criticizing her. She could feel their eyes on her. They were all staring at her. She was determined not to give in. She raised her head, attempting to act as if nothing significant had happened. But secretly, she was terrified.

So when she saw someone she knew, she flew instantly to their side.

"Lady Holland!"

The buxom woman turned around in surprise. Pamela could count on Lady Holland. She would protect her.

From the day Pamela had entered society as a debutant, Lady Holland had always doted on her as if she were her own daughter.

"Please help me! I've been tricked. I swear on the Moirai that I would never do something like that. You believe me, don't you?"

She gazed pleadingly at the noblewoman, an injured expression on her face. She thought that would be enough to win over kindly Lady Holland. She was sure she would drape an arm around her shoulder and tell her what a poor, mistreated thing she was.

Lady Holland smiled just as Pamela expected. Relieved, she smiled back. But the next moment, she froze.

"Excuse me, who are you?"

Pamela gasped.

There was a horridly amused glint in the eyes of the supposedly kind woman.

As Pamela stood rooted to the ground, someone bumped into her. She stumbled and fell. In that short interval, Lady Holland had vanished out of sight.

"Oh, I'm so sorry," came the cool apology from a noblewoman with a fan held over her mouth. The slender woman with the dark-blond hair twisted in a knot was Countess Emanuel, who was friendly with Constance. Pamela was instantly on guard.

As she'd feared, the countess remained where she was and began talking to Pamela with hardly a pause for breath.

"You see, I was truly happy for Miss Grail. She's such a dull girl, with nothing at all to make her special, but she's not a bad person. As the Grails put it, she's sincere. And that's a very rare thing indeed in this world of ours. You understand that, I'm sure. That's why what you did makes me a little angry. Yes, just a little. But it all turned out to be quite amusing, so I forgive you."

Having said that much, she reached out a hand to Pamela, who was unable to get up on her own.

"After all, it appears there are plenty of people quite eager to waltz with you. I don't even need to lift a finger."

Pamela glanced around in surprise. She was surrounded by a large crowd. The quiet melody suddenly picked up its pace. A tune in triple time rang out brightly across the hall—a waltz. The blood drained from Pamela's face. Waves of laughter rippled toward her.

The people peering at her *excitedly* were all over a certain age. Those who were closer to her own age were watching from the outside, as if they didn't know what to make of this peculiar atmosphere that was so different from an ordinary ball.

Even Pamela had never experienced anything like this.

Ordinary balls were terribly boring and formulaic. The gossip and teasing were cute child's play. She found a night out at a questionable pub on the wrong side of town with a group of commoner boys much more thrilling. That was why she had come up with her scheme in the first place. She thought she could twist this group of predictable idiots around her little finger.

As the countess walked past Pamela, she whispered in her ear.

"In my hometown, we make thieves put on a pair of burning shoes and dance until they die."

※

"Oh, it's starting, it's starting!"

"I haven't seen this in ages."

"Must've been ten years since the last one."

"I wonder how long they'll *last*."

"Oh, I do hope she's still got some spirit in her by the time my turn comes."

"This has always been the true pleasure of a ball. But it really has been ages. Everyone's been so timid these past ten years."

"They didn't want to attract the wrong kind of attention and end up with their head on the block."

"Like what happened ten years ago."

"That was just awful."

"Shhh, don't bring it up."

"Yes, but tonight really was a shock. It was just as if—"

"Yes, as if—"

"Just as if Scarlett Castiel had returned from the depths of hell."

Constance Grail

Age sixteen, "sincerity" is her motto. Hazelnut hair, pale green eyes. Plain and dull. Cheating fiancé, who makes her almost dissolve into tears. Asks for help in a pinch and summons a serious bully... **←new!**

 Scarlett Castiel

Sixteen when she died. Eternally sixteen. Black hair, amethyst eyes. Beheaded in Saint Mark's Square for attempted assassination of Crown Princess Cecilia. "What's yours is mine, and what's mine is mine" is her motto. Seems to have a good memory.

 Neil Bronson

Probably seventeen or eighteen. Son and heir of the Bronson Company. Connie's fiancé. A stylish, pleasant young man. Deemed a despicable slime for cheating on Connie with Pamela. Would have held a press conference if he lived in another age.

 Pamela Francis

Probably fifteen or sixteen. Platinum blond. The Zouzou of Connie's generation. Considers kissing child's play, cheats with Neil. A rich baron's daughter. Likes to use people and torment them. Ultimately is tormented herself.

 Brenda Harris

Probably fifteen or sixteen. Pamela's shadow. Or maybe the most terrified subject in Queen Pamela's reign of terror.

Mylene Reese

Probably fifteen or sixteen. Connie's friend. Viscount's daughter. Insensitive, loves gossip.

 Viscount Hamsworth

Probably in his late thirties. Host of the ball at the Grand Merillian where it all went down. So portly, you'd think he was under a curse to become a pig. Single. Apparently very rich. Seems like a cruel joke, but he's also a priest.

Countess Emanuel

Probably in her mid-thirties. Seems gentle, has a nasty tongue. Dotes on Connie somewhat. Has a scary hometown.

©Yu-nagi

When Connie opened her eyes, the sun was already high in the sky. The light was soft, and the air was clear. A little bird was chirping outside the window.

She felt as if she'd just woken from a vivid dream. Yes—as if she'd brought Pamela Francis to her knees in some sort of argument…

No, that would be impossible.

After all, this was Pamela she was talking about.

Connie closed her eyes and arched her back, stretching.

Yes, that would be impossible. She was sad to admit it, but Constance Grail was a plain, insignificant nothing.

In this gloomy mood, Connie opened her eyes again. Somebody's face was directly in front of her own.

"…Huh?"

The person's amethyst eyes were like enticing pools, and her hair was a veil as black as night.

"…Huh?"

Although the girl was bewitchingly beautiful, Connie felt extremely uneasy.

Wasn't this her own bedroom? She glanced around. There was the familiar ivy-patterned wallpaper, and beside the bed was the nightstand with the golden handles and cabriole legs. There was the love seat and the coffee table with the glass top. And there in a corner of the room was the dressing table with the attached bureau.

Outside the window, she could see colorful spires. Although the Grail domain was nothing but green fields and forests, here in the capital, they were surrounded by buildings. Of course, when the social season ended in early fall, the domain would probably be brilliantly red and orange, too.

Anyway, to Connie, the capital looked the same as it did every year.

"So you've finally woken up, have you, Constance Grail? You slept through yesterday, you know."

However, on ordinary mornings, she did not hear a voice as clear and delicate as a chime.

After a pause, Connie screamed.

"Aaaaaaaaaaaaaaaaaah!"

The girl in front of her backed away with a shocked expression. But Connie was still in a panic. The events at the Grand Merillian came flooding back to her. It was as if every time she blinked, she was seeing a different scene in a play.

W-wait a second...

It wasn't just images. The mood, the temperature, the voices, the smells...everything was so fresh and clear. It couldn't be—

"It was a dream, but it wasn't a dream?!" she shouted incoherently.

"What are you talking about? Are you still asleep?" came the grumpy response.

No, Connie felt relatively alert. Her memory told her that she had met this person in the hallway between the grand hall and the conservatory and that she was a noblewoman. But she wasn't certain. She must still be half asleep. This must be a dream. Or was it? She decided, very timidly, to ask.

"Um, would you mind telling me...who you are?"

In any case, she knew one thing. From the intimidatingly perfect features and the refined, elegant bearing to the alluring figure and daring dress, this was obviously not a friend of Connie's.

The girl narrowed her eyes, and her red lips formed a half-moon smile. "Me? I'm Scarlett," she announced. "*Scarlett Castiel.*"

Scarlett Castiel?

Connie's jaw dropped.

"Now wait just a minute. Scarlett Castiel was executed ten years ago."

"*Oh, stop it! Do I look alive to you?*"

Judging by her tone, the girl seemed amused by Connie's comment. Connie examined her. True, her exquisite face was otherworldly, but that probably wasn't what the girl meant. The slope of her jaw and neck was delicate, and her chest was voluptuous. Her waist was slender—and her feet were literally *not* touching the ground.

For some reason, she was floating lightly in the air.

When Connie saw that, she fainted.

"*You sleep too much.*"

Awakened by this exasperated comment, Connie opened her eyes to find the same girl peering down at her, hand on her hip.

"*And to think, you fell asleep in the middle of a conversation with me…! I've never been so offended in my life!*"

But you're not alive, Connie thought. Instead of saying that, she said stiffly, "I fainted."

Those amethyst eyes…that hair as glossy as onyx… Her beauty took Connie's breath away. All of it fit perfectly with descriptions of the famous Scarlett Castiel. Her features seemed right, too.

Still, ten years had passed since Connie saw the real Scarlett. And she'd only gotten one look. Although she remembered her being extraordinarily beautiful, her memory of Scarlett's precise features was vague. It was the execution itself that had made a stronger impression, since she'd never before seen one. After it was over, she'd crawled home and stayed in bed for three days and three nights. For Connie, the name Scarlett Castiel meant the worst trauma she'd ever experienced.

"B-but why the Grand Merillian...? I thought Scarlett Castiel's ghost haunted Saint Mark's Square..."

The rumors of a headless young lady wandering the square every night in search of her missing appendage were so famous, they were considered one of the Seven Mysteries of the Capital. When Connie told her that, Scarlett tilted her head.

"Saint Mark's Square? Oh, you mean where I was executed? I haven't been back there once since becoming like this. I hardly remember a thing about the day I was executed."

Interesting. Connie was relieved to hear those words from the so-called Scarlett. On that day, the square had bubbled over with the worst of humanity. It was better if she didn't remember.

"But the Grand Merillian, now that's where that idiotic Enrique and his scheming Cecilia humiliated me! Just thinking about it makes my blood boil!"

"How can you be so disrespectful to our prince?! And his s-scheming? What did you say...?!"

And what unbelievable slander against the celebrated Cecilia, who was so merciful that people said she must be the second coming of Saint Anastasia. But the girl saying such terrible things went on as if she couldn't care less.

"Anyhow, when I came to, I found myself in the Grand Merillian, but for some reason, I couldn't go into the grand hall. Whenever I tried, I'd be pushed back. I suppose there are some limits on what the dead can do."

Scarlett tilted her head like she was trying to remember something.

"I don't remember exactly when I became like this, but I should probably thank you for being able to go in there. No one can hear me when I talk. I can't even exchange glances with most people. You're the first one who ever noticed I was there."

"Miss Scarlett..."

The fleeting smile on the girl's face sent a pang through Connie's heart. She couldn't get another word out, but the girl nodded anyway, as if to say she understood.

"You may be plain, and you may not have a single outstanding characteristic, but you should feel proud of yourself for noticing me!"

"Hmm, that isn't quite right," Connie answered soberly. That wasn't why she'd been silent. But she remembered something the girl had said to her just before she entered the grand hall where the ball was taking place.

"I've got you to thank, girl."

Connie hadn't really understood, but it seemed that after she talked to the girl, she'd been able to enter the hall. Now it made more sense, but she still had another question.

"Why are you here in my house?"

She must have followed her home.

After she got to go inside the grand hall, did she think she could go wherever she wanted or something?

Connie's doubt must have showed on her face, because the girl calling herself Scarlett planted a hand on her hip and glared down at her.

"Clearly, it's because I haven't yet been paid for my services."

"Paid for your services?"

"You haven't forgotten already, have you? Or did you genuinely think I'd rescue a complete stranger without getting something in exchange?"

The girl giggled. Her face had a ferocious beauty to it, like a lioness chasing down prey. At that moment, a string of words flitted across Connie's memory.

"I'll help you. But in exchange…"

She felt as if a bucket of cold water had been thrown over her. She hadn't heard the end of that sentence. But she knew that all across the land, in times ancient and recent, people who made deals with strange creatures usually paid with their life. Connie hugged her shivering body and stuttered, "I d-didn't hear you…!"

"What?"

"I r-really didn't hear you! I don't know what happened! Please spare my life…!"

But even as Connie pleaded with her, the girl laughed hysterically.

"Nice try."

The world turned black with despair. Tears pooled in Connie's eyes.

Father, Mother, please forgive me for leaving this world before you—

Her life had been as unremarkable as her looks. Connie slumped dejectedly.

Scarlett Castiel approached Connie, her presence overwhelming her. Standing there with that sadistic smile on her lips, she looked every bit the wicked woman she was rumored to be.

"I saved you, and I won't take no for an answer!"

At that moment, poor Constance Grail thought that Scarlett was going to lead her into the afterworld just like Atropos, oldest of the three Fates, cutting the thread of life.

"Constance Grail, prepare yourself."

Connie squeezed her eyes shut and steeled her will. But it was not death that awaited her.

Her future, it turned out, was to be a little different than she'd imagined.

"From here on out, I demand that you devote your life to making sure I get my revenge!"

Connie blinked at the unexpected words.

"...Revenge?"

Scarlett edged closer, rage burning in her amethyst eyes. *"Yes, revenge. You and I are going to send every single one of those outrageous beasts who drove me to the executioner's block to hell."*

"Um, that's..." Connie staggered backward in the face of this extraordinary being. She gulped. "And who in the world could that be...?"

She couldn't just say yes so easily. She didn't even know who Scarlett wanted revenge on. Depending on the situation, Connie might not be up to the challenge by herself.

"I don't know."

"What?"

"I was framed, you see. I was executed for a crime that Cecilia set me up for. A person like me would never have done something so pathetic."

Scarlett narrowed her eyes in disgust.

What did she just say? At a loss for words, Connie stared at the source of this outrageous statement.

Executed for a crime of which she was innocent?

In other words, she'd been falsely accused?

"And that, Constance, is why I need you to act in my place to discover the true criminals and make their lives hell!"

How could this be? Connie's heart was pounding fast. Until this very moment, she had believed that Scarlett Castiel was a horrible person. She had total faith in a rumor that was plausible. What a fool she had been!

"So then it's not true that you forced Princess Cecilia's entire birth family to kneel at your feet...?!"

She wasn't only incredibly beautiful. She also came from a bloodline so noble, the royal family often married their princesses off to the dukes of Castiel. Add that she had been engaged to the crown prince, and she must have been the envy of many. All those feelings no doubt fueled the rumors. Connie was certain Scarlett had always been isolated. The least she could do was discover the real Scarlett and give her the understanding she deserved...

Connie squeezed her hands into fists and smiled sympathetically. Scarlett gave her a puzzled look.

"Oh, no, I did that."

"...You did?"

"What?"

"...N-nothing. Um, then what about wielding your power over Cecilia and throwing her in prison for lèse-majesté?"

"That did happen. Although she didn't learn her lesson in the least."

"...Then what about the story of you throwing red wine on her and tearing her dress off in the middle of a ball?"

"I didn't take off her undergarments, so that's not so bad, is it?"

"…Slapping her across the face with all your strength in public?"

"What's wrong with that?"

Connie took a deep breath. "You've done quite a lot, it seems!"

"Nothing that amounts to much."

"It does amount to much! I'll admit execution was an overly harsh punishment for those crimes, but you should have expected to be locked up, at least!"

"What did you say?! Just who do you think I am?!" Scarlett barked, scowling.

"I apologize—you are Miss Scarlett Castiel!"

"That's correct. I am a very grand personage! Who cares if I pester an insignificant viscount's daughter?!"

"But you did end up getting executed!"

Now she'd done it.

Connie had a bad habit of letting her tongue slip exactly when it shouldn't. The blood drained from her face. She was so terrified, she couldn't even look at Scarlett. Her eyes darting everywhere but at her, she screwed up her last bit of courage.

"A-also, about helping you get revenge—"

She was going to say it wasn't a good idea.

But before she could even get the words out of her mouth, they were rejected.

"What about the debt?"

Scarlett's tone was as calm as a placid sea.

"Your family is in debt, aren't they? What do you plan to do about that, now that you've broken off the engagement?"

She hadn't broken it off. Connie hadn't. Her Royal Highness Scarlett had broken it off.

But the truth was, the result was the same. The incident at the ball had lost her family the support of the Bronson Company. She had discarded her family's reputation and her fiancé, leaving only shame and debt.

Connie's shoulders drooped dejectedly. The more she thought about it, the more she felt like she was suffocating.

"It's not as if I couldn't help you."

Connie looked up. She must have had a very desperate look on her face. Scarlett smiled in amusement.

"You are going to help me get revenge, aren't you?"

"Uh…"

"And surely this would never happen, but for a sincere Grail to fail to return a kindness—well, I couldn't imagine anything more insincere."

"What would you like me to do?" Connie answered reflexively.

The most wicked woman in the world smiled with satisfaction.

When Connie walked down the stairs to the living room, the family's maid, Marta, came running toward her, looking worried. Apparently, as soon as Connie got home from the ball at the Grand Merillian, she had collapsed in bed and stayed that way until now. According to Marta, that is—Connie had no memory of any of it.

The members of the Grail family had found out what happened the morning after the ball, but by then, thanks to the strenuous efforts of Viscount Hamsworth, the church had already approved the dissolution of Connie's engagement to Neil Bronson. Scary.

Marta said that as head of household, Connie's father was on his way to the church to complete the necessary documents. Connie let out a low, involuntary wail.

Her father, Percival Ethel Grail, was the veritable personification of sincerity. He probably never imagined in his wildest dreams that his daughter's fiancé might be unfaithful. She wouldn't be surprised if he'd burst a blood vessel or two from the shock.

Worried, she asked Marta how he was doing. Marta sighed deeply.

"Oh, the master was horribly angry. At one point, he even threatened to challenge the young gentleman to a duel. It was only thanks to the mistress's words that he returned to his senses."

It seemed he had ultimately decided that since Connie had settled the matter with Neil herself, it would be insincere for him to interfere any further. *Thank you, principle of sincerity. Thank you, Mother.* Connie's mother was always the one who held the family together.

"But before we worry about that, Miss Constance, shall I make you some milk porridge? You haven't eaten a bite since yesterday."

"Oh, that would be wonderful! I'm absolutely starving! ...Also, has anything arrived for me?"

The last part was an order from Scarlett. She'd said that by now *all the letters should have arrived*, so she had better go and get them. Given that the order was coming from the one and only queen, Connie nodded right away, but secretly she was confused. Since she was shy, she had only a handful of friends, and she couldn't imagine them going out of their way to write her a letter about what had happened.

She glanced at Marta. As predicted, she was as surprised as if she'd seen snow in July. Connie nodded knowingly.

"I'm sorry to ask such an odd question. Please forget I said anything."

"No, it's not that...," Marta said, apparently struggling to get the words out before going to fetch her mail.

Connie carried the armload of letters into her room.

"What is this?!" she shrieked.

"You see? I was right." Scarlett smirked.

According to Marta, servants bearing personal correspondence had been arriving at the house constantly since the day before. Connie wasn't boasting, but she'd never received so many invitations in her life.

"You've given them something to talk about. To think, for a chaste nobleman's daughter to do something of that nature in public!" Scarlett added.

But Connie hadn't done it. She'd say it a million times—she, Connie, hadn't done it. The queen in front of her had.

Scarlett wanted to see the invitations, so Connie sat down on the love seat and spread them on the glass-topped coffee table. She guessed there were at least twenty. Scarlett inspected each one carefully, then suddenly yelped in delight.

"Here it is! I knew it would be there. Just look at those frills and gold leaf. Emilia Caroling is still as tacky as she was ten years ago!" she said, pointing to a particularly eye-catching card. Connie picked it up. The sender's name was written on the back.

"…The Baroness Godwin?"

"Godwin? Don't tell me Emilia married Douglas Godwin! That enormous butterball? And to think she used to call him a pig on two legs!"

Scarlett snorted.

"Anyhow, Constance, you're going to Emilia's ball. That woman loves to talk, and she loves to see other people in trouble. If you ask the right questions about what happened ten years ago, I have no doubt she'll start twittering like a canary in heat."

Scarlett's biting words broke the momentary silence in Connie's bedroom.

"Are you a complete idiot?"

Connie cowered. Scarlett's chilly gaze was directed at the reply to Lady Godwin's invitation that Connie had just written.

"It seems this will be our last chance to view the camellias—what the hell is this?"

"Um… It's a seasonal greeting?"

What else could it be? But Scarlett's face went blank. When she did that, her picture-perfect features drew the eye even more, like she was some sort of finely made doll. As Connie was absently contemplating this fact, lightning struck again.

"What kind of fool writes about wilting flowers as a social nicety?"

"Um…!"

"Camellias ultimately fall with their petals intact! In classical literature, they were used as a metaphor for decapitation! It would be bad enough to talk about them blooming, but here you go bringing up their ill-fated end! You might as well come out and challenge the host of the party to a fistfight!"

Connie was at a loss for words.

"And your handwriting is despicable! Rewrite that immediately."

"As long as she can read the words…"

"What did you say?"

"Nothing, nothing at all!"

Connie scrambled to pull a fresh sheet of writing paper from her bureau and dip her feather pen in ink. No sooner had she begun to write, however, than a barrage of criticism flew at her: *"Be careful! You just dropped an ink spot right there!" "How could you possibly choose your words so poorly?!" "That word looks awful! Start over!"* As she struggled along, holding back her tears, she heard someone bang the knocker on her door.

It was Marta, asking for instructions.

"Miss Kate, daughter of Baron Lorraine, is here. Shall I show her up?"

"Kate? I'll go right down."

Kate Lorraine was one of Connie's few friends. Connie stood up happily, then noticed the pitiful balled-up ruins of her letter-writing attempts covering the floor. When she turned around, the devil with the beautiful face was grinning impishly at her.

She hesitated for a second before turning back toward Marta.

"Actually, I'm too busy to go down right now. Can you show her up?!"

The moment Kate opened the door, she threw her arms around Connie, shouting her name.

"I heard you'd hardly left your bed. I've been so worried about you!"

Kate's chestnut-brown hair tickled her face. She was so soft, and she smelled so good. Connie couldn't help smiling at her friend, whose eyes were so wide with affection that they seemed about to fall right out of her face.

"I'm fine now. I just ate a whole pot of milk porridge and licked the spoon clean."

"Glutton. I don't know how you eat so much and don't gain weight. I'm jealous…," she said, pouting. It was true that Kate might be a little rounder than average, but Connie, with her washboard figure, was jealous of Kate's chest. Today, for instance, even though she was wearing a drab, high-necked dress, her chest looked about to burst right out of it.

"Are you really all right, though?" Kate asked, throwing Connie a worried look from the love seat. Connie was confused for a second—then realized what she was talking about.

"Don't tell me people are already gossiping?!"

Needless to say, she was talking about the incident at the Grand Merillian.

"Yes! You'd think a hurricane came through in December," Kate murmured.

Connie's face tensed. Even Kate, who was as unconnected socially as Connie—even less so, to be honest—knew about it. Which meant she could probably assume that by now, all of society knew about the Grail family scandal.

"You probably haven't heard, since you've been in bed, but yesterday Pamela returned to her domain. They said it was so she could rest, but I'm sure the truth is she slunk off with her tail between her legs because the future looked so dark. I've always known that little home-wrecker was a coward."

It was strange how calm Connie felt even as she listened to Kate talk about the topic she most wanted to avoid—Pamela Francis. She probably had Scarlett Castiel to thank for that. But someone else was on her mind...

"What about Neil?"

Kate frowned. "He doesn't seem to be faring very well, either. I heard that a number of big business deals that the Bronson Company had lined up on the condition that Neil married into your family fell through. Neil hasn't been charged with adultery, but the church is confining him for corrupting public morals. Sir Damian has been going around to all his customers with head bowed."

Connie's heart ached a little when she heard that. Just a little. She shook her head to clear away the sympathy and got back to the main topic.

"Um, so then what about me…?"

How did people view the primary force behind hurricanes? In response to Connie's terrified question, Kate nodded with the utmost gravity.

"Poor Constance Grail has proven that even a lamb will dash at a hunting dog if it's mad enough. That was the topic of the editorial piece in the noble edition of the *Mayflower* this morning. Congratulations, Constance Grail. You're the 'it girl.'"

What a horrible way to make her debut in the papers. Connie pressed her hand to her forehead and stared at the ceiling. But as she was reeling from the news, Kate noticed the wretched state of her desk.

"Well, that's unusual."

"What?"

"Sorry, I couldn't help looking. This is an invitation to Lady Godwin's ball, isn't it? And you're going? You always used to say no to such things. What changed?"

"Nothing, it's just that…"

What could she say? Connie glanced at Scarlett, who until now had been watching them as quietly as a statue. Just as she'd said, Kate didn't seem to see her. What to do? She doubted Kate would believe her if she told her the truth. But what could she tell her instead?

Listen, Kate, I suddenly gained the ability to see the ghost of the infamous Scarlett Castiel. Or I guess I should say she possessed me—she still does—and actually, she says someone set her up, and the two of us plan to find out who the criminal is. And by the way, that's why I'm going to Lady Godwin's ball, but I'm fine; don't worry about me…

No, that wouldn't go over very well. Connie rejected the idea immediately. She didn't want to be estranged from one of her precious few friends.

As Connie wiped the cold sweat from her face and desperately searched for an excuse, Kate suddenly gasped and clapped both hands over her mouth. Then her eyes started darting around nervously.

"I—I do see how you could feel that way! Y-yes, I think it's a great idea! Go have fun! There's sure to be lots of beautiful people at Lady Godwin's ball! And y-you never know—you just might meet a handsome, kind, unmarried prince on a white horse there…!"

"What? Oh, no, that's not why I'm going…"

"It's fine, Connie! My cousin Stacy was just saying that these days, women are allowed to be a little more forward. And the novel I finished the other day said that the only way to heal a broken heart is to find a new love!"

Yes, Kate definitely seemed to be misinterpreting her motives. But since she couldn't think of a good excuse, she just nodded and said uncertainly, "Right… I'll give that a try…"

It wasn't long before Kate exclaimed that she had to be going. Scarlett watched her hurry off with a puzzled frown.

"What do you think she was up to? Gathering information? Ugh. You'd better watch out for her, Constance Grail."

"Oh, no, I'm certain she only came to check on me because she was worried!"

The Lorraines were new money who had only recently risen from petty officers to their current position as barons. Kate's mother wasn't of noble birth, and she had lots of children, so the family was by no means wealthy. Kate's personality also probably had something to do with the fact that the only ball she'd ever attended was her debut. Other than that, she stayed home helping her mother with chores or piecework. Of course, the Lorraines did have a few maids and butlers, but they couldn't afford many. Connie knew it must have been hard for Kate to slip away to check on her today.

Connie was proud to call the kind, thoughtful Kate Lorraine her oldest friend. But even after she explained that to Scarlett, the latter looked suspicious.

"Um, let me think… Kate is for me like Miss *Lily* was for you—"

"*Lily?*" Scarlett tilted her head in adorable confusion, which made Connie tilt her own head.

"…Um, hadn't you been close with the marquess's daughter, Lily Orlamunde, since you were both young? I don't want to sound presumptuous, but if you could think of Kate like Lily…"

According to the rumors, Lily Orlamunde was the one friend Scarlett had truly accepted.

That didn't mean she was a criminal like Scarlett, of course. She had spoken up for Cecilia when Scarlett hurled absurd criticisms at her and tried to dissuade Scarlett from acting so cruelly, and she had sought to reform Scarlett's wicked ways until the end. She was known to be so fair-minded, people called her The White Lily of Charity.

Scarlett nodded. *"Oh yes, Lily. I'd forgotten all about her. She must be married by now, no?"*

"Y-yes, she married three years ago."

"Only three years ago? That took a while."

Young ladies in this land were generally expected to marry between the ages of sixteen and eighteen. Lily had been past twenty-five when she announced her engagement. However, there was a reason for that.

"It seems that Miss Lily grieved quite deeply over your death. She blamed herself for not stopping you from committing your crimes and pledged to pay for your sins herself. Everyone tried to stop her, but she spent years devoting herself to charitable work."

The Orlamunde family had always had close ties to the church, and Lily had apparently drawn on those connections to help orphans and tutor young children. It was extremely unusual for a young noblewoman to engage independently in such activities, rather than as a proxy for her husband, and Lily Orlamunde's self-sacrificing work was said to have eased the bitter opposition noblewomen faced if they became involved in social issues.

Connie could hardly bear to tell this beautiful moral tale without breaking down in tears, but Scarlett, whose connection to Lily was far more personal than her own, seemed uninterested.

"Oh, is that so?" she said, sounding bored. *"And who did Lily marry?"*

"Earl Randolph Ulster of the House of Richelieu. But—"

"Randolph?! That straitlaced prig?! She married my nemesis?!"

For once, Scarlett raised her voice. Connie shuddered in surprise.

"And you say he's called Randolph Ulster?! That stubborn mule is still a count? Ten years ago, everyone said he'd become duke as soon as he came of age. Did he do something bad?"

"Oh, no, nothing like that. According to the rumors, Lord Randolph asked the current duke if he could wait a while to take over…"

Some of the higher noble families held several titles. Randolph's family was one of them—they were dukes, but they also held the Earl of Ulster title. This was called a subsidiary title, and it was typically given to the successor to the higher title before they received that title, as a matter of convenience.

"But what about…?"

"Hmph, as usual, it's impossible to figure out what that man is thinking. But never mind. We must go speak with Lily right away. She's a smart girl, so I'm certain she'll have much more useful information for us than Emilia."

"B-but that's impossible."

"You'll be fine. If you don't know her, I'll think of a way. That's my specialty, after all."

"No, it's not that; it's just…impossible."

"What's impossible? Do you mean to disobey—?"

"No!" Connie finally shouted. "Lily is dead!"

Scarlett was silent. A hush fell over the room. Unable to stand the tension, Connie looked down. After a pause, Scarlett asked, *"When?"* Her voice was strained.

"A year ago."

"Was she sick? Was there an accident?"

"No, I heard…she killed herself."

Rumor was she'd used poison. And she hadn't done it at the Ulster residence but at her own family chapel.

"You're lying."

"It's true. It was even in the papers."

Lily's suicide had livened up the capital gossip for quite some time. It had happened just after she married the Earl of Ulster, so all sorts of speculations about her untimely death had circulated. The Royal Security Force had investigated it as a possible murder but in the end had rejected that theory and declared it a suicide.

"No, I'm certain it's a lie."

"Miss Scarlett…"

Connie glanced at her, her chest tightening. She was ashamed that until a short while ago, she had never doubted that Scarlett Castiel was a veritable devil in women's clothing. After all, she had enough of a heart to grieve her friend's death, didn't she?

"It's a lie. I mean…," Scarlett practically shouted, hugging her shaking body. *"I mean, someone as wicked as Lily would never kill herself!"*

"…What?" Had she heard that right? She must have imagined it. Yes, she had to have. "Miss Scarlett?" she asked, just to be sure.

"What?"

"Miss Lily was your friend, wasn't she?"

Scarlett scowled emphatically. *"My friend? Don't say such awful things. I'd rather dance a polka while standing on my hands on the Cliffs of Hangara than get chummy with a girl like her."*

"B-but everyone says Miss Lily was the only person who kept visiting you even after you were locked up…"

According to the rumors, all the other members of Scarlett's clique turned on her at the drop of a hat, but Lily Orlamunde braved the curious stares of their acquaintances to stick by her friend until the very end.

"She kept visiting me...? Oh, that!"

Scarlett's suspicious gaze suddenly cleared. She arched her well-shaped eyebrows, and a second later, her voice rang out like a gong.

"About that! It makes me furious even to think of it! Yes, that cur did come to see me! She looked at me there behind the bars, and she ridiculed me! 'You really bungled this one, didn't you, Scarlett?' she said. Who the hell did that wicked girl think she was?"

※

"You really bungled this one, didn't you, Scarlett?"

Those were the first words out of Lily's mouth the day she came to see Scarlett on the pretext of a "visit."

Scarlett, who was fed up with being stuck in a cold stone cell, scowled at Lily. She had known this seemingly innocent girl as long as she could remember, and their exchanges had always been ironic. Every last thing about Lily irritated Scarlett. And the feeling was probably mutual.

Lily wasn't quite as beautiful as Scarlett, but she was certainly blessed with good looks. Her platinum-blond hair fell in a perfectly straight cascade against her nearly translucent white skin. Although her features weren't especially striking, they were as regular as a statue's.

She had a cold, almost artificial beauty, but the gentle smile that constantly played around her lips and her polite demeanor softened the impression. The truth was, her pale blue eyes were always as cold as ice, but Scarlett was likely the only person who ever realized that.

"That's why I always said you ought to avoid doing anything so obvious."

She sounded like a teacher scolding a slow student, which irritated Scarlett.

"What are you talking about? I can't help it. Everything I do attracts attention."

If she took one step, she was surrounded by hangers-on, and if she said a single word, the whole room fell silent to listen. That was everyday life for Scarlett. Asking her not to stand out was ridiculous.

"Tell my father to get me released from here immediately," she said, throwing a disgusted glance around her cell.

There was a bed, although it was so hard she could barely sleep on it. There was a desk and chair as well. No windows, but the guards would light the lamp if she asked. Her cell was simple but always clean.

For prisoners' quarters, it was probably top class, but to Scarlett, it was worse than a pigsty. She couldn't bear to spend another day there. She was sure her father, the duke, would do something to help. The House of Castiel was more powerful than any other family in the kingdom, save the royal family.

Lily gave an exasperated sigh as she watched Scarlett.

"You really are an idiot," she said.

"What did you just say?"

"You have an excellent memory, but unfortunately, you lack the ability to piece together information. That's what we call a wasted gift. Listen to me. If it were possible to secure your release, it would surely have already happened without the assistance of the Duke of Castiel, and moreover, you probably wouldn't have been imprisoned to start with."

"…But they can't keep me locked up here forever, can they? It's not as if I actually poisoned that woman."

"Oh, I'm sure you didn't. But that is precisely the problem. The problem is that an individual exists who is capable of entrapping a member of the Castiel family. And the even bigger problem is that after all this time, you still don't know who that individual is."

Scarlett couldn't contradict her. She had already been imprisoned for two weeks. By now, she understood her predicament—although she didn't want to admit it.

"I came today to say good-bye. I'm washing my hands of this affair. The situation is truly maddening, but it appears to be beyond me. I'm sorry, Scarlett. I really did want to help you, but…" Lily paused for a moment, tilting her head in consternation. "I care far more about saving my own neck than yours."

So saying, Lily Orlamunde flashed a smile lacking even the smallest hint of regret.

※

"And that's the whole truth. I certainly can't imagine an impudent woman like her killing herself, can you?"

Having listened to this account, Connie rested her hand against the wall of her room and let her head droop.

"You say she did charitable work because she felt so much regret over my death? Ha. I'll bet you anything she did it out of self-interest. After all, she'd been telling me since we were little how strange it was that girls and women couldn't live in the same way as boys and men. She thought it made more sense to have a meritocracy, regardless of gender. I thought that was an odd thing to say, but in the end, she used me to get what she wanted. I don't mind a little impudence, but she went too far!"

For her whole life, Connie had idolized The White Lily of Charity—loyal to the wicked Scarlett, yet always filled with dignity and integrity. But now...

"When it came to harassing Cecilia, that wicked creature was far worse than I was."

"Miss L-Lily was worse than you?"

"Oh yes. But she never dirtied her own hands. For example, if Cecilia seemed to be enjoying a conversation with Crown Prince Enrique, I'd slap her silly then and there for not knowing her place. But that would be the end of it."

"...The end of it...?"

"Lily, on the other hand, wouldn't do anything. She would simply look down with a sad expression, then murmur something admirable like, 'Poor Scarlett.' And what do you think would happen next? Her admirers would act all on their own. And that's not all—everyone present would begin to feel hostile toward Cecilia."

"Terrifying."

"It is! It's very sly, don't you think? Sly and scheming! She's not the kind of person you would want as a friend, is she? Lily Orlamunde was a levelheaded, brilliant, infuriatingly careful girl."

Connie grimaced, but Scarlett already seemed to be thinking about something else.

"…Yes, it's very odd."

"Odd?"

"Yes, odd. Odd and abnormal."

"…What is?"

"I can't imagine that Lily would kill herself. But if she did, it could only have been because something happened that she could not bring under her control."

Scarlett's amethyst eyes shimmered as she mulled over the implications.

"Try to imagine it. Does hail fall in the middle of summer? Yes, it may happen once in ten years. But it would never happen twice."

"…What do you mean?"

"I mean this must have something to do with my revenge. You think so, too, don't you, Constance Grail?!"

No, I don't, Connie thought to herself. But Queen Scarlett was brimming with so much confidence, Connie didn't say a word.

※

Several days later, Connie was standing in front of a certain orphanage, dressed in a maid's uniform.

There was a guardhouse near the front gate, so she stated her business there and asked for the doorkeeper. An elderly woman in a navy-blue nun's habit appeared. Connie silently repeated the lines she had been made to practice over and over the night before. Would she be able to say them well enough? Her legs were shaking. But when she glanced at Scarlett beside her, she looked so utterly unruffled that Connie steeled her will and opened her mouth.

"P-pardon me for coming without an appointment. I am a maid at the Marquess of Orlamunde's house. My name is *Lettie*."

She told the elderly nun that her mistress, the Marchioness of Orlamunde, wanted to make an offering of letters from the children at the orphanage on the anniversary of her daughter Lily's passing. In response, the woman smiled and readily agreed.

"I'm sure the children would be delighted to do that. They simply adored Miss Lily."

She gave no sign of suspicion about Connie's maid disguise, which stung a bit.

Connie had borrowed the clothes from Marta, telling her that she was going to Kate's house to make raspberry pie. Kate loved baking, and Connie's role was to assist her in the Lorraine kitchen and taste test her creations. She often borrowed maid's clothes that she could get dirty for this purpose, so she was able to leave home wearing the outfit without anyone suspecting her.

Scarlett was the one who had come up with the name Lettie. Needless to say, Scarlett was also the one who'd devised the entire plan.

The Maurice Home for Orphaned Children had originally been a public hospital. Many years of use finally rendered it too dilapidated to be a home for anyone, but after it closed, a church bought the building and turned it into an orphanage. The Orlamunde family had donated an immense sum of money to remodel the facility. That was one reason the orphanage had been the center of Lily's activities until her death.

Children were frolicking around the courtyard with its decorative fountain, the younger children shouting happily while the older ones wrote letters on the stationery Connie had brought.

Apparently, Lily had taught the children at the orphanage to read and write. In one corner of the courtyard was a well-used blackboard and chalk. Connie had forgotten about this aspect of Lily's work because the picture Scarlett had painted had made such an impact, but she really did think it was a wonderful endeavor.

While she waited for the children to finish their letters, Connie played with the younger ones who couldn't yet write. Of course, she put her all into it. When they played tag, she chased the children down and caught them up in her arms, then raced around holding them. When they played hopscotch, she showed off her trick of standing with her back turned and kicking the pebble with her heel into the square. In a matter of minutes, she had won the children's admiring gazes and the nickname of Hero. Even Scarlett had to admit that Connie was good at this.

When the children tired of playing, Connie asked them a question.

"Was Miss Lily kind?"

Connie had two important jobs to do at the orphanage.

"Yes!"

"Did she ever seem sad? You know, like she was worried about something?"

"No, never!"

"Really?"

One was to try to find out what had happened to Lily. That mission had just ended in failure. As Connie sat with her shoulders slumped in disappointment, she noticed that several of the older children who had finished writing their letters were watching her.

They looked somehow…scared. Strangely bothered by this, Connie was about to go over to them when Scarlett warned her against it.

"We don't have time to waste on distractions."

So the first mission was a fiasco. As for the second…

Connie wiped the sweat from her face. Then, *pretending* to slip, she dove into the fountain.

"I'm so sorry, but all we have are nun's habits. Well, we do have clothes for small children, but…"

"Oh, no, this is absolutely fine. I'm terribly sorry for causing you trouble."

In fact, that had been her aim to begin with—but she didn't say that. She simply changed out of her drenched maid's uniform and into the nun's habit with the embroidered name of the Maurice Church, collected the thank-you note from the orphanage director and the letters from the children, said her thanks, and left.

Although the sixth month of the year, Mars, was usually very rainy, the sun's rays were growing stronger every day as summer approached. That was especially true on a clear day like this one, and Connie felt the humid heat beating down on her as she walked along clasping her package.

"Now to buy the flowers."

Scarlett, on the other hand, looked cool as a cucumber. Connie guessed that she couldn't sense the heat.

"What? Right now?"

The sopping wet maid's outfit was bulkier and heavier than she'd expected, and she was worn out from playing with the children. The truth was, she wanted to go home. However, the young lady from the House of Castiel had other plans.

"Listen to me. The more time passes, the easier it becomes to see through this sort of lie. The secret to success is to finish everything up and exit the scene before you've been found out."

She nodded knowingly, as if she was speaking from experience.

"From the Maurice Orphanage, you say?"

The man looked up and scowled suspiciously at Connie.

She had come from the orphanage to the Orlamunde residence. More precisely, to the guardhouse where visitors without an appointment were received.

As for the wet maid's outfit, she'd hidden that in an alleyway across the street.

"Y-yes. I'm a maid there. My name is Co—I mean, Lettie."

She held up an envelope with the Maurice Orphanage seal on it. It contained the thank-you note she'd just received from the orphanage director. She explained that the children had desperately wanted to write letters to their beloved Miss Lily and that today she hoped to offer up their letters along with a prayer for Miss Lily. She showed off the bouquet of white flowers she'd just bought as proof.

The man took his time examining the envelope and Connie. The envelope was unmistakably from the orphanage, and the nun's habit with the insignia embroidered on the sleeve was probably the same as the ones that other nuns had worn when visiting the estate. Still, Connie felt so nervous, she worried her heart might fly right out of her mouth. With measured movements, the guard took a bundle of notes from his desk and pulled one out. Then he carefully compared it to the envelope, using a magnifying glass. After a few moments, he looked up and asked Connie to wait while he went to fetch someone from the house.

"...M-my heart was in my mouth the whole time."

Now that it seemed she would be safely admitted to the mansion, Connie—who had been sure a security officer was coming to arrest her at any moment—breathed a sigh of relief. But her heart was still pounding, and her whole body was covered in sweat.

"That went very well, I'd say."

Oblivious to Connie's emotions, Scarlett looked as excited as a child whose prank had succeeded.

After a brief wait, a butler with salt-and-pepper hair arrived at the guardhouse.

"The lady of the house is not well today and is unable to see you, but she sends her gratitude for your thoughtfulness in offering a prayer. I will show you to the chapel in her stead."

"Oh, it's Clement!" Scarlett explained. *"He looks well."*

The butler led Connie into the estate of the Marquess of Orlamunde.

The House of Orlamunde was among the most proper and pious of all the old high-noble families. Many popes hailed from their distinguished lineage, and it was said that several generations earlier, the Marquess of Orlamunde had experienced a surge of religious faith and ordered a chapel built on the grounds of the mansion, which was highly unusual.

There were several small gardens partitioned by hedges on either side of the stone pathway leading to the main building. The butler led Connie along a stream flanked by a carpet of grape hyacinths to the chapel on the edge of the gardens. The main building was farther down the same path.

Everything was just as Scarlett had said it would be: The current marchioness was very *fastidious* about purity and never fraternized with the so-called *lower classes* if she didn't have to. She would probably come up with some excuse to avoid receiving Connie in person. However, she would most likely allow her to enter the chapel on the edge of the gardens. She was as famous for her *compassion* as for her fastidiousness. She wasn't likely to harm her reputation by chasing off a nun who had come to offer prayers for her daughter.

When they arrived in front of the chapel, the butler sifted through the bundle of keys hanging at his waist, selected one, and opened the door. A cool breeze drifted from inside.

"May I offer up these flowers as well?" Connie asked.

"Of course. I'm sure the young mistress will be admiring them from heaven."

He told her to stop by the guardhouse on her way out, then left.

The chapel was small and dim. There was an altar but only enough room for a few people to worship there. Sunlight streamed in through a round stained glass skylight overhead. Dust glittered in the shaft of light. A painting of the Moirai, symbols of the church, hung on one wall. It depicted the famous myth of the three Fates.

Clothos spun the thread of life, Lachesis wove it, and Atropos cut it.

In other words, human fate was all a matter of the Moirai's whims. The painting was faded in places, but it made masterful use of light and shadow. No one who saw it could help but feel overwhelmed by its magnificence. Connie, too, reflexively brought her hands to her chest and bowed her head.

So this was where Lily Orlamunde had taken her own life.

"*It's probably behind the memorial frame— Hey, what are you doing?*" Scarlett asked, interrupting Connie's prayer. Connie looked up and was met by an exasperated stare.

"*Tell me, why do you think we came all the way here?*"

Obviously, to find out the truth about Lily's suicide. But wouldn't it be heartless to come to the place where she'd ended her life and not even offer a prayer? When Connie brought up that point with Scarlett, she snorted dismissively.

"*Idiot. Praying won't make Lily happy. If she were here, she'd probably snap at you to hurry up and figure out what really happened. I know Lily. I'm certain she left a clue here somewhere. And she probably hid it in some spiteful place no one would think of.*"

"You mean, like behind the memorial picture frame…?"

"*Yes. After all, who would think to flip over and expose this side of the people's saint?*"

Scarlett laughed boldly. She was right—but…

"This must be some kind of sin…"

"*Just as she would have liked it.*"

Scarlett shrugged. *Takes one to know one*, Connie thought and grimaced, but Scarlett ordered her to pull down the picture immediately.

The blood drained from her face in earnest this time. She'd come this far, though, so she didn't have much choice. Saying no had never been an option—in fact, it hadn't been an option since the moment she met Scarlett at the Grand Merillian.

She steeled herself. Thankfully, the picture was small enough for her to be able to grasp both sides of the frame. Still, her hands were shaking at the irreverence of it. What she was about to do felt somehow outrageous. Actually, since it was a crime, it *was* outrageous.

Her face pale, she reversed the painting. Her eyes widened.

"This is…"

A yellowed envelope was stuck to the back.

Her heart thudded unpleasantly in her ears. What was going on? Was it really a clue left behind by Lily Orlamunde? Maybe it was just a suicide note or even some sort of appraisal of the painting. Whatever it was, Connie hesitated to touch it, given she was a complete stranger. Her heart beat faster.

As she hesitated, she heard a noise outside. She jumped. The footsteps did not pass by but drew closer to the chapel.

Someone's coming!

The door creaked. *What should I do?* Her mind went blank. *What should I do? What should I do?* She couldn't move. She had no idea how to get out of her predicament.

"*Hide it! Hurry!*" Scarlett screamed.

Connie's hand jumped to yank the glued-on envelope off the frame and slip it down her dress. She practically threw the picture back onto the wall just as the door creaked open. She gasped when she saw who it was.

The man was solidly built and so tall, she had to look up to see his face. He had ocean blue eyes and hair trimmed short. His skin was deeply tanned. His shoulders were broad and muscular, and his face showed no trace of softness. His presence was so overpowering, she physically shrank from him. This frightening figure looked down on Connie with an ill-tempered expression.

"*You?!*" she heard Scarlett exclaim.

"*What are you doing here, Randolph Ulster?!*" Scarlett asked in a high-pitched voice as she took in the young man.

Randolph Ulster?

Lord Ulster? Otherwise known as His Highness the Grim Reaper? The Randolph Ulster who was a friend of the crown prince and therefore had been at odds with Scarlett? The one who had then married Lily Orlamunde?

The blood drained once again from Connie's face. Had he seen her

©Yu-nagi

putting the picture back? No, she didn't think so. Her eyes darted around, panicking. She unconsciously glanced at the picture.

"Look straight ahead, or he'll catch on to you," Scarlett hissed.

She craned her neck up at him. His masculine features and muscular build were set off by a black military uniform with a standing collar. In his hands, he held a bouquet of white lilies. When he saw Connie, he narrowed his eyes.

"Sorry. You're from the Maurice Orphanage?" he asked, studying the embroidered insignia on her habit. He spoke flatly, like someone used to giving orders. A chill ran down Connie's spine.

"…Yes."

"Brings back memories. My wife took me there a few times. I don't believe I've met you before, though."

"My name is Lettie. I've only just begun working there."

"Is that so? By the way, there was a redheaded boy I often used to play with there. George, I think it was. How is he?"

How am I supposed to know?!

Of course, she couldn't say that, so she paused for a moment to take in his words, then hesitantly replied.

"O-of course he…"

"Wait a second. He's talking about the orphanage we just visited? George had brown hair. Tony was the red-haired one in that age group," Scarlett interjected.

Connie glanced at her. Unlike her usual mocking expression, her face was serious at the moment. Strangely enough, as Connie stared into her bottomless amethyst eyes, the wild beating of her heart slowed, and she regained her composure.

"…Oh, you must mean Tony. We also have a boy named George, but his hair is nearly black."

Randolph blinked in surprise. "Ah, of course, Tony. Pardon me."

"We all make mistakes. Well, I'd better be getting back…"

She started toward the door, but as she passed Randolph, he stopped her.

"It's not safe to be out on the streets alone, Sister. If you don't mind, I'll accompany you to the orphanage."

"—Oh, you d-don't need to do that! I have several stops to make, and it's not very far anyhow! I appreciate your thoughtfulness, but I'll be fine. Good-bye!"

Before reaching for the door, she turned toward him, lifted the skirts of her habit, and curtsied. Then she hurried out of the chapel. Gradually picking up speed until she was running almost as fast as possible, she crossed through the gardens and flew out the gate without so much as a glance at the guardhouse. She slipped down a vacant alley and rested one hand on the hedge, letting out a long breath.

"That was terrifying! What a frightening man! You don't think he saw through me, do you?"

"I'm not sure. At least, I don't think you left any tracks for him to follow..."

Scarlett looked up at the Orlamunde residence.

"But that man has always had a strangely sharp nose for trouble."

※

The altar held a bouquet of baby's breath and a bundle of letters written in childish hands.

Randolph set his own bouquet of flowers next to them and, without offering a prayer, turned on his heel. As he did, he sensed something odd about the picture on the wall. Staring at it, he noticed it was very slightly off-kilter. As if someone had put it back up in a hurry.

Without a moment's hesitation, he reached out and took it down. Nothing looked unusual about the wall behind it. Which meant...

He turned the picture around. As he suspected, he could see that something had been glued to the right-hand corner, perhaps about the size of a letter. The small traces of paper still stuck to the glue were not discolored, which suggested the object had been removed very recently. And somewhat forcibly. He looked down at the floor. When he found a shred of paper the size of a fingernail clipping, he knit his brow and sighed softly.

"You say a nun was there?" asked Kyle Hughes, a subordinate of Randolph's, when he returned to the drawing room of the main house. His tone was as casual as his appearance. Like Randolph, he was wearing a military uniform, but he had unbuttoned the stiff collar just enough to look relaxed without being uncouth.

"She was dressed like one, at least," Randolph said bluntly, sitting down on a sofa. It seemed the Marchioness of Orlamunde still hadn't made an appearance.

"What do you mean?"

"Have you ever met a nun with perfect pronunciation and not a blemish on her hands, who curtsies like a lady when she says good-bye?"

"...I see your point." Rudely resting his elbows on the table, Kyle bit into a cookie that had been set out for guests. "Everything's a mess these days, what with the incident at the Grand Merillian the other night and all."

"...Speaking of which, have you found out anything about the girl who broke off her engagement?"

When he first heard about the incident, Randolph hadn't been very interested, so he hadn't looked into it. But he figured that Kyle, who liked gossip, would know something. As predicted, Kyle grinned.

"Don't be shocked—but it was the Grail girl."

"Grail? Those beacons of sincerity?"

Randolph knit his brow at this unexpected information.

Kyle laughed dryly. "Yes, the ever-sincere Grails."

The family were typical nobles, known to anyone in the higher social circles.

"Have you ever met her?"

"We've never spoken, but I've seen her a few times."

"Hazelnut hair and green eyes, was it?"

"Yes—have you met her yourself?"

Randolph gazed out the window. The drawing room was the pride of the Orlamunde house, with a row of tall, thin windows overlooking the gardens. He could glimpse the stone chapel through the trees.

"I just did."

※

The maid outfit Connie had hidden in the alley was still right where she'd left it. She asked Scarlett to keep watch for her, then quickly changed back into it in the shade of a tree. Despite the early-summer sun, she shivered at the touch of the cold, wet fabric.

Scarlett told her to throw away the nun's habit, but Connie hesitated to be so callous toward the goodness of the orphanage staff. All the same, she couldn't return it in person wearing her disguise. As a last resort, she decided to leave it at the door along with money to have it washed.

"…Miss, what are you doing?"

As Connie was attempting to squeeze the habit between the heavy iron bars of the gate, unusual for an orphanage, she heard someone calling her. She turned around to see a group of familiar faces. They were the older boys who had written letters for Lily at the orphanage. From the trowels and hammers in their hands, she guessed they were returning from apprenticeships at some factory or another.

Their expressions struck her as odd. All of them looked frightened. They were afraid—of Connie? She remembered that they had had the same look earlier that day. When Connie was asking the younger children about Lily, they had clearly looked nervous. What could they be worried about?

A boy with fiery red hair took a step forward, as if to guard his companions. He glared at her, his expression intentionally stiff.

"Kiriki kirikuku."

Connie could see that the children were watching her with bated breath. The words must have some important meaning for them. Connie panicked. She had no idea what they meant.

"Ki, kirikuki?"

Was it a foreign language? Could they tell she was flustered? Gradually, the tension lightened until finally the children began exchanging relieved looks. "I told you so!" "Tony's just a worrywart." "Shut up, who cares?" they said, jostling one another.

One, a boy with black hair, ran over to Connie.

"Miss, did you give our letters to Miss Lily?"

She nodded, and the boy smiled. She wondered if she had imagined the tension of a moment earlier. Connie smiled back.

"Hey, what was that you said a minute ago?" she asked the red-haired boy, who was scratching his head.

He hesitated for a moment, then looked her straight in the eye and said softly, "...A spell."

"A spell?!"

That sounded scary. Did kids these days cast spells or something?

"Yes. It's supposed to show you who the bad guys are. Miss Lily taught it to us."

Connie gasped, then blinked slowly. "...When?"

"Before she died."

The boy with red hair—Tony—looked like he didn't quite know what to say.

"Miss Lily said that if *something* happened to her, we should say the spell to anyone who came around asking about her."

Midday was long past, and the crimson sun was sinking low in the sky.

"And she said if they reacted even a tiny bit, then that meant they were very bad people."

Saint Mark's Bell tolled in the distance, signaling the closing of the palace gates. It would take a while before the area got dark. The half circle of the sun was directly behind Connie and the kids. In a while, the lengthening shadows would melt into darkness.

Night was coming.

When Tony spoke again, he looked as if he was going to cry.

"She said if that happened, I was supposed to take everyone and run away."

Marta looked quite surprised to see Connie return in wet maid's clothing. Connie said she'd fallen in the road, but she doubted that Marta believed her. She sensed that Marta wanted to ask her something, but she wouldn't have been able to answer her if she had.

From start to finish, not one of Constance Grail's actions that day had been sincere.

She went silently to her room. For some reason, she was utterly exhausted.

She still had the envelope with her. Scarlett, who had been quiet until now, finally spoke up.

"Let's open it."

Connie nodded. By this point, she wasn't about to insist that it was insincere to read other people's letters.

As she opened the seal, she glimpsed something gray. A key. It was entirely utilitarian, without a single decoration. The top part was round, with a hole in the middle, and the end was jagged like a piece of a gear.

"There's something else inside," Scarlett said.

Connie turned the envelope upside down. Something white fluttered onto the floor. A scrap of paper. Small letters were printed on it, as if it had been torn from a book. Several words had also been written on the paper with a pen. Connie squinted. The letters were sloppy, as if they'd been written in a hurry. In places they were blurry, but she could just barely make out the words.

This was the sole clue Lily Orlamunde had left behind. It consisted of a single sentence.

Destroy the Holy Grail of Eris.

"The Holy Grail of Eris…?"
Connie's soft voice faded into the dimness of her room.

Constance Grail

Age sixteen, wants "sincerity" to be her motto. Carelessly becomes Scarlett Castiel's accomplice in revenge and honestly wishes she could pull out. ←**new!**

Scarlett Castiel

Extremely pissed off, eternally sixteen years old. Desperately wants revenge but, ridiculously enough, doesn't know who to take it on, which is like raising an arm to hit someone and being unable to lower it, bingo wings swinging. ←**new!** Now that everyone she knew is married, dead, etc., she feels like Rip Van Winkle.

Kate Lorraine

Sixteen. Baron's daughter. Fluffy chestnut hair and eyes. Plump, well-endowed. Not bad-looking but doesn't have a boyfriend. Only knows about love from novels.

Emilia Godwin

Formerly Emilia Caroling. Scarlett thinks she's an ostentatious idiot. (Look who's talking.)

Randolph Ulster

Twenty-six. Black hair, cerulean eyes. Also known as His Excellency the Grim Reaper. Vaguely terrifying.

Kyle Hughes

Coworker of His Excellency the Grim Reaper. Vaguely playboy-ish.

Lily Orlamunde

Probably twenty-four or so when she died. Believed to have committed suicide by poison in the chapel of her family home. Has the slightly embarrassing nickname The White Lily of Charity. Apparently not at all white-lily-like in reality. Wicked but seemingly wants to improve women's social standing. Strictly speaking, last name Ulster, but everyone still uses Orlamunde because she died less than a year after marrying. Left a bewildering message when she died, throwing everyone into chaos. ←**new!**

Also, something about kiriki kirikuku.

Countess Emanuel's ball was a smashing success.

Needless to say, the topic on everyone's lips was the *hunt* that had taken place at the recent ball in the Grand Merillian. All the attendees were dying to hear the funny story about the wounded fox that the hunters had pursued in turn. The most hilarious part was that, according to rumor, Pamela Francis's hair had turned as white as an old lady's in a single night.

Of course, everyone knew that was just an embellishment to make the story better. But that also meant it was now considered acceptable to treat Pamela in this way.

And so Emilia laughed to her heart's content. In the end, that cheeky little brat had been reduced to a dog with her tail between her legs.

The person no one could make sense of was Constance Grail. Everyone at the party was raising a fuss about how that insignificant viscount's daughter was just like Scarlett. And that was no joke. Scarlett Castiel had truly been without parallel.

She was the worst of the worst—but she was also special in a way that no one else was.

Anyway, it didn't matter. Emilia shook her head to clear away the distracting thoughts. Why waste time thinking about someone who was dead?

In life, the survivors were the winners. Emilia believed that very much. It meant she was a winner. She had snatched happiness for herself. More happiness than Lily Orlamunde ever had, although Emilia wouldn't even have been able to kiss her feet ten years ago, let alone Scarlett Castiel herself.

Emilia's ball was coming up soon. She had sent an invitation to the overly sincere Grail girl. If the figure at the eye of the storm showed up, there was no question Emilia's ball would be a success. Her snobby guests would praise her to the skies.

Ten years had passed since Scarlett was executed. Ten years had passed, too, since Emilia had married her husband as a means of escape. She had given birth to two sons in that time. That should be enough to fulfill her wifely duties. Wasn't it about time for her to spread her wings as a woman in her own right?

"Good evening, Emilia."

The abrupt greeting came from Aisha Huxley. Her face was made up with heavy eyeliner and dark-red lipstick. She was still as skinny as a stick. Ten years ago, her freckled face had always been turned sullenly downward, but people change. There was no trace left of the strange girl who had once blindly worshipped Scarlett.

"Good evening, Aisha. Oh my!"

A tall, handsome man was standing next to Aisha. Aisha giggled in satisfaction at Emilia's momentary stunned silence, tilting her head as if to ask, *Notice something?*

"My special friend," she said triumphantly.

All Emilia could manage was a stiff "oh?"

Like Emilia, Aisha was married. She had one son and one daughter. Aisha was the daughter of the Earl of Spencer, if Emilia remembered correctly, but she had married into Viscount Huxley's family. Which put her in approximately the same position as Emilia herself, a baroness. In fact, the Godwins were better off financially, and when it came to looks, she thought herself more attractive than the sickly, skinny Aisha. So why…?

She watched the man as she sipped a cocktail in the grand hall. His even features naturally drew the eye, as did his elegant attire. She couldn't help following every move he made with her eyes.

Aisha hadn't told her anything about the man. Emilia had never seen him in society before. He must be some low-ranking quasi-noble. Perhaps he was even a commoner. This thought did nothing to raise Emilia's spirits. It was humiliating. To think that someone like Aisha had snagged such a good-looking man! *I can do better than she can—*

Before she knew it, she had handed her empty glass to a waiter and followed the man upstairs.

She found herself in an abandoned hallway. Just as she was about to call out to him, she noticed that someone had beaten her to it. She slipped into the shadow of a pillar.

The woman wasn't Aisha. She was younger and prettier. *Isn't that the only daughter of the Marquess of Grafton, who owns the wharf in the suburbs of the capital? Kiara, I think it was.* Emilia smiled wickedly. Just as she suspected.

A man like that would never take Aisha seriously.

Emilia watched the scene with the relish of a child plucking the wings from a butterfly.

The woman nestled up to the man and sighed into his ear:

"Kiriki kirikuku."

When he heard the words, the man narrowed his eyes and smiled. His bony finger traced her earlobe. They gazed into each other's eyes, and when his face was close enough to kiss her, he whispered something. The woman nodded. He kissed her, the smile still on his mouth. Her forehead, her cheeks, her neck. Then he grabbed the neckline of her plunging gown and brought his lips to her chest.

He could hardly contain himself, it seemed. The woman's exposed white breast was tattooed with an image of the sun. Emilia had heard that Miss Grafton's conduct wasn't exactly pristine, but now she wondered if she was an actual whore.

Instantly losing interest, Emilia was about to sneak off when she glimpsed something shiny.

A little bottle?

With a well-practiced gesture, the man pulled a vessel the size of his pointer finger from her cleavage and stepped away from her. The woman rearranged her disheveled gown, still smiling.

Then, as if nothing at all had happened, they turned their backs on each other and walked off.

What in the world just happened?

No sooner did the question occur to Emilia than it vanished again. Her priority right now was Aisha. What mattered was that she'd caught Aisha's gentleman meeting secretly with a beautiful young woman. She must tell Aisha about it right away. As a friend, of course.

She looked up. Kiara Grafton was walking innocently toward her. Although Emilia had recognized her, they'd never talked. Their eyes met for an instant, and then, without so much as a nod, she walked past.

As she did, Emilia inhaled a saccharine, flowery scent.

I know that smell...

She looked over her shoulder at the woman. What was that scent? She traced the memory and, after a moment, arrived at an answer.

Oh yes, Paradise!

She was certain that's what they'd called it ten years ago.

Emilia Godwin

Probably twenty-five or -six. Has children. Thinks survivors win in the game of life. Unclear whether she knows what happened ten years ago. Wants her day in the sun. Calls Aisha a friend, but definitely not a friend.

Aisha Huxley

Probably twenty-five or -six. Skinny as a stick. Has debuted in society in the worst sense.

The Handsome Man

Introduced as Aisha's lover. Pursued by Emilia because he's handsome, but she gave up after finding him with a younger woman. Took a small bottle from the woman and vanished.

Kiara Grafton

Has a sun tattoo on her chest. Was making out with the handsome man but walked off casually after giving him the bottle. What the hell is this business with kiriki kirikuku? Gives off a saccharine smell.

Destroy the Holy Grail of Eris.

Those were not peaceful words. But whatever could the *Holy Grail of Eris* be?

Connie didn't have a clue. Thinking there might be some hint in the text, she examined the scrap of paper again, but the only things written on it had to do with the climate and geography of the kingdom. It seemed to have come from some sort of tourist brochure produced by the city hall. The kind of thing you could pick up anywhere.

"Do you have any idea what this means?" she asked Scarlett.

"Not a clue," she answered, shrugging. "But in the Myth of Faris, Eris is the goddess of discord and strife. She is a wicked deity said to have once driven a kingdom to utter ruin. Back when I used to go out on the town undercover, Eris was the name I used."

Although she added the last bit casually, Connie latched on to it. It was scary how well it seemed to suit her.

The Kingdom of Adelbide where Connie lived had once been a territory of the Faris Empire, a monumental aggressor that had at one point been on the verge of swallowing up the entire continent. Faris had taken advantage of turbulent times to seize control of governance, and because of Adelbide's location in the east, it had been named the Principality of East Faris. Later, when the empire began to decline, the Grand Duke of Amadeus claimed the title of New King and renamed the territory Adelbide, becoming its founding father. This happened about a few centuries earlier.

This was also the era in which the Grail family's own founding father, Percival Grail, had lived. This history explained why so many things—including Adelbide's language as well as much of its culture and customs—were rooted in those of the former empire. The Myth of Faris was among them.

"I think the Holy Grail comes up in the old myths, too, as some sort of sacred object that brings happiness and prosperity to the land. It was originally a vessel of good harvests, with healing powers."

Ruin and prosperity, strife and healing. Connie felt as if the Holy Grail of Eris must possess two completely opposite natures.

"You mean…this evil goddess brings blessings?" Connie asked.

But then why would Lily be telling them to destroy it?

Scarlett drew her brows together in thought but seemed to arrive at no answer. She sighed, apparently giving up.

"What about the key?" Scarlett asked.

Connie shook her head listlessly, looking at the simple skeleton key in her palm. P10E3, the model number needed for reproducing the key, was imprinted on the top part, but the all-important crest of the workshop that had produced it was missing. Without that, it would be impossible to search for the vault or storehouse it opened. Nothing was working in their favor.

"Normally, you'd think…," Connie began, crossing her arms and choosing her words carefully, "…that this is a key to the Holy Grail of Eris, and that's what we're supposed to destroy."

Normally, of course.

"Yes. But unfortunately, Lily wasn't normal."

She was absolutely right. Connie gripped her head in frustration.

Connie felt like she was going to get a fever from thinking so much—or maybe she already had one.

It was past noon by the time she woke up; all the exertion of the previous day was partly to blame. Sunlight beat down into her room. She touched her forehead, but it wasn't hot. Bewildering.

With nothing else to do, she went down to the living room. As she was sipping a cup of hot tea, the servants suddenly began rushing around. It seemed an unexpected visitor had arrived.

After a few minutes, Marta, the head maid, came into the room. For some reason, she looked furious, and her already-stout form seemed even more puffed up than usual with indignation.

"Marta, what's wrong? Judging by your face, has Father gone and done something intolerably sincere again?"

"We have a guest."

Connie knew that. That was when she started to feel uneasy. Why had Marta come to her about it? Who was this guest? She had a bad feeling. Her mouth suddenly went dry, and in an attempt to calm herself, she brought her cup to her lips.

"Sir Neil Bronson is here."

Connie spewed out the sip of tea in her mouth. Marta held up a handkerchief for her.

"Neil?!"

"Yes. He said he wanted to apologize to you. What shall I do? Would you like me to kick that shameless, fetid pustule straight out the front door? Or shall I punch him in the face? Or perhaps you'd like me to chop him to pieces?"

"What horrid choices you've given me!" Connie exclaimed, but the truth was that she *didn't* want to see him. She had no idea how to act toward him now. She didn't need his apology. An apology wouldn't bring her back to blissful ignorance of his unfaithfulness.

She decided to turn him away. Just as she was about to say so, however, an unexpected voice rang in her ears.

"Oh, it's fine. Just meet with him."

Scarlett sounded as casual as if she was telling Connie to go say hello to an old friend.

What?! She shot her a reproachful glance, but of course no look from Connie could make Scarlett flinch.

"After all, you're still bothered by the fact that he cheated on you, aren't you? You really ought to talk it out. You won't feel better until you do."

"Ugh."

She had no retort for Scarlett's surprisingly sound advice.

"Also," Scarlett continued, *"I had a look in your closet just now, and you haven't got a single proper dress in there even though Emilia's ball is just around the corner. The Bronson Company carries dresses and accessories, don't they? This is the perfect opportunity for you to extract something from Neil Bronson in place of monetary compensation."*

Connie pushed her stray hairs into place and headed for the drawing room. Neil was already waiting for her. His eyes widened when she came in.

"…I didn't think you'd actually meet with me."

Connie felt exactly the same way.

"You really are a sincere Grail."

To tell the truth, I had no desire to see you, she thought—but didn't say that. Instead, she smiled and looked away.

Neil seemed to have lost a few pounds since she last saw him a few days earlier. The exhaustion was evident on his face.

"I heard you were under confinement…"

"I am. I received special dispensation to leave the house to visit you," he admitted.

"…Oh, I see. I'm sorry I kept you waiting. You waltzed in here unannounced."

She figured she could get away with this much sass, but when she looked at him, he was smiling uncomfortably, like he'd accidentally put salt in his tea.

"I know it was rude of me, but I thought you'd turn me down if I asked first."

Then he apologized.

"What I did to you was inexcusable. I've ended things with Pamela. She's paid plenty for her crime. I think right now, she's probably in the provinces, reflecting on what she did."

"*Idiot!*" Scarlett suddenly broke in. "*That sort of woman would never admit she's done something wrong. You'd be a fool to think she's learned her lesson!*"

There was something peculiarly convincing in the boldness of her declaration. Connie glanced at her. *Interesting.*

The girl standing in front of her had been executed—and apparently still hadn't learned her lesson.

"Father offered financial assistance as the very minimum in terms of compensation, but Viscount Grail wouldn't take it."

Connie froze in surprise. She hadn't heard anything about that.

Scarlett scoffed. "*Of course he did. You're a businessman. When things go wrong, you offer a bribe. What do you mean, assistance? The very thought of a commoner with the veneer of baronet giving a handout to a viscount is unbelievable! Know your place, man!*"

Connie wasn't sure if her father had shared the same sentiments as Scarlett, but she could see why he hadn't told her about it. And why he'd refused the offer.

He hadn't wanted to burden Connie any more. She looked down, burdened instead by a sense of responsibility.

"You wouldn't consider forgiving me, would you?" Neil squeaked out.

"…What?"

"No, you don't have to forgive me. But I do hope that you will direct your anger at me alone. I beg you not to bring the Bronson Company into it."

"…What?!"

"Ever since the ball, the masses have started to boycott the company. Someone broke the glass in our headquarters, too. This is all your doing, isn't it, Constance?"

"…What?!?!"

"I'm not trying to interrogate you. You have a right to be angry. It's only natural. I'm the one in the wrong here. But you're going too far. This issue is between you and me. I want you to leave the business out of it. My grandfather is bedridden from the shock."

Connie herself felt like retreating to bed in shock.

She couldn't even speak. Her chest was bursting with sorrow and anger. Did Neil really think she would do something like that?

Did he think she was that kind of person?

Connie bit her lip and stared straight ahead.

"...I didn't do it."

She felt like she was reliving the incident at the Grand Merillian. She was being interrogated for a crime completely without grounds.

"But..."

The difference now was that she had the will to fight back. She was sad. She was hurt. She was furious. But strangely enough, she was not afraid.

"I swear on the name of Percival Grail the First, I did not do it."

Constance Grail looked Neil Bronson straight in the eye and flatly denied his accusation. Neil gasped.

For a member of the Grail family, swearing on the name of Percival Grail the First was equivalent to putting their life at stake. It was something they almost never did—and always meant when they did do it. Neil had known the Grails long enough to know that.

"Then why...?"

For a moment, his face had been uncertain, but it quickly twisted in distress.

"Oh my!" Scarlett exclaimed, floating into the air. "The Bronsons do rely on the lower nobility for their business."

A giggle spilled from her lips, ripe and red like fruit.

"Perhaps he didn't apologize in quite the right way. Even after three generations, I suppose he might not truly understand what it means to deal with the nobility."

Confused, Connie shot Scarlett a questioning look. She grinned.

"The masses aren't mad for Constance Grail. They're simply irritated that a family of **upstarts** is trying to twist the eminent nobles around their fingers. Now they've *found a wonderful cause to cover up their nastiness. Perhaps the situation roused their lower-noble complex? Humans are frightening creatures."* She giggled.

Connie wondered if she was right. The truth was, she didn't understand it. But since she couldn't let his false accusation stand, she parroted Scarlett's words.

"That's just…," Neil said, going pale. Since he didn't try to argue with her, however, she assumed it must ring true for him. The criminal wasn't Connie but rather his own customers—he couldn't hide his shock at this revelation. His face was so white, she thought he was going to keel over then and there.

There was only one thing she could say to him in this situation.

"…Is there anything I can do?"

An awkward silence passed.

"What? You want to help him?" Scarlett scoffed.

"You'll help me?" Neil said at exactly the same time. Connie shuddered.

"I mean, the Bronson Company hasn't done anything wrong."

They'd simply been caught up in the storm. Connie didn't know what everyone else thought, but at the very least, the Grail family logic—or rather, her own—told her that was the case.

"…This is disgusting. He's made this mess himself, and you don't need to fix it for him."

Of course, Scarlett was correct that Neil Bronson was unquestionably the guilty party here, and if she wanted to, she could punch him in the face right this second. She could smash that innocent-looking nose right into the floor. Constance Grail—and only Constance Grail—had every right to do that.

"…Constance," Neil said, looking at her in confusion. Connie shook her head as if to say, *Don't take this the wrong way.*

"I'm not doing this for you. I'm doing it for the people who are suffering because of your actions."

All of this had begun with the incident at the ball, so in a sense, Connie did bear a scrap of responsibility.

Scarlett's eyebrows were practically at her hairline.

"…You're *such* an idiot! What on earth can a fool like you do to help him…? Oh, it's intolerable…but it can't be helped. Who's your best customer, little upstart?!" Scarlett shrieked, poking him. Needless to say, he didn't notice her. Connie had no choice but to translate.

"Um, who is the Bronson Company's most valued customer?"

"The Countess of Custine…," Neil answered, looking suspicious at the abrupt question. Scarlett instantly began spouting off.

"So that show-off is still alive, is she?! Well, that makes things easy. You deal in Lucca silk, don't you? Take the very best of it and have a dress made up at a good place—the Moonlight Fairy would be perfect. Be sure to have it embroidered. Make it as intricate and ostentatious as possible. Have them use plenty of gold thread, too. When it's complete, get down on one knee and offer it up to her, begging for her mercy. Make sure you sound pitiful."

Scarlett stared into Neil's face.

"You're fairly good-looking, so you ought to do it yourself. It's important to be obsequious. She may very well whisk you off to her bedroom, and you must be prepared for that. She's rumored to be very skilled in that *department, so if you're lucky, she'll take you to paradise. That should be enough to smooth things over. Old hags like her have a fair amount of influence…and sweet little Constance Grail doesn't have to lift a finger!"*

The Countess of Custine sounded terrifying. Connie grimaced but nevertheless suggested this to Neil as a method of apology sometimes used by nobles. When she got to the part about the bedroom, she kept her eyes glued to the floor.

As for Neil's virtue, that was a matter for the Countess of Custine and the gods alone to decide.

"…I see. I'll bring it up with Father," Neil replied, then gazed at Connie with what seemed to be a conflicted look.

She looked straight back at him.

Neil was the first to look away.

He bowed deeply to her. "I truly am sorry."

As she watched him, Connie made up her mind to tell him something she'd never shared with anyone.

"Do you remember the first time we met?"

He had been wearing a shirt with a stiffly starched collar and an ivory vest. She could tell at a glance that the young man Damian Bronson had brought to the Grail house was elegant and handsome, and that made her feel terribly timid.

She'd scarcely been able to greet him properly, but Neil hadn't smiled or made fun of her for being so plain and dowdy. Of course, she didn't know what he'd been thinking—and she'd kept her eyes down, because she didn't want to know.

As she cowered there, unsure what to do, she heard someone speaking to her. *"Me too."*

The words sounded uncontrived, as if they'd flown unbidden from his mouth.

Connie looked up in surprise. Neil had the same awkward expression on his face as she did. *"Actually, I'm nervous, too."*

Connie blinked, and then they both smiled at the same time.

That had probably been enough for her to fall in love.

"At that moment, I thought to myself how lucky I was that such a wonderful person was going to become my husband. But you probably didn't share this sentiment… At first, I didn't believe the rumors about Pamela, and it hurt, but now I understand a little. It's not entirely your fault that things turned out like this. It's fine. I'm over it."

The next words came naturally.

"Good-bye, Neil Bronson."

She had loved him, but not enough to cry over. So she was fine. She grinned. Although the tip of her nose did tingle just the slightest bit.

"…I completely missed my chance to ask for a dress," Connie mumbled as she watched Marta evict Neil from the premises with feigned politeness. Scarlett narrowed her eyes as if she couldn't care less.

"Excellent decision not to take a dress from a tasteless man like that. I'm sure he would have sent you something horrid," she declared. Her indifferent tone was so thoroughly Scarlett-like that Connie just stood there sniffling, unsure whether to laugh or cry.

※

Kate Lorraine lifted the brass boar's-head knocker and rapped it on the door. After a moment, the familiar face of the Grail family's maid, Marta, appeared. Kate held out the present she'd brought with her.

"I baked a raspberry pie," she said.

Raspberry pie was the Lorraine family specialty, and it could be made only in the month of Mars. It was her friend's favorite, and she hoped it would lift her gloom over the broken engagement. She'd spent the whole morning holed up in the kitchen baking it.

Marta gave her a bewildered look. "Raspberry pie? But Miss Connie just baked one with you a few days ago."

"She did?"

There was a silence. Marta's expression grew steadily more suspicious. Kate widened her eyes and clapped her hands, scrambling to save the moment.

"Oh yes, right! The thing we did the other day! That's what you meant! I forgot all about it! Yes, Connie and I baked a raspberry pie together at my house!"

※

"...And?"

Kate was looking fixedly at Connie.

"When exactly did I bake a raspberry pie with you?"

The buttery, flaky, slightly salty crust was a perfect match for the filling of raspberries simmered with sugar to jammy perfection. It wasn't too sweet or too heavy, and Connie always ended up demolishing the whole thing.

Sitting before this bewitching baked good, Connie paused her fork in midair.

"No, um, I mean…"

She glanced around nervously. Kate frowned in exasperation at her careless friend.

"It's so like you to miss these details! I did tell Marta you came to my house, but I don't know if she bought it!"

"Tha—"

"But what's this all about? Since you used me as your alibi, I assume you're going to explain yourself?"

"Uh…"

She couldn't exactly tell her the truth, which was that she needed a maid's outfit to fool the innocent people at the orphanage. Connie grimaced, searching desperately for an excuse.

"Um, it's just that I wanted to be by myself…?"

Unfortunately, the explanation that came out of her mouth was unbelievably shabby. She was doomed.

"Really now," Kate said, squinting at her. Her voice was scarily devoid of emotion.

"Um, Kate…," she said reflexively, but no more words followed. As Connie was panicking over what to do next, Kate broke the silence with a loud sigh.

"Oh, it's fine."

Connie looked up, surprised by her friend's calm tone. Kate was frowning at her. Her eyes were filled not with anger or accusation but instead with pure concern.

"I won't ask you any more about it until you're ready to talk. So you'd better tell me if you need help."

"Kate…"

Her heart was full of both remorse and affection.

Kate smiled mischievously.

"But next time, I'm not going to cover for you!"

*   *   *

Evening arrived before she knew it.

Connie examined herself in the mirror: There was the dull hazelnut hair, the green eyes, and the entirely ordinary face. Nevertheless, wearing a pale blue dress, with her hair up and a hint of makeup on, she looked quite a bit more eye-catching than usual.

"We managed to make you presentable, I think."

Scarlett smiled with satisfaction. She had turned the house upside down looking for clothes and jewelry, and what she found seemed made-to-order for Connie. Normally Connie had the maids do her makeup, but tonight she followed Scarlett's instructions to the letter. She'd applied emerald powder to her eyelids and a brighter-than-usual blush to her cheeks. She topped her light-colored lipstick with honey. Now she was finally ready.

Tonight was the night of Emilia Godwin's ball.

"Oh, my dear, you look even prettier than usual tonight!"

Percival Ethel Grail's imposingly bearlike face dissolved into an indulgent smile. He praised his beloved daughter for a few more minutes before a distant look suddenly came into his eyes, and he murmured in a voice thick with emotion.

"To think that my shy daughter stood up to Neil Bronson, and now here you are going off to a ball on your own initiative... Watching you grow into such a kind, strong young woman is just...just...!"

Overwhelmed with feeling, he dabbed his eyes and looked up at the ceiling. His wife, who seemed to have appeared at his side out of nowhere, rubbed his broad back and whispered soothingly to him.

Connie's mother, Aria Grail, was a beautiful woman, with green eyes and wavy golden hair. When she saw her daughter looking so different from usual, she brought her hand to her cheek and tilted her head.

"My, my. Make sure you don't have too much fun tonight, now."

Connie stiffened, wondering what, exactly, her mother meant. But Aria just smiled gently.

"Connie!"

"Oof!"

In a flash, Connie's little brother, Percival Layli, had thrown his arms around her stomach. He was almost ten, and with his mother's aquamarine eyes and golden curls, he was as pretty as an angel.

He looked up at his sister with sparkling eyes.

"Ooh, you look so pretty today!"

What was that supposed to mean, *today*? She didn't know how to take that. Of course, since Connie was a lady, she would never poke at a thicket where she knew snakes were hiding.

"I heard about Neil Bronson. I'm glad you got rid of that terrible man! I'll knock him out for you next time I see him! Bam! Just like that!"

"Uh…"

"And don't worry about the money. I'm sure that if you do the right thing, the three Fates will show us the way forward."

Connie nodded at her brother, but she felt suddenly uncomfortable— even though the old Connie would have unquestioningly agreed with him.

"Connie?"

Layli was a good boy. A *sincere* boy.

Her expression must have become suddenly harsh, because Layli was looking at her uncertainly. Snapping back to the present, Connie ruffled his soft curls and smiled. "It's nothing," she said.

A moment later, Marta came in to tell her the carriage was waiting.

"Are you ready, Constance?" Scarlett asked melodically. Their ride was outside the open doors.

The sky was dark and heavy, as if it had been blotted out with a thick layer of black oil paint. Connie's hem fluttered in the night breeze.

Scarlett turned toward her with evident pleasure.

"And now, the beginning of a delightful night!"

Her amethyst eyes sparkled as brightly as if a treasure chest were buried in their depths.

※

Emilia Godwin was in excellent spirits.

The hall was filled with a pleasant din, and her guests were overflowing with praise for her. The reason, of course, was Constance Grail. The girl of the moment had made an appearance for the first time since the incident at the Grand Merillian—here at Emilia Godwin's own ball. Constance had chosen Emilia for this honor, despite the fact that Emilia was neither a countess nor a viscountess, but only a baroness. This tickled her pride immensely.

That wasn't all. She wasn't sure where they'd heard about it, but *a certain someone* had also asked to attend the ball. It must have been ten years since they had talked. Her heart was aflutter. Emilia had always secretly looked up to this person who was consistently fair and never looked down on anyone because of their low rank.

She had Constance Grail to thank for all of this. So when the girl came over to greet Emilia, she couldn't help blinking. What a disappointment. True, she looked a bit more elegant than Emilia remembered, but she was still the ordinary kind of girl you could find just about anywhere.

Her fashion sense wasn't bad. She carried herself quite beautifully as well. Of course, she was nothing like Scarlett… Suddenly, she realized she was comparing this insignificant girl to Scarlett Castiel and froze. Why had the thought even occurred to her? As she stood there trying to suppress her discomfort, Constance Grail curtsied to her. Emilia gaped.

The gesture was just like Scarlett's.

The shape of her fingers when she held up her hem…her perfectly straight back…the timing with which she moved her foot back…her expression when she cast her eyes down and lifted her face…all of it was a mirror image of Scarlett. That woman had been wicked inside, but on the surface, she was more graceful than anyone else on earth.

"Good evening, Emilia Caroling."

Her voice had always been as airy as a chime, and her first words were as predictable as a script.

"What a lovely dress you have on tonight. It sets off your sunflower locks perfectly."

Emilia had taken that to mean that *only* her dress was lovely, and she had always had a complex about her hair, which was more like yellow paint than gold. For that reason, she'd hated Scarlett's standard greeting. She'd hated it and found it so frightening, she would shrink away from Scarlett whenever she heard it.

"Thank you for inviting me tonight, Lady Godwin."

What unpleasant memories. Emilia bit her lip and decided to cheer herself up by taking it out on the girl standing in front of her. That's why she had invited her in the first place. The nail that stuck out got hammered down. The only ones who survived were those who didn't flinch when they were hammered. Which category did this girl fall into? Would she break like Pamela Francis, or—?

"What a lovely dress you have on tonight. It sets off your sunflower locks…perfectly, Lady Godwin."

Emilia looked at her in shock. She had precisely the same innocent smile on her face that Scarlett used to have.

※

Had she made some sort of mistake? Connie racked her brain.

She was certain her curtsy and manner were presentable, thanks to Scarlett's ruthless training, and she'd perfectly carried off the greeting that Scarlett had promised had always made Emilia *so happy* in the past.

So why had Lady Godwin gone white as a sheet and walked off without saying a word? Scarlett burst out laughing when it happened.

"She's still as cowardly as ever," Scarlett announced, although Connie wasn't sure what she meant to imply. Connie glanced at her, but Scarlett just shrugged and looked innocent. *"All I did was make it easier for you to get information from her later."*

But if this method was causing her to run away, wasn't Scarlett getting her priorities wrong? Of course, Connie could never say that to Scarlett's face.

For a while after that, Connie was treated like an exotic animal in a show tent.

The gentlemen's greetings somehow had a whiff of poison to them. The young women whispered among themselves loudly enough for her to hear. The noblewomen dropped sarcastic comments as they passed her.

As they'd planned ahead of time, Connie let Scarlett manipulate her like a puppet. From her restraint when people talked behind her back to her responses to the sarcastic comments and the timing of her smiles, she relied on Scarlett for everything. Otherwise, she might have broken down under the pressure.

"*I think you passed,*" Scarlett said, surveying the ballroom as if she were trying to imprint it permanently in her memory.

It had occurred to Connie before that Scarlett had a good memory. Now she was certain of it. She must have some sort of grand palace in her mind where she stored her memories. She was meeting most of the guests at tonight's ball for the first time, but without exception, she remembered not only their names and faces but every other point that came up in conversation, from their domains to their hobbies.

Connie was taking a break from chitchat to have a glass of chilled fruit water when she spotted Emilia Godwin in a corner of the ballroom. She was talking to a noblewoman Connie didn't know. The woman was skinny as a stick. Neither of them was smiling. Both were holding fans over their mouths and glancing repeatedly in her direction. Emilia looked as if she had seen a ghost. Bewildering.

"*...Is that Aisha Spencer? Why, she's changed completely,*" Scarlett muttered. "*I didn't know those two were friends. But this is a good opportunity. We'll go talk to both of them at once.*"

Connie didn't really want to, but she didn't have much choice. Just as she took a step in their direction, however, she was interrupted by loud voices.

"What did you say?" The strained voice rang out across the ballroom. "Would you mind repeating that one more time?"

"I'd be happy to tell you a hundred times, Teresa. I'm quite appalled by your husband. It seems he'll never tire of spending his nights at the whorehouse. The women in the Ladies' Association can't stop gossiping about him. They say Kevin Jennings is giving noblesse oblige a bad name. My husband works with him at the royal palace, and even he is keeping his distance. I do wish you'd do something about it."

Two noblewomen were facing off. The one with the tense expression was average-looking, while the one who was berating her was a beautiful woman with defined features.

"Who are they?" Connie asked.

"Teresa Jennings and Margot Tudor. The two of them came over to greet you a few minutes ago—don't you remember?" Scarlett replied smoothly. Now that she mentioned it, Connie did remember them, mainly because the combination of the strong-willed beauty and the self-effacing woman in her shadow seemed unusual. She hadn't remembered their names, of course.

Their exchange wasn't loud enough for everyone at the ball to hear, but Connie and the others nearby were all witnessing the tense exchange.

Beautiful Margot sneered condescendingly at plain Teresa.

"But of course, that might be impossible—for you. You really ought to make a little more effort to win his affection."

Teresa's face went white as wax. Her lips trembled slightly, and she looked down. After a few moments, she mumbled, "…And how is Linus?"

Her voice was very quiet, and Connie couldn't read the emotion in it. "What?"

"Hasn't he been…working an awful lot of nights lately?"

"…That's because your husband is always out having fun at night. My husband has to pick up the slack for him."

Teresa raised her head. Her expression had brightened, but not in a pleasant way.

"Oh, is that what he told you? Then three nights ago, he must have said he was working again."

"…What are you trying to say?"

"Did he give you that bouquet of sea holly like he said he would? He told me that as long as he brought you presents, you didn't complain about him working nights, so I'm sure he must have. They were such unusual flowers, with thorns and blue petals. He ordered them just for you, you know."

The blood was draining steadily from Margot's beautiful face.

"Shall I tell you exactly what I mean?"

Teresa Jennings smiled triumphantly.

"We're having a secret love affair."

Connie shuddered. What a terrifying world this was! She thought she might as well head over to talk with Emilia and Aisha now—but no sooner did she look back in their direction than a very unladylike noise escaped her lips.

Aisha had vanished, and a black-haired man had appeared seemingly out of nowhere to take her place. He had a compact, muscular figure and masculine face. He asked Emilia something, and she pointed toward Connie with her fan.

His cerulean eyes turned in her direction. For an instant, Connie was pierced by the gaze of Randolph Ulster.

Eeeek!

Naturally, he was not in his military uniform tonight.

Nevertheless, his black formal dress was simple to the point of austerity. It made Connie think of mourning weeds, and in that sea of showy attire, he stood out glaringly. She couldn't help interpreting it as an expression of inner attitude.

Which is to say, he hadn't come tonight to enjoy the dancing. He had come to slaughter some prey or another in a bloodbath.

S-S-S-Scarlett, I need you…!

Connie involuntarily took a step back and clung to Scarlett. But Scarlett herself looked nervous. "I—I can't help you! I've never gotten along with *that man!"* she shrieked, then vanished. She was shockingly fast. Before Connie even realized it, she was nowhere to be seen.

So this is what they mean when they say it's all over.

Randolph took a step toward her, then another. Connie spun on her heel, but his deep voice reached her before she could flee.

"Good to see you again, Sister."

With a sense of doom, she turned slowly around.

"Y-you must be mistaken…"

"Mistaken?"

She nodded convulsively.

"I see. In that case, let me introduce myself. My name is Randolph. Randolph Ulster."

She knew that.

"I'm C-Constance Grail."

"I know."

Unfortunately, the mood was nowhere light enough for her to remark that she'd had exactly the same thought.

"Let me ask you point-blank. What are you trying to do?"

"Wh-what are you talking about?"

Of course, she knew exactly what he was talking about. She knew all too well. She just couldn't say it. She couldn't say, *I'm currently helping Scarlett Castiel exact revenge.*

"What did you steal from the Orlamundes' chapel? The suicide note of the deceased lady? Or—?"

"No, um, it's…"

Her eyes darted around the room. No excuse came to mind. Cold sweat dripped down her body. She was silently screaming for help. *S-somebody save me!*

"Oh, fine!"

Apparently unable to stand it any longer, Scarlett had reappeared from who knows where. Fuming, she shouted, *"I suppose there's no other way! Step back, Constance!"*

What's happening?

She felt *something* enter her body. The last time, she'd felt like she was being hit with a mallet, but this time, it was like she was being pushed into a corner of her own body. And she was still conscious.

"If you're so certain, then of course you must have some evidence?"

Someone was borrowing Connie's mouth to speak. The extremely confident voice sounded like hers and yet was unrecognizable. She guessed that her expression must look different, too. Her chin was tilted up, and she was glaring straight into the terrifying face of Randolph Ulster.

Randolph had been stone-faced up till now, but for just an instant, she saw his cerulean eyes lose their focus.

"Or could you be calling an innocent young girl a thief? That's hardly behavior worthy of His Excellency the Grim Reaper. I've never been so insulted in all my life. If you don't take back your accusation immediately, I might run to the Ladies' Association in terror and tell them the impeccable Randolph Ulster simply won't leave me alone."

"You're most welcome to do that, provided you come with me first to the Maurice Orphanage so the director and children can tell me you're not the Lettie who works for the House of Orlamunde."

H-he knows—! Connie cowered, but Scarlett smiled fearlessly.

"I'll have to turn down that invitation. As they say, all of us have a doppelgänger or two in this world. I'm honored that you asked, but I'm not so cheaply won. I would never agree to a date with a gentleman upon our first meeting."

He must not have expected her to be quite this defiant. He pressed his lips together in shock.

It must be over now—wasn't it? Her heart was in her mouth. Just as Randolph frowned and began to speak again, she heard the sound of glass breaking. This was followed by a series of screams.

Connie looked around in surprise. Teresa, the self-effacing noblewoman who had been arguing with Margot a few minutes earlier, was curled on the floor, her hand on her cheek. Someone must have hit her. Blood was streaming through her fingers and dripping from her chin.

A spot of fresh red blood bloomed on her collar.

Margot was looking down on Teresa, panting. She was holding a broken wineglass. She must have hit Teresa with it, because red rivulets were streaming down the jagged edges.

"This woman…"

Margot's eyes were bloodshot, and her voice was shaking with anger.

"This whore is to blame…!"

Randolph Ulster was the first to move in the hushed ballroom. Rushing to the side of the fallen woman, he lifted her in his arms with no concern for bloodying his formal clothes and examined the wound.

"The cut doesn't appear to be very deep. However, there's a chance that glass fragments are lodged inside. It should probably be washed immediately. Someone get a bottle of disinfectant and a clean cloth. The doctor will take some time to arrive. We can perform first aid while we wait."

Several manservants rushed to his side and politely hauled Teresa away. The maids ran to the laundry room. Connie heard someone being scolded for standing around and ordered to send a fast horse for the doctor right away.

"Margot Tudor," Randolph said in a completely emotionless, businesslike voice. She was standing rooted to the spot, but her shoulders twitched when he called her name.

"You probably know this, but you've inflicted bodily harm. As a person charged with enforcing the law, I cannot overlook your offense. I will draw up a report while I wait for my subordinates to arrive. Lady Godwin, I'm sorry to trouble you, but is there an empty room I may use? If possible, I'd like a female attendant as well."

Under the influence of his tranquil demeanor, the uproar in the ballroom gradually calmed. Connie heard someone whispering behind her.

"…It's over already? He's spoiled our fun!"

"Have you forgotten? This is what happens whenever that boy shows up."

"I heard he's in the Royal Security Force now, but he's still doing the same thing he did ten years ago. He's like some kind of watchdog."

"Seems his new job has made him even more straitlaced."

Having finished giving orders to the servants, Randolph returned to Connie's side. Given the circumstances, he seemed disinclined to continue interrogating her, but his eyes said he wasn't done yet.

"About our conversation earlier…"

Connie looked around the ballroom. It was in terrible disarray. A trail of blood dotted the floor, following Teresa's path out of the room. The music had stopped, and the younger ladies were gathered together, pale and anxious. The older guests displayed a mix of emotions. Some were worried, others looked pleased, and still others looked bored that it was over already.

Connie had never been to a ball like this before. That sort of argument never happened. No…she shook her head. Something like that *had* happened. Just the other day at the Grand Merillian. Blood hadn't been shed, but Pamela Francis had been driven into a corner with vicious words. By whom? Scarlett Castiel, of course. Not by Connie. But…

A warning bell rang in the back of her mind.

Just then, a low voice seized Connie's heart like a pair of talons.

"Can you honestly say you had nothing to do with it?"

Naturally, the ball came to a premature end.

As the guests departed one after another, Connie searched for Emilia. She found her sitting on a bench in the courtyard outside the conservatory. She looked utterly exhausted. And with good cause. As the hostess of the ball, she most likely would have to go to the Jennings household and explain what had happened, and on top of that, the on-site investigation by the Security Force had only just begun.

As Connie walked toward her, she glanced up.

"You're just like her." She turned away, as if in resignation. "It's funny, because you don't look like her at all."

"…Like Scarlett Castiel?"

Perhaps because she was surprised to hear that name come out of Connie's mouth, Emilia jerked her head up. Then she smiled self-mockingly.

"I'm sure I'll be scolded for saying that to an ordinary girl like you…"

Connie heard longing and hatred and envy in her voice and, behind that, perhaps just a hint of affection for the departed. Without really meaning to, she asked Emilia a question.

"…Do you know why Scarlett had to be executed?"

"Because she tried to poison Crown Princess Cecilia," she declared, as if that was completely obvious.

"But…"

Until recently, Connie had believed that explanation. But the executed woman herself had told her it wasn't true. Yes, Scarlett was appallingly prone to tricking and entrapping people, but she had been genuinely angry when she told Connie that.

Emilia stared at Connie as she stood there clenching her fists and trying to think of some counterargument.

"…You really do remind me of her."

With that, she stood and gazed up at the white moonlight seeping through the clouds.

"In the seventh division of inmest Mars, at the old Montrose residence. The invitation will be in the hat of Earl John Doe," she mumbled, as if to herself.

"What…?"

Ignoring Connie, Emilia hurried off toward the ballroom, as though completing her duty.

Before she disappeared, however, she turned toward Connie and whispered, as if she were reminding a forgetful child, "In life, the survivors are the winners. Take care that you don't lose your place out of carelessness, Constance Grail."

"You want me to sneak into the Castiel residence?"

Connie sounded shriller than she'd intended.

John Doe meant someone with no name, and Earl John Doe was what everyone called the host of a masked ball that had been held for decades—or so Scarlett told her. The role of host rotated among members of the high-noble ranks, but since they were always called John Doe, the ball itself was called the Earl John Doe Ball.

"Yes. The seventh division of inmest Mars is the Old Farish way of saying Mars seventeenth. That's less than a week from now. Which means we have to sneak into my house as soon as possible."

Connie blinked in confusion. "…Your house?"

"Yes, my house."

"…The Castiel house?"

She didn't understand how any of this was related to the Duke of Castiel.

As Connie continued to blink in confusion, Scarlett gave an exasperated sigh. *"Do you ever listen? I told you it's a masked ball where people conceal their identity. Do you have a mask?"*

Of course she didn't. And she might add that she'd never needed one before this moment. Her silent objection must have shown on her face, because Scarlett snorted.

"As I suspected. That's why I plan to lend you mine… Y-you leave me no choice, so I'll let you use it as a special favor. I hope you realize what an honor that is!"

"What?! But I don't need it. I mean, we don't need to sneak in there—"

"Were you going to say you could just buy a new one? Idiot. You probably don't know this, but masks are far more expensive than one would imagine."

That *would* be a problem for a debtor like her. She didn't know what to say.

Scarlett wasn't done. While guests at the ball hid their identities behind masks, they tacitly understood who was who, for the most part. They only *pretended* not to know.

Apparently, Scarlett was a regular at the Earl John Doe Balls, lover of nightlife that she was. Therefore, if Connie wore Scarlett's beloved mask, she was more likely to be approached by someone who knew about the circumstances surrounding her death.

Connie was convinced, but carrying out the infiltration was another matter. Scarlett seemed to think of it as merely popping by her old house to pick something up, but from Connie's perspective, it was flat-out breaking and entering, plus theft.

Instead of commenting, she changed the subject. "...Do you really think Emilia Godwin doesn't know anything?"

"Probably not," Scarlett said breezily. *"Despite appearances, that woman is a coward. The only thing she's good at is running away. I have no doubt that ten years ago, if she sensed danger, she would have run in the opposite direction from the truth. Anyhow, she's not particularly smart. It's quite possible that even if information was dropped at her feet, she didn't notice it."*

"Then why did she invite me to that ball?"

"Even she must realize that someone knows something. The Earl John Doe Ball is ideal for gathering information. Those parties have always been packed with fools who fear no gods."

In other words, Emilia must have been saying that she'd give Connie an opportunity in exchange for not hanging around her anymore. Having explained that much, Scarlett paused, and an uncharacteristically innocent smile spread over her face.

"Plus, this could be a good chance for you, Constance!"

"A good chance?"

"Yes, to pay off your debts. I told you that you still had prospects, didn't I?"

Scarlett *had* said something like that on the day she asked Connie to help her reap revenge.

"It's not as if I couldn't help you."

In other words...this ball was a perfect opportunity for someone like her who had so few chances to meet men.

But...

"I can hardly imagine warming up to someone if we've both got masks on..."

Connie crossed her arms and silently mulled over the issue, a serious look on her face. Scarlett furrowed her brow in exasperation.

"Idiot. Did I ever say you were supposed to look for a new fiancé? Listen to me. People who go to dances with masks on usually have some sort of secret to keep. Men and women both. So here's what you do. You find someone, anyone, and take advantage of their weakness to extort some money from them."

A soft rain was falling.

Connie had just put out the oil lamp. She stared up at the expanse of darkness on the ceiling above her bed. The sound of the rain echoed through her body, hounding her.

She couldn't see Scarlett. Apparently, she had recently learned how ghosts *sleep*. That didn't mean she was really sleeping, of course. But if she closed her eyes and told herself to fall asleep like she had when she was alive, she would apparently lose consciousness. Oddly enough, when that happened, Connie couldn't see her. Although that didn't seem to mean she had disappeared.

"Can you honestly say you had nothing to do with it?"

She suddenly heard Randolph Ulster's voice in the dark. When she closed her eyes, the miserable scene at Lady Godwin's ball rose in her mind's eye. Everyone was looking at Connie. Looking with fear, anxiety, exuberance...and malice.

"Take advantage of their weakness to extort some money from them."

It was possible that Scarlett wasn't as terrible a person as the rumors made her out to be. But she certainly wasn't a good person. She viewed right and wrong in an entirely different way than Connie did.

The rain continued. Connie pressed her interlocked hands to her eyes and sighed.

Unable to sleep, she got up, thinking she'd go have a cup of warm milk or something, and walked down the west stairs leading to the kitchen. She noticed a candle was lit in the stand. Someone appeared to be bustling around down there. She approached the noise suspiciously.

"Father...?"

Percival Ethel was standing in the hall, fully dressed. Her mother was standing next to him in travel clothes. What was going on?

Hearing her voice, Connie's father turned toward her.

"Is that Connie?" he asked, looking somehow stern. "I know this is sudden, but I am returning to the Grail domain. Aria will be coming with me. I'd like you and your brother to stay here."

"At this hour...?"

And in the rain? But her father simply nodded and went on as if that didn't matter.

"A post horse has just arrived from the domain. For the past several days, it seems the usurers have been clamoring for their money. Most likely, that's because our prospects for returning it have evaporated— although the deadline is still a ways off. It seems some young folks who tried to resist them today were assaulted. Fortunately, people were nearby and came to their rescue, so they escaped with only minor injuries."

He fell silent for a moment. Connie could see the pain in his eyes.

"If they're going to hit someone, they ought to hit me. If they're going to curse at someone, let them curse at me. I don't know why they don't. It would be infinitely better that way. But I suppose that would be meaningless to them. The truth of the matter is, this is what hurts me most, and I'm at a loss for what to do."

Ethel sank back into silence. Aria quietly wrapped her arms around him.

A moment later, a manservant announced that the preparations were complete.

Ethel brushed Connie's cheek with his large, rough hand.

"Take good care of Layli."

※

Percival Layli had been sulking all day. The moment he opened his eyes, he learned that his parents had returned to the domain, but when he asked why, no one would tell him. His sister seemed to know something. Layli was the only one who'd been left out. That wasn't very sincere.

His smoldering dissatisfaction suddenly exploded on his way to the courtyard to practice fencing with Cid, one of the family's servants.

If no one in this house will tell me what's going on, then I'll find out for myself!

"…I forgot something in my room. I'll be right back, so would you start getting ready without me?"

Layli was ordinarily a well-behaved child, so Cid didn't question him.

But instead of going to his room, Layli slipped out of the house.

※

"Layli has shut himself up in his room?" Connie asked, confused.

Cid hung his head as he apologized. His face was pale.

"He snuck off the grounds. I realized right away and ran after him… I caught him talking to someone on the street. I think he may have found out what happened in the domain. That's most likely why he's upset. I'm very sorry, Miss Constance. I am prepared to be punished for what I've done."

"Oh, no, that's not necessary—"

"I should have gone with him when he said he was returning to his room. That would have been the proper thing. He's so young; I shouldn't have let him out of my sight. If my useless neck will do you any good, I will offer it up on the spot—"

"Did you even hear what I said…?!" Connie couldn't help shrieking.

Meanwhile, the pale-faced Cid had pulled his short sword from its holster. She desperately tried to convince him no punishment would be necessary but, failing to succeed, finally promised to turn the matter over to her father when he returned if Cid would only wait until then.

Having delivered this plea, she hurried off toward Layli's room.

"Layli, I'm coming in."

He hadn't responded to her repeated knocks, so Connie finally pushed the door open.

Percival Layli was sitting on his bed with his arms around his knees and a blanket pulled over his head. He didn't react when Connie called his name.

He looked terrified. As Cid suspected, he must have heard what happened in the domain.

When Connie placed her hand on his arm to calm him, his little shoulders shivered. Connie blinked. Had she surprised him? But something was strange. He wasn't surprised. He was—

Connie forcefully grabbed his wrists. He resisted. But he had only the strength of a young child. She rolled up his sleeve, and he let out a squeal of pain.

His thin white arm was marked with maroon bruises, as if someone had grabbed him hard.

He hunched over further in fear.

"…When I went outside, a person suddenly came up and started talking to me."

He said that a man with a scar next to his eye had grabbed his arm and yelled at him.

"If you don't return the money," he'd said, *"I'll make the people of your domain pay. Every night I'll rip off a toenail or carve out an eyeball or slice off a nose. And it's all the fault of your family—no, you—for not paying your debts."*

What an awful thing to say! She felt her gut go cold, then hot. Anger, sadness, and helplessness swirled in a burning mass in the pit of her stomach.

"Everything will be fine, won't it? As long as we're sincere, it will all be fine, right?"

"It will be fine, Layli. Of course it will. You haven't done anything wrong."

Perhaps because her words soothed him, Layli dissolved into sobs. Connie drew his small body toward her and stroked his soft curls over and over. It was true—her brother hadn't done anything wrong at all.

The ones in the wrong were that man and the usurers who had hired him and, if she took it a step further, Pamela, who had destroyed their prospects of returning the money at the Grand Merillian, and Neil—and Connie.

It went without saying that the origin of all their problems was a certain friend of her father's, and if only Percival Ethel Grail hadn't taken on responsibility for his debt, none of this would ever have happened. There was no free pass that said it was to be expected because they were Grails. To put it bluntly, her father was a fool. An enormous, incurable fool.

But there were plenty of incurable people in the world. Scarlett was one of them. She was a horrible, wicked girl who had defended the first punishment dealt at a ball in ten years, pulled the wool over the eyes of innocent orphanage workers, and planned a theft from a marquess. Connie was a victim. She had simply been wrapped up in things. She couldn't have avoided it.

After all, Connie had always strived to be sincere.

And see? This word, *sincerity*, had done a wonderful job of protecting Connie's heart.

But could Connie truly say she was sincere? Really, truly? Could she say she hadn't covered up the uncomfortable truth and used the mask of the victim to escape?

When Connie returned silently to her room, Scarlett was waiting.

"Well, well, I was certain you'd collapse in tears," she said.

Maybe she would have in the past. She would have ignored her helpless self and instead moaned about the absurd situation she found herself in. But all her crying wouldn't fix Layli's swollen arm, or heal the wounds of the residents of her family's domain who had been attacked, or reduce the amount of money her father owed.

She had been too happy-go-lucky to realize that before, even though it was completely obvious.

Over and over, she heard a reproachful voice asking her if she really had nothing to do with it. She bit her lip.

She did have something to do with it. It wasn't *only* Scarlett's fault. Maybe it had started with her, but Connie had chosen her own actions after that. No matter how many excuses she told herself, she knew what she'd done was wrong.

Connie let out a long breath. She had no idea what expression was on her face at that moment. But when Scarlett looked at her, she smiled excitedly as if she'd just discovered something unusual.

After all…

After all, she'd realized something. Connie's sincerity and her father's sincerity weren't the same. Even if many people suffered in the end, like they would this time, her father's understanding of sincerity did not budge. If someone appeared before him asking for help, he would absolutely do the same thing again.

Even if it wasn't the right thing to do as a father or as the lord of the domain, at the very least, it was the right thing for the human being Percival Ethel Grail to do. Because even when things got as bad as they were right now, he would never, ever use the word *sincerity* as an excuse.

Ethel's sincerity wouldn't save Connie and her family. That made her frustrated and angry, but she still felt a little jealous of him.

Connie could never be like that. That wasn't what sincerity meant to her. For her, it easily became an *excuse*. She silently apologized to Percival Grail the First.

I'm sorry...but I can't swear on your name anymore.

There were things she wanted to protect. And people. She would do anything for them. She would *dare*! She would become a wicked woman if she had to. She was ready to take the blame now. She didn't care if she was punished for it.

"So what are you going to do?" Scarlett asked in her usual casual tone. Connie had already made up her mind on how to answer.

"I'm going to the Castiel residence."

On that day, Constance Grail threw away the shield of sincerity.

Constance Grail

After various events, has given up on being sincere. Sixteen years old and fully prepared to seek revenge, break and enter, and commit theft.

Scarlett Castiel

Finds Emilia useless.

Kate Lorraine

Feels a little sad that her friend is keeping secrets from her. Nevertheless, covers for her. Kind and a good cook, but still no boyfriend.

Neil Bronson

Driven by filial piety to storm the Grail house but instead gets a thrashing himself. Still leaves with a gift, so the Bronson Company might be okay in the end. Possibly pounced on by Countess Custine. ←**new!**

Percival Ethel Grail

Probably in his early forties. "Sincerity" is his motto. Looks like a bear.

Aria Grail

Probably in her late thirties. Golden hair and green eyes. Connie's mother, generally considered beautiful. Feels guilty for not passing down her beautiful face to Connie. Not born a Grail, so unclear whether she is sincere.

Percival Layli Grail

Almost ten. Golden hair and aquamarine eyes. A little angel with his mother's good looks.

Emilia Godwin

Ecstatic about her party until things go terribly wrong. Cowardly. Senses she should keep clear of Connie's problems and therefore tells her about the Earl John Doe Ball to get rid of her. Doesn't know what happened ten years ago and doesn't want to know.

Aisha Huxley

Was whispering about something with Emilia.

Randolph Ulster

Terrifying. Even Scarlett says she can't handle him. Always hits Connie's heart right where it hurts.

Teresa Jennings

In her late twenties. Ordinary-looking. Gets carried away and admits she's having an affair with Margot's husband. Is then hit with a wineglass and sheds blood.

Margot Tudor

In her late twenties. Beautiful. Attempts to harass Teresa about her husband's visits to the brothel but gets a shock in return. Her pride in tatters, finds herself attacking Teresa with a wineglass.

©Yu-nagi

The middle-aged doctor told Teresa that she'd have a mark on her cheek for a while but that it should heal with time.

Just as Randolph Ulster had said, Margot's glass hadn't made it past the shallow layers of her skin. Teresa felt depressed about that. She'd rather the scar remained for the rest of her life. If it had to happen at all, she wished the mark would stay there as an ugly reminder of Margot Tudor.

Then I could torture that awful woman for the rest of my life.

Teresa and Margot had been friends since childhood. If beautiful Margot was the sun, gloomy Teresa was no more than the shadow she cast. Margot's mere presence was enough to steal everything from Teresa. Her first love. Her dearest friends. Her partner at the debutant ball. She didn't know if she did it out of malice. But in the end, Margot inevitably stole the things Teresa wanted most.

Even Linus Tudor.

Teresa had met him before Margot. He had come to Adelbide ten years ago from the neighboring kingdom of Faris. The Tudors were a subsidiary family with roots in Faris, and because the current Duke of Tudor did not have children of his own, he had adopted Linus to carry on the family line.

He had sweet, even features and a soft manner. He spoke with an elegant Farish accent—and Teresa had fallen for him at first sight.

But of course, Margot had stolen him from her. Teresa had long suffered beneath her friend's oppressive presence, but when Margot and Linus's engagement was announced, she felt her heart finally shatter. Deeply wounded, she married another man—her parents' choice—but she never stopped caring for Linus. The truth was, she had always loved him.

So she was elated when, six months or so earlier, he had come to her saying she was the one he'd liked from the start. She knew it!

She'd always suspected that Linus felt the same about her.

Now she gazed in rapture at him as he stood before her. He'd come to see her in secret, because he was worried about her injury. Needless to say, she was overjoyed as she showed him into the back study. Her husband had spent a short time in the study after returning from work but had already left for the brothels.

Even after what had happened, Linus Tudor's love for Teresa was unchanged. He smiled at her as gently as ever. *That smile alone is worth getting injured*, she thought to herself. Even if the wound never healed…

"Did you give Kevin his dose today?"

Linus's voice brought Teresa back to her senses. She answered with a broad smile. Kevin. Kevin Jennings. Rule-abiding, high-strung Kevin. Her mind-numbingly tiresome husband, who had never once whispered that he loved her.

"When Kevin is here…" Linus had told her with deep sorrow when they first started seeing each other. *"When Kevin is here, it's difficult for me to come see you."*

Teresa felt the same. Kevin got in the way. So the ever-thoughtful Linus taught her a method for getting him out of the house.

Kevin Jennings was pathologically methodical and rule-abiding. Even in the sphere of everyday life, he could not relax unless all the rules were followed. And they used that against him.

Every day when Kevin returned home, he drank a cup of black tea in the study. He wouldn't touch it until it was completely cool, so he always let it sit untouched for a while after the maid prepared it. *That's* when she did it.

The clear liquid was stored in a bottle the size of her forefinger. When she removed the cap, the saccharine scent of flowers rose to her nostrils.

Teresa didn't know what it was. *"Paradise,"* Linus had said with a smile.

Gradually, her quiet, scrupulous husband became increasingly emotional, until eventually he began visiting the brothel every night. Teresa was thrilled by this new reality.

Ahhh—now I can see Linus again.

For Teresa, that was all that mattered.

Yes, she thought, handing Linus the empty bottle. He refilled it and handed it back. This magical little bottle was to thank for clouding Kevin's sharp eyes and allowing Teresa to meet with Linus.

"Is that all? You don't have any more?" Linus asked.

That was an odd question. He'd told her just a drop was enough—and it was true—so stockpiling reserves would be pointless. When she told him as much, he smiled.

"You're not putting it in the teapot or the pitcher, are you? Only this cup?"

He must have noticed Kevin's empty teacup, because he picked it up and peered inside.

"You must never drink this," Linus had told her, so of course she had only put it in her husband's cup.

As she nodded, she heard something hard hit the floor. The ceramic cup shattered across the rug.

Teresa blinked slowly and looked at Linus.

"Honestly, I never thought the two of you would do something like that."

He smiled cynically, as if he hadn't just hurled Kevin's cup on the floor.

"It would have been bad enough if you'd played those silly children's games ten years ago, but to do it now? You really let your guard down, my dear. Is this all the fault of that young lady who made the fuss at the

Grand Merillian the other night? Grail, was it? We must teach a lesson to those who don't know their place."

He tilted his head as if the problem was simply too much for him.

"In truth, I'd planned to set up Kevin's successor, but with this scandal, that will be impossible. Well, I suppose it's all for the best that the trouble-maker has been removed. For a while there, I didn't know what would happen. Thank goodness you married Kevin Jennings."

Linus took a step toward Teresa and wrapped his arms around her waist.

"I have you to thank for everything, Teresa."

He was smiling radiantly. Teresa reflexively smiled back at him. His smile spread wider. He brought his face closer to hers as if he was going to kiss her. She closed her eyes.

But instead of a kiss, she felt *something* sink into her stomach.

"Oh…?"

Her stomach burned as if she'd been branded. The heat was followed by a pain that took her breath away. She tilted her head and looked down. The handle of an exquisitely carved dagger was protruding from her lower abdomen. A red stain spread across her dress as she watched.

What's happening? she wondered in a daze.

"Take my hand," she heard a soothing voice say. Linus. Linus's gentle voice. He guided her shaking hand to the hilt of the dagger.

"When I said I wanted to end things, you pulled out a hidden knife and tried to kill us both. Unable to land your blow on me, you turned the knife on yourself. I tried to stop you but missed by just a hair. Honestly, it's a bit played out. But that's what makes it so perfect. It sounds just like you, don't you think?"

But Teresa didn't understand his words anymore. She felt only the heat and the pain. Hot, searing pain. She could not speak.

"I'm sorry, Teresa. I meant it when I said I liked you more than Margot. After all, you were so much more miserable and unattractive and pitiful than she was. If it weren't for the surrounding circumstances, I might even have overlooked this."

The world is tilting. The world, the world is at the wrong angle—no. It's me who's tilting.

Her body was thrown down onto the rug like a pendulum torn from its support. She landed with a dull thump, but she could no longer feel the pain. Her shaking arm reached reflexively for him.

Kneeling beside her, Linus peered into her face. His face was beautiful. His irises were bluish silver. They were as beautiful as the sea beneath the moon. She felt she was falling into his eyes. For the first time, she noticed that he had two black dots like stars beside his pupil.

"But…"

He combed his fingers through her hair. She could no longer move her body. But when she moved her eyes, she saw a small birthmark on his wrist. No, not a birthmark. A sun.

A tattooed sun.

Tears spilled from her wide-open eyes and down her cheeks.

After checking Teresa Jennings's carotid artery to make sure she was dead, the man stood up and stretched. Then, as if he'd forgotten, he smiled a terribly kind smile.

"But then, if you overlook the little details, sometimes you fail. *Just like ten years ago.*"

Teresa Jennings

Actually a complicated woman. Egged on by her love, Linus, she puts "something" in her husband's tea. Murdered by Linus.

Linus Tudor

In his late twenties. Originally from Faris. Blue-gray eyes. Two black spots in one eye. Sun tattoo on his wrist. Murdered Teresa.

Kevin Jennings

Scrupulous and methodical. Doesn't feel right unless all the rules are followed. Given "something" to drink by Teresa. Called a "troublemaker" by Linus.

Litton's shop had been quiet all day until the young girl came flying in.

"Please help me!" she cried.

Litton was a middle-rank dressmaker who also took on laundry and delivery of clothing. Of course he had all sorts of customers, but the Castiel family put in the most orders—for the shared uniforms worn by the lowest of their lowly maids, who didn't even have uniforms with their own names on them.

In the Castiel household, all the waiting women were given uniforms with the family crest. Litton was in charge of sewing the uniforms and going to the dormitory for live-in servants once a week to exchange fresh uniforms for dirty ones to wash.

"When I woke up this morning, my clothes were gone! I'm certain Mathilda did it!"

It seemed the girl was a live-in maid for the Castiels.

"Which department are you in?" Litton asked, flipping through the register he'd pulled from a drawer. It wasn't unusual for maids from various houses to come on their own to his shop to order extra uniforms, especially the ones who lived in dorms with many young girls. They gave various reasons—someone had spilled tea on them, someone had slashed their skirt—and he sympathized with them for undergoing this rite of passage. Still, as a matter of routine, he always checked their name and position before handing over the new uniform.

"I'm a washerwoman."

His hand paused over the register at this unusual answer. Washer-women didn't last long. A young girl was doing well if she stayed on the job three days. Aside from the old-timers, turnover was high. Writing down all their names was such a pain that he'd stopped trying long ago.

Oh, whatever.

Litton scratched his head and selected an indigo uniform from the shelf. He handed it to the girl, who thanked him with a smile.

She had hazelnut hair and green eyes and the average sort of face you saw everywhere.

Vanessa was using an iron to smooth the wrinkles on a piece of linen she'd just put through the wringer. The iron was hot and heavy and would burn the clothes if she let her attention wander for even a moment. She had to stay bent over and focused on her task the whole time. Lately, her overworked back had begun to hurt her when she stood up. When she was a girl, everyone had tried hard to master their skills. The young girls these days hardly lasted three hours, let alone three days.

The bell rang, and a girl in an indigo servant's uniform—an unfamiliar face—arrived to pick up the finished linens. That happened a lot. New washerwomen were always coming in to replace the old. She knew that, but she still couldn't contain her irritation.

"What happened to Cassie?!" she asked sharply.

The wringer clanged. You had to yell if you wanted anyone to hear you in this place. That was the second reason washerwomen never lasted.

"She said her head hurt!"

"She must have meant her head was empty!"

Girls these days were always pretending to be sick. She piled the mountain of neatly folded linens in a basket, grumbling the whole time. It must have been heavier than the new girl thought, because she staggered backward under the weight.

"Watch your step! I won't forgive you if you drop those!" Vanessa snapped. She'd have to start all over again if that happened.

"Yes, ma'am!" the girl replied. Her voice was energetic despite her small size. That appeared to be the only impressive thing about her. But lots of girls were like that.

"Rule number one of the washerwomen: Be your best and don't make a mess!"

"Yes, ma'am!"

Another lively response. In that case, the problem was whether she'd last three days—or three hours. Vanessa looked her over again.

She had hazelnut hair and green eyes. And a face that only looked more commonplace the longer she stared at it.

※

Constance Grail charged across the second-floor breezeway, hiding her face behind the basket of laundry. The elevated passage was terrifying and long, and she couldn't see the end. Who could find their way around this house—this palace?

After a while, she saw a glimmer of light and heard playful voices. Below her was a cylindrical atrium. She peered down into it and saw a red-faced elderly gentleman flirting with several young women.

"*Ugh. It's that old skunk, Jared,*" Scarlett announced. She looked as if she'd just seen a worm. When Connie gave her a questioning look, an affectionate smile spread over Scarlett's beautiful face.

"*My dissolute uncle. He used to visit sometimes when I was alive. I guess he's still hanging onto life, though I can't imagine why.*"

Connie was too scared to probe for details. Scarlett gave her an innocent look.

"*Turn left up here,*" she ordered. "*Now right.*"

Then, "*Climb those stairs.*"

After that, "*Go straight, then just keep going.*"

Eventually, they arrived in a long, narrow gallery. The white plaster ceiling was covered with religious paintings, and the walls were crowded with ornate mirrors and artwork. Jewelry, precious ornaments, and sculptures of famous people adorned the pedestals.

"See that bay window at the far end? Walk over to the suit of armor just in front of it."

Connie could make out what looked like armor at the far end of the room. She had readjusted the basket in her arms and was mentally preparing herself for her next task when she heard someone calling her.

"What are you doing in here?"

She turned toward the threatening voice. A figure was standing in the door.

It was a man with pale golden hair, reddish-purple eyes, and a cold, beautiful face.

"*...My brother,*" Scarlett mumbled, sounding dazed.

Which meant this must be Maximilian, the soon-to-be master of the Castiel house. Connie had heard the rumors about him. People said he was a very proper man, both like Scarlett and unlike her. If she remembered correctly, his wife was a high noble from Faris.

He was eyeing her suspiciously. Scarlett whirled around to face Connie.

"Tell him that Jared called for you."

"Hmm? Oh, um, Sir Jared called for me."

"What?" Maximilian said, narrowing his eyes.

"He said I was to come see him."

"That pig. I thought I told him that if he touched another one of our staff, I'd have him castrated... But I do say, it seems his taste has... changed."

Did members of the Castiel family receive some sort of special training in how to eviscerate ordinary people? Feeling slighted by his fascinated but not malicious tone, Connie lowered her head.

"Please, I beg you to overlook my offense—"

"Are you an idiot, girl? Just go back to your post. I'll deal with the pig."

©Yu-nagi

With that curt command, Maximilian spun on his heel and strode away. Connie breathed a sigh of relief as she watched him recede into the distance.

As Connie continued to proceed through the sea of paintings and sculptures, each a perfect window onto its era, Scarlett muttered, "He's not like me at all, don't you think?"

Connie looked over at her, confused.

"Tell me the truth. His hair is different, his features are different…and his personality is, too, right?"

Of course, she was talking about Maximilian.

"I thought there were some similarities," she blurted out.

"What?"

"Huh?"

Surprisingly, Scarlett was gaping at her. "…Such as what?"

"Oh, nothing, just the way you both treat everyone else like the lowliest of servants."

And the way they both called other people *girl* or *boy*. Also, how they reflexively used the word *idiot*. Come to think of it, they were practically twins.

Scarlett looked as if she'd been caught off guard.

"No one's ever said that to me before," she replied in an unusually injured tone.

"They haven't?"

"No. I mean, my brother has blond hair and different-colored eyes from me, and he's smart and serious."

This fluent list of differences seemed to be something Scarlett had come up with a long time ago. That was surprising. Could Scarlett Castiel really think that?

"Also, we have different mothers."

Connie stopped in her tracks.

"Oh, you hadn't heard? My father's first wife left him. I'm the daughter of his *second wife. Ten years is longer than you might think, after all."* Scarlett's lonely voice echoed down the chilly gallery. *"Have you heard of Cornelia of the Starry Crown?"*

Connie nodded. That was the name of the last empress of Faris, who ruled when the kingdom was still a sprawling empire—and when it fell into ruin.

At the time, the rulers of Faris made a practice of marrying the chiefs and royalty of the lands they conquered, bringing them into the imperial bloodline in an attempt to indirectly control their territories. Needless to say, the imperial family itself had to maintain its pure Faris heritage, so high-ranking noble families who swore allegiance to the empire were chosen for intermarriage. Although they were derided for their *"impure blood,"* these families were said to hold great influence.

Cornelia's father was the youngest son of the emperor. However, he fell in love with a lady of impure blood, of all things, and the two of them as good as eloped. Their daughter was Cornelia Faris. She was called "the Starry Crown" because she was the first successor to the imperial throne in the empire's history to possess as many different bloodlines as there were stars in the sky.

Later, territories including the Principality of East Faris—which later became Adelbide—revolted, and the empire fell apart. Members of the imperial family were executed one after the next, but Cornelia escaped the massacre because she was off studying in the neutral Republic of Soldita. From there, she went into exile, and no one knew where she ended up. One theory speculated that she stayed in the republic and married the son of the sovereign.

Connie was by now in front of the suit of armor made from dully gleaming steel. Scarlett pointed to the helmet.

"It's in there."

Removing the helmet wasn't all that difficult. It wasn't attached to the breastplate but instead simply set on top of a dummy.

With a clang, the face of the wax dummy appeared. Connie stared in surprise. On the top half of its expressionless face, covering the nose and sunken eyes, sat a black mask.

It looked as if it were fashioned from the starless night sky—but most likely the material was jet.

"In a remote village in the Republic of Soldita was said to live a young girl descended from Cornelia of the Starry Crown. The story was true, and if she had lived in better times, I don't doubt that valiant warriors would have come from all across the continent to swear their allegiance to her on bended knee," Scarlett mumbled. *"Crownless Aliénore—she was my mother."*

※

The mask that Connie took from the Castiel residence was neither too big nor too small. It fit her face perfectly.

Originally, jet was used to make mourning ornaments. Perhaps that was why Scarlett had selected a pitch-black mourning dress with a tight, high neck for Connie to wear to the evening's festivities.

The old Montrose residence was a luxurious mansion set on sprawling grounds outside the capital. The Earl of Montrose himself had been accused of treason several decades ago and the family stripped of its title. Plans had been made several times to tear down the old mansion, but each time, those involved had died mysteriously, and as a result, no one dared go near the residence anymore. It was a venue with quite a history.

"Your invitation?" asked a man wearing a clownishly smiling mask that covered his entire face and a shroud-like, inky-black overcoat. His tone was businesslike as he held out a white-gloved hand. Constance glanced at him before replying.

"It's in the hat of Earl John Doe."

There was a brief pause before the man placed his hand theatrically on his breast and bowed.

"Welcome, unwelcome guest."

The gate creaked open. Connie straightened her back and stepped into this abode of vice, rampant with demons and demonesses of all descriptions.

The lights in the salon flickered strangely. Only a scattering of candles had been lit in the gorgeous chandeliers hanging from the ceiling, casting scant light on the shadowy room beneath. Far fainter than the light of oil lamps, the candlelight served not to illuminate the figures of the guests but rather to further obscure them.

Censers wafted exotic-smelling incense through the room, where several tents had been erected. They were covered in transparent silk and periodically emitted the chatter of coquettish voices. The intimate goings-on of the men and women inside were projected on the tent walls as black shadows from which Connie quickly averted her eyes.

In one corner of the hall, a large, swarthy man was holding forth in a language Connie didn't understand. In front of him, beautiful foreign children were dancing in circles to a mystical melody. The masked guests watched as if entranced. Scarlett snorted.

"Some taste they have."

Wondering what she meant, Connie looked back at the crowd and saw that the large man was now talking to one of the masked guests. The words she could overhear were all unfamiliar. She gave Scarlett an inquiring look, but she only prodded her along to greet the host.

The host, it turned out, was a *woman*. She was lying in a slovenly pose across a velvet sofa in front of the fireplace, wearing a dress so low-cut and filmy, it looked more like an undergarment. In one hand, she held an ebony fan. Connie couldn't tell exactly what her face looked like because of the delicate butterfly mask covering her eyes, but she appeared to be no older than Connie's mother. Her most striking feature was her lips, as red as if she'd just taken a sip of blood.

"So it's Deborah's turn to host tonight," Scarlett observed, sounding amused. Apparently, they were acquaintances.

The glamorous Deborah turned toward Connie as if she'd just noticed her presence and slowly smiled. "And what is your name?"

Scarlett smiled languidly. It was the arrogant, attractive smile that Connie knew so well.

Without Connie's noticing, a crowd had formed around them. Their curious, clinging gazes tracked her from behind their masks. Normally, that would have been enough to make her shrink. Tonight, however, Connie felt eerily calm.

Deborah narrowed her ashen eyes. Connie did not look away as she spoke.

"Please call me Eris."

Out of the corner of her eye, she saw Scarlett watching with amusement, one hand on her cheek. Eris. The pseudonym Scarlett had been so fond of using—and a fragment from the note Lily Orlamunde had left behind.

The crowd fell silent, and stillness descended.

"Well, well, I haven't heard that name in quite a while."

Not surprisingly, it was Deborah who broke the silence.

"We had a guest by that name ten years ago." She sounded as if she was recalling a pleasant memory, her mouth hidden behind her ebony fan. "But she was a careless girl. Before she knew it, her head was separated from her body…"

The fan snapped shut.

"Are you quite certain your head is attached securely?"

The tip of the fan swirled toward Connie, dancing in the air. It pointed at her neck, which was tightly swathed in black fabric. Someone shrieked. Now who was it who had told Connie to wear a dress that completely hid her neck? Who had said it would be just perfect for tonight's ball?

Amid the tension, Scarlett let out a peal of highly amused laughter.

Connie could hear people whispering. Of course, they were talking about the suspicious guest who went by the name of Eris—a ghost.

No one, however, seemed willing to approach her directly. At a loss for what to do, Connie made her way over to the buffet laid out on tables by the wall. An old-fashioned bell was hanging in the corner. When she looked around, she realized there was one in each corner of the salon. She was gazing at them curiously when she heard Scarlett sigh with exasperation.

"I can't believe you're able to eat at a time like this."

If Scarlett had let her, Connie would have explained that she'd been too nervous to get down much of anything for dinner. She was examining the morsels of meat and chicken on skewers when she smelled a saccharine, flowery scent. When she glanced around, she spotted a woman drinking a vividly colored cocktail. She looked several years older than Connie and was wearing a rose-colored dress with an open back.

"How nostalgic. It's Jane," Scarlett whispered.

Jane? Connie couldn't see her whole face because of the mask, but her cleanly sloped nose and glossy, puckered lips were very seductive.

At this point, Connie realized she had a significant problem. Because of the masks, she didn't know who anyone was. So if she met someone suspicious, she would only be able to remember them by the parts she could see. But she suspected that if she were to meet them somewhere else without their mask on, she wouldn't know who they were.

"Lady Eris, wasn't it?"

Connie jumped at the abrupt question. Screwing up her courage, she turned around and felt the strength drain from her.

No matter how she wished to deny it, the portly figure before her could only belong to Viscount Hamsworth.

"My word, that beautiful mask is certainly one of a kind. But I'm equally certain that if you were set free from it, your bare face would be equally beautiful. I feel most fortunate to have met you here—and most frustrated."

"Oh, um…"

"Then again, this is amusing in its own way. Which is to say, I myself am enjoying the momentary freedom of having hidden my true identity tonight."

It wasn't exactly hidden. In the case of the viscount, not hidden in the least. To the contrary—the viscount could only be the viscount. Sensing Connie's lukewarm gaze, her unmistakable conversation partner nodded.

"Pardon me for not introducing myself. Please call me Ham—so long as I am hidden by the moon, that is."

Except he wasn't hidden.

Afraid her inner voice would burst unbidden into public, she slapped a hand over her mouth, but the viscount didn't seem to notice.

"It's been quite a while since one of our balls was this well attended," Hamsworth said, casting a leisurely gaze around the room. "As the old proverb goes, a leaf hides best in the forest. I wonder what sort of rotten leaves they've brought in tonight."

The idly chatting masked crowd...the swaying tents...the lovely foreign children...

"Wouldn't you agree?" The viscount looked at Connie—but their eyes did not meet. For some reason, he was looking toward where Scarlett was standing. For an instant, Connie shuddered, wondering if he could see her, but it seemed to be mere coincidence, because he turned back to her as if nothing odd had happened.

Just as she was about to respond to him, the bells in the four corners of the salon began clanging.

The guests froze and looked at one another in confusion. Connie turned reflexively toward Scarlett.

"Why are they ringing?"

"It's—" Scarlett said, her expression turning serious. There was a clamor near the entrance and shrill shouting. What was going on?

"The military police!" someone screamed.

"Run! The Royal Security Force will expose us all!"

No sooner had Viscount Hamsworth heard the words *military police* than he vanished, with such astounding speed that Connie wondered where he might have hidden his barrel-like form.

She stood in a daze. Expose them? True, the masked ball was not exactly proper, but attending didn't seem like a crime on its own.

"I knew it was strange!" Scarlett said, scowling. "You can try to cover it up with an exotic theme all you want, but those children were obviously out of place. I'm certain they were being sold as slaves!"

Slaves. The trade had spread freely during the days of the Faris Empire, but when Adelbide was founded, it was abolished.

"That new-money pig said as much a moment ago when he asked you about the rotten leaves. This ball was no more than a front for trafficking in human lives!"

Connie thought back to the darling faces of those tender young children. The masked guests had practically been licking their lips as they watched them dance. It had been an auction of sorts.

"Enough chitchat. You and I had better get out of here fast. Fortunately, I've been to the Montrose residence quite a few times, and if I remember right, there was a hidden passage around here somewhere."

The salon was in an uproar. The guests with a sharp sixth sense had already disappeared. No doubt the Security Force had had quite a clash with the host outside the entryway.

After a short delay, the ruckus drew steadily closer to the salon. Finally realizing what was happening, the remaining guests went pale and began to scatter. Connie, too, scurried to follow Scarlett's directions.

Suddenly, out of the corner of her eye, she spotted something swaying. Her body went stiff, and her legs froze beneath her.

It was a woman. A young woman. A woman not much older than Connie. She slowly toppled to the floor, a fountain of blood spraying from her. Connie stared in shock.

She couldn't take her eyes off the blood as it soaked into the carpet. But no one approached the victim. To the contrary, they avoided her as if she were an inanimate obstacle. Connie's heart pounded. No one was coming to her rescue.

No one was going to save her.

The instant Connie realized what was happening, she spun on her heel.

"Constance?!"

She pushed her way through the crowd surging in the opposite direction.

"What do you think you're doing?!" Scarlett screeched, but Connie could no longer hear her. The fallen woman had her full attention.

She knelt beside her and lifted her in her arms. The woman's eyes were wide open and unfocused. Blood was running from her right arm. The wound was gaping open in a straight line, like a cut. Despite the quantity of blood pulsing from it, the gash looked surprisingly shallow—but it was rapidly turning black.

This seemed bad to Connie. She grabbed a pitcher of water from the table and dumped it on the girl's arm to wash away the clotted blood. Then she tore off a strip of her mourning dress and tied it as tightly as she could at the woman's shoulder joint. Connie realized that the rose-colored dress was the same one that the woman Scarlett had called Jane had been wearing. She had a tattoo of the sun on her chest.

"Can you even hear what I'm saying?! You're acting awfully saucy for Constance Grail!"

Scarlett's panicked shriek brought the din back to Connie's ears.

"I told you the military police are coming! Get out of here this instant! Forget about this woman! Do you even know her?! I don't think so! You have nothing to do with this situation!"

"Scarlett?"

"What?"

The woman was still unconscious. But she wasn't dead. She had a heartbeat.

I can save her.

Connie bit her lip and looked up. "I'm sorry, but I can't just abandon her…!"

This had nothing to do with sincerity or being a Grail. It was simply her own willfulness.

Scarlett caught her breath and said nothing. After a moment, she grimaced. "You idiot, Connie…!" She looked on the verge of tears. "I wash my hands *of this! If they catch you, it's over! Even if you haven't done anything, they'll chop your head off!"*

Her emotions were painfully evident in her tone and expression. Connie's chest tightened, and she felt tears well in her own eyes. But still, she could not abandon the woman. She held back her tears and said in a strained voice, "I'm sorry, Scarlett, I'm sorry…!"

"If you have time to apologize, you have time to escape, you obstinate mule!"

Military police dressed in navy uniforms flooded into the room. The remaining guests struggled in vain as the masks were torn from their faces, and they were arrested one after the next. The censers were stomped to pieces, the tents were ripped, and the screams and shouts echoed.

"What are you doing?!"

Before she knew it, a military policeman had grabbed Connie's arms from behind and yanked them over her head. A squeal escaped her mouth at his merciless violence. The policeman ignored her cry, however, and pulled even harder to make her stand up.

Her bones made a creaking sound. She held her breath—and then something like static electricity shot through her, and the pain vanished.

The man released her arms in shock. Her support gone, she dropped to the floor with a thud.

"What the…?"

The man looked back and forth between his hands and Connie, his brow furrowed.

"You asked me what I'm doing?"

Scarlett's form flickered between Connie and the policeman, speaking with overwhelming presence.

"I'm the one who should be asking you that, you lout!"

Her exquisite amethyst eyes flashed. Goose bumps rose on Connie's skin. The salon felt suddenly cold. A jolt of unspeakable fear ran through her.

"Who the hell does this girl think she is?"

The man pulled a saber from the holster on his hip and brandished it. Connie gasped as the dull sheen of the blade flashed in her direction. Just as she squeezed her eyes shut, however, a different deep voice took command of the situation.

"How rash of you to pull your saber on a defenseless lady. Or is that how your unit operates?"

The man's tone was chillingly high-handed, but the heavy bass notes were unforgettable. Connie opened her eyes in surprise.

"Lieutenant Commander Ulster?!" the man blurted out before raising his hand in a salute. "Why are you here...?"

"I happened to be nearby on other business. Don't worry—I'm not trying to steal the credit from the Gaina Unit. However, if I were your commander, I would order you to stop the idle chitchat and see to the wounded first!"

Randolph looked pointedly at the unconscious woman, and the man hurried to lift her in his arms. Although he gave Connie a dissatisfied glance, he stalked off without another word.

Randolph shifted his gaze to Connie, who was still crumpled on the floor, and delicately raised one eyebrow.

"You again, Constance Grail?"

He took a step toward her, then another. Each time, his jet-black cloak flapped open to reveal a flash of vermilion lining. His features were so sharp, she was sure they'd cut her hand if she touched them, and as always, his face was as expressionless as if it were stamped in place.

He truly does look the part of the Grim Reaper, Connie mused with a strange sense of detachment.

"Just to be sure, I'm going to ask you a question." Randolph narrowed his cerulean eyes coldly. "Did you have anything to do with the human trafficking going on tonight?"

She shook her head. But would he believe her, given the circumstances?

"I didn't think so."

She looked up at him, perplexed by how quickly he'd accepted her word. His face was as emotionless as ever.

"In that case, there's no need to arrest you—but a coincidence thrice over is an inevitability. Don't you think it's about time we have a heart-to-heart?"

No, that would be impossible, Connie thought. She glanced to Scarlett for help, but she just looked away sulkily. Apparently, she was still fuming over Connie's refusal to flee earlier.

"Unfortunately, at present it would be difficult to prosecute you for the theft at the marquess's residence. To start with, I don't even know what you stole. As for your use of a false name at the orphanage and illegal entry into the marquess's residence, my guess is the violated parties won't want to raise a fuss over it. The marquess in particular takes great care with regard to appearances. Even if I were to arrest you, they would likely drop the charges."

If Scarlett wasn't going to help her, Connie's only option was to say something on her own.

"Still, you'd probably like to avoid having a criminal record, wouldn't you?" he continued. "Will you tell me what was going on? If I feel satisfied with your answer, I won't pursue the matter further. I don't think that's such a bad offer."

Suddenly, she remembered Scarlett's words.

"Take advantage of their weakness to extort some money from them."

That reminded her that Randolph Ulster was the son of the Duke of Richelieu—a family that ranked just as high as Scarlett's. In other words, he had money.

Connie gulped.

Of course, she wasn't going to threaten him. She had no idea what his weakness was, and anyhow, if she did something like that, he'd probably slice her in two on the spot. But...

But maybe she could negotiate with him.

Randolph wanted information. Even if she didn't tell him the full truth, perhaps she could skillfully skirt it...

"...What's the matter?" Randolph was peering at her, his brows furrowed.

No doubt her expression was peculiarly grim. "Did you hit your head in the chaos?"

"Oh, no, it's just, I wanted to n-n-n-n…"

"N-n-n-n? Yes, I'm quite sure your head is—"

She interrupted his worried inquiry by shaking her head. Then she took a deep breath and said, "Negotiate. Can we negotiate?"

"…Negotiate?" he repeated.

Scarlett was staring at her in shock.

Randolph brought his hand to his chin, puzzling over something. After a few moments, he nodded as if he'd figured it out.

"I did hear that the Grail family had taken on some debt. You're saying that if I want information, I've got to pay for it?"

"Um, yes…"

He'd seen right through her. Immediately. Tears sprang to her eyes.

She knew she was being extremely impudent. But her relationship with His Excellency the Grim Reaper could hardly get worse, and whatever he thought of her, if there was a shadow of a chance he'd say yes, she wanted to take the gamble—that was the honest truth. Except that had been shot down immediately.

Would he shout at her that she should know her place? Would he sneer at her like she was a maggot?

Connie shrank in fear at the possibilities, but his reaction was not at all what she expected: He simply agreed.

"That would be acceptable."

"What?" she asked, despite having made the request herself.

"But you're no slum-dwelling informant. You're a noble. If you receive a hefty sum of cash, people will likely begin to ask questions. What to do…?"

He appeared to be considering the question, his finger still on his lip. Presently, he arrived at a conclusion.

"Constance Grail. Are you prepared to weather a scandal?"

She tensed beneath his sharp gaze but forced herself to return it and answer decisively, "…I'm used to scandals by now."

Connie had abandoned sincerity, and she was ready to do anything. No request could shock her. She'd show him!

"In that case, the fastest approach would be…"

She was so lost in her own sentimental drama that she nodded reflexively to his next words without even thinking.

"…an engagement."

"That's exactly what I was hoping you'd say… Huh?"

Only after carelessly agreeing did the strangeness of it hit her.

"Is it now? Then we'll do that."

"…Huh?"

"Of course, once some time has passed, we'll break it off. But in the meantime, the Grail family can pay off their debts, and I can keep an eye on you. I wouldn't call it the ideal solution, but it's certainly reasonable."

"…Huhhhh?"

"Oh, yes, about that moneylender Elbadia…"

He was on to a new subject. The switch was so fast, Connie could hardly keep up. By *that moneylender Elbadia,* he must mean that detestable, unscrupulous usurer.

"Word reached me of the troubles in the Grail domain. It was more than I could countenance, so I took care of it. Those scoundrels likely won't be throwing their weight around anymore. I thought we might find some skeletons in their closet, but as it turned out, we didn't. I might have been a little rough on them."

"Um, th-thank you…?"

Randolph gave her a confused look. "For what?"

"Um… Good question…"

She didn't know herself. But she had more important things to worry about.

"I can't exactly say it's fortunate, but you've just broken off your engagement, and I only lost my wife two years ago. No one is likely to think it strange if our engagement drags on for a while. For my own reasons, I'd be grateful if we could extend it as long as possible, but I won't force you.

I was concerned that you might not be prepared for the scandal that is sure to come when a young lady breaks off two engagements in a row, but since your resolve is firm, I see I had no need to worry."

He sounded so matter-of-fact about it all, he might as well have been reviewing a task with a subordinate. Everything he said made sense. It made sense, but nevertheless…

…something about it felt odd.

It wasn't what she had been imagining at all.

Connie couldn't hide her confusion. Meanwhile, behind her, Scarlett was raking her fingers through her hair.

"I swear, that man never follows the standard script! That's why I never could handle him…"

There was a reason Randolph Ulster was called His Excellency the Grim Reaper.

As a member of the Royal Security Force, the investigative unit charged with cracking down on crime in the kingdom, he always wore black clothing, and the sight of him mercilessly mowing down criminals was as frightening as the Grim Reaper. But the real reason for his nickname had to do with his personal life.

When he was six years old, his parents had perished unexpectedly in an accident. Several years later, his sickly older brother drew his final breath on his sickbed. When he was sixteen, Scarlett—a girl in the same generation and social class as him—was executed, and to top it all off, his wife killed herself less than a year after they married. This much death could hardly be considered a coincidence. There must be an angel of death hovering over Randolph Ulster's shoulder, stealing the life of everyone close to him.

The rumor spread until he received the unwelcome nickname of His Excellency the Grim Reaper.

©Yu-nagi

"I see... So that's how you plan to clear Scarlett Castiel of the false accusations."

The interview Randolph conducted in a drawing room of the old Montrose residence was truly impressive. He didn't apply so much pressure that she felt he was interrogating her. Nevertheless, he skillfully drew out her answers, highlighted her contradictions, and sharpened his questioning when he noticed her acting flustered.

Before she knew it, Connie had confessed the whole story to him. She even admitted to dubious matters such as seeing Scarlett's ghost. She felt she deserved praise, however, for avoiding at all costs the word *revenge*. Beside her, Scarlett sat slumped with her hand on her forehead. Connie wished she could do the same.

"...Ten years ago, I was on a secret mission abroad. When I received the news, I remember thinking it was a foolish, unexpected way for her to die."

At the word *foolish*, Scarlett—who had been listening with eyes closed—gave a start.

"But I wasn't interested enough to be suspicious. That was wrong of me."

At these words, spoken with no feeling whatsoever, Scarlett floated lightly into the air and gazed down on Randolph with an atrociously beautiful smile. *I bet... I bet she's thinking about how she can make him cry*, Connie thought.

"Do you have any idea what the Holy Grail of Eris is?" Randolph asked matter-of-factly.

"The Holy Grail of Eris?" she echoed in surprise. "W-wait just a moment now."

"What's wrong?"

"Do you believe me?"

The truth was, she herself still felt like she was making the whole thing up. Could anything sound more ridiculous than her claim that she could see the ghost of a girl who had been executed ten years ago?

Randolph turned to her and nodded. "Certainly, it's a preposterous tale, because of course I can't see Scarlett myself."

"Uh-huh…"

"The truth is, I don't have enough information yet to decide whether or not I believe you. But for me, the situation I most want to avoid is that everything you're saying now is a lie, and in fact someone else is behind it all."

Connie stared at him in surprise, but he just shrugged as if nothing was amiss.

"That's just one possibility. But if you act unpredictably again, I want to be prepared to deal with it. I'm acting on a hunch, not as part of an official investigation. Whatever the reason, it wouldn't be right for me to spend too much time with a girl of marriageable age in a personal capacity. I need some pretext of decency."

She knew exactly what he was getting at. But she wanted him to consider her point of view. That pretext of decency had gotten them into a very strange situation.

"If you *are* trying to prove Scarlett Castiel's innocence, then I suppose you can do as you please. Of course, I can't countenance any crimes, but I commend your desire to help another person, even if they're dead."

"Um, th-thank you…?"

Randolph paused for a beat, then gave her another puzzled look. "For what?"

What was this, déjà vu? Connie was starting to feel dizzy.

"Anyhow, as far as my personal impression goes," Randolph went on in his usual dispassionate tone, "every now and then, you have an expression that reminds me of Scarlett Castiel. So much so, in fact, that I can't help wondering if she's the one speaking to me."

Although his face was as blank as ever, there was something nostalgic—well, perhaps not nostalgic but at least reflective—about his words. A few minutes earlier, he had said he had no interest in Scarlett, but that also meant he felt no enmity toward her. There was something strange about a man who could maintain that much distance from a woman who, for better or worse, had a powerful ability to draw people to her.

"Um, Your Excellency?"

Connie wanted to ask him one last question. It was of great importance to her.

"Are you a-angry with me…?"

"Angry?"

On the night of Emilia's ball, he had reprimanded her so piercingly, she had been left speechless. That had been only one factor in her change of heart, but if he hadn't said it, she likely would have taken longer to come to the same conclusion.

"Oh, that," His Excellency the Grim Reaper said, nodding casually. "You seemed so vulnerable. You'd give yourself away at the slightest poke. Couldn't help it."

"You couldn't help it?"

"Yes."

"…You couldn't help it…?" She tilted her head in confusion. How unexpected.

"Anyhow, is there anything else you're keeping from me?"

Lily Orlamunde's key came to mind. She'd told him about taking the envelope from the chapel and about the note inside. She'd mentioned the scrawled message about the Holy Grail of Eris. He'd said he didn't know what it meant.

But just as she'd been about to tell him about the key, Scarlett had pierced her with an ice-cold glare, so she'd hurriedly swallowed her words.

Now, as she hesitated again over whether to tell him, Scarlett spoke up.

"*Absolutely not. Do not tell him about the key. We don't yet know if we can trust this man.*"

Connie paused for a second, then dropped her eyes and mumbled, "No, nothing."

Randolph nodded with almost disappointing readiness.

"I see." He turned slowly toward her. He appeared to be trying to decide whether to say something. "…You may not realize this, but for the sake of your future, I feel I ought to tell you."

Those cerulean eyes, as blue as a cloudless sky, took her in.

"Constance Grail—*Miss* Grail."

She had a bad feeling about this.

Randolph's face remained solemn.

"You're, well—you're lousy at lying."

※

Teresa Jennings was dead.

Rain as fine as silver threads had been falling since morning. The newspaper article said that when Teresa's lover told her he planned to leave her, she had tried to kill both him and herself. The lover, Linus Tudor, had survived unharmed but was not in his right mind, and he had returned to his native land.

Connie filed away these facts quietly in her mind. She did not tell herself it had been her own fault, as she might have before. They had their own problems, and it was none other than Teresa herself who had made the decision. Teresa was responsible for what had happened. Just as Constance Grail was responsible for abandoning sincerity and choosing her own path. But…

But she did have a tiny bit to do with this. She couldn't let herself forget that.

The constant patter of rain swathed the city in a gray veil of mist.

Randolph was waiting outside the house. Although he wasn't wearing his uniform, he had on a black jacket with a stand-up collar and black pants. His umbrella, too, was black from top to bottom. He really did look the part of the Grim Reaper.

Today, he would go to his church and take an oath of engagement with Connie. It was essentially a meet and greet. More than a formal ceremony, it was a chance for him to acknowledge that from now on, he would be part of her family. Piles of paperwork still had to be filled out before they could publicly announce the engagement, and they planned to find various excuses to avoid it until ultimately the marriage was canceled.

Connie's parents still weren't back from the domain, but she had received their permission by letter. Apparently, Randolph had tested the waters with them as well. At first, they had questioned her, but recently they seemed to have given up on having a say, probably since her mind seemed made up.

"I've asked Viscount Hamsworth to be our witness," he told her. The viscount happened to belong to Randolph's neighborhood church. "He's really too degenerate to stand witness to a holy oath, but considering the whole engagement is false to start with, I thought he'd be perfect for the job."

"I see...," Connie said.

She must have looked down, because Randolph blinked and asked, "What's the matter?"

"...Nothing, it's just... About the engagement..." She couldn't help sounding evasive, given what she was about to say. "Are you certain you want to do this, Your Excellency? When I thought it over, I realized you weren't getting much from the arrangement..."

For her part, Connie would be avoiding prosecution for a crime and having her family debts taken over. But what about Randolph? She had been too flustered before to realize it, but he seemed to be on the losing end of the deal. Lily Orlamunde had died two years ago. That wasn't a short span of time, but it wasn't particularly long, either. Some people would probably enjoy making a fuss over that fact. Plus, they weren't even of the same social rank. Randolph was currently an earl, and his family held a dukedom. He hadn't said anything to her, but she suspected his family must oppose the match quite strongly.

His Excellency the Grim Reaper turned slowly to Connie, his face as emotionless as ever.

"To admit my childish feelings," he said in a tone that suggested he was about to tell her something very important, "I don't care for marriage."

"You don't?" Connie blurted out. Could Randolph Ulster be one of those people she'd heard about lately who wanted to be single for their whole life? But then what would happen to the enormous Richelieu domain? If he didn't marry, he wouldn't have children to inherit his fortune. He must have guessed the reason for her surprise, because he continued speaking.

"Ever since my father passed, my uncle has ruled our domain. He has a fine son whom I suppose might as well take over from his father. The Earl of Ulster has no direct control over a domain, so not having a child poses no problem."

In other words, he wasn't interested in inheriting the family domain. Still, that seemed like a poor reason not to marry. Anyhow, he'd already been married to Lily Orlamunde. Connie wondered if her suspicion showed on her face. He glanced at her.

"I know it's not much of a reason..."

He paused and seemed to hesitate for a moment but ultimately shrugged as if he'd changed his mind.

"...but it's a secret," he concluded.

"A secret?"

"Yes."

His answer was too decisive for her to probe any further.

"Anyhow, I've been saying publicly that I'm not interested in taking over the dukedom for a long time, but some people are still pushing for me to do it. Quite a few are scheming for me to marry their daughters. So, as you might guess, this plan suits me as well. A fiancée will keep the riffraff away. I'll be only too happy if people say I'm an inappropriate choice for the lord of the domain."

Huh.

Still looking serious, he wrapped up his explanation.

"In other words, from my perspective, this arrangement will bring nothing but benefits."

What an odd man he was.

Nevertheless, she felt as if a strong breeze had just blown away all her uncertainties, leaving a clear sky.

He reeks of alcohol.

As soon as the door opened to the room where Connie and Randolph were waiting for the priest to administer their oaths, she grimaced.

It was like a barrel of wine had just walked in.

Deathly pale and clearly hung over, Hamsworth was gripping a pitcher into which he repeatedly vomited.

"Uh, so…have ya…*blergh*…said your…?"

No, they hadn't said their oaths yet. What was he trying to say anyway? More importantly, what were they going to do about this?

Connie glanced up at Randolph. His Excellency the Grim Reaper looked the same as ever as he thanked the viscount for coming. Was that all they needed to do? Well, it was only a temporary engagement, so maybe everything would be fine.

Despite the rocky start, they managed to get through the oaths, and afterward, Hamsworth collapsed, exhausted, into the guest chair. Connie couldn't help feeling sympathetic for the chair as it creaked beneath him.

Her business finished, she was preparing to say her good-byes when the viscount reluctantly lifted his head and looked in her direction. His gaze wandered for a moment before he narrowed his eyes ever so slightly and smiled with amusement.

"May the gods protect *you all*," he said.

Randolph accompanied Connie back to her house, then continued on to the Royal Security Force headquarters where he worked. He'd told her he had the day off, so she assumed he must be a workaholic.

Connie was strolling in the courtyard admiring the rainbow of flowers— fragrant pure-white gardenias, marigolds like little suns, pale purple clematis—when Scarlett interrupted her thoughts.

"…*So what are you going to do now?*"

"What?"

"It seems you have no intention of helping me anymore."

"What?!"

Scarlett was sulking. She'd been in a bad mood ever since the incident at the old Montrose residence, and apparently, she still wasn't over it.

"Why would you say that?" Connie asked. Scarlett looked down at the ground theatrically.

"After all, your debt is taken care of…"

So that was the issue. Connie couldn't help smiling. Scarlett scowled. Connie smiled even more.

"Listen to me, Scarlett."

Although less than a month had passed since they first met, to Connie it felt like ages.

"Ever since Pamela yelled at me at the Grand Merillian—no, since even before that," she began. It had started when her father took on the debt. And when Neil chose Pamela over her. "Every time something bad happened to me, I'd accept it as inevitable, but at the same time, there was this voice screaming inside my head. *Somebody help me!*"

Why? Why me? Someone! Please, someone!

"But of course, nobody ever did."

Somebody help me!

"Fine, I'll help you."

Except for one person.

"And now that I think about it, there's something I've never said to you."

There really was no good reason. Maybe she'd been thinking Scarlett had an ulterior motive in her quest for revenge. But still…

Scarlett looked suspicious, but Connie stared into her eyes.

"Thank you for helping me," she said.

Scarlett had saved her.

The amethyst eyes gradually widened.

"Now it's my turn to help you, isn't it?"

She smiled brightly. Scarlett pursed her lips like she was angry. When she spoke, her tone was scolding—but at the same time, she seemed to be savoring the moment.

"...*You idiot, Connie.*"

Connie looked up. The rain had stopped, and the sun was pouring down on the city as if it had just been resurrected. Connie shaded her eyes against its brilliance and smiled at the sky.

Soon it would be Diana, the seventh month of the year.

Constance Grail

Has traded sincerity for stubbornness. Sixteen, and unexpectedly engaged to Randolph Ulster. ←new!

Most likely acting on knee-jerk reflex. Has recently become fully committed to helping Scarlett get revenge. Was overly chummy with Scarlett in the heat of the moment, but Scarlett didn't say anything, so she figures it's probably fine.

Scarlett Castiel

Troubled by the fact that Connie hasn't been very obedient lately. Also, she got a little too chummy in the heat of the moment, but Scarlett isn't so petty that she'd scold her for it, and anyway, sh-she can do whatever she wants…! Decided to be equally friendly in return.

Maximilian Castiel

Around thirty. Light-blond hair, reddish-purple eyes. Scarlett's brother by another mother. Apparently serious and smart, unlike Scarlett. Still treats everyone like his servant.

Aliénore Shibola

Scarlett's mother.
Called Crownless Aliénore.

Cornelia Faris

The last empress of the Faris Empire. Called Cornelia of the Starry Crown because her veins ran with the blood of the kings and chiefs of the many lands Faris had conquered—as numerous as the stars in the sky.

Randolph Ulster

A truly unpredictable man. Recently engaged to Connie. Apparently has a lot going on. Seems to be good at his job.

Deborah Darkian

In her late thirties.
Host of the most recent Earl John Doe Ball.

Viscount Hamsworth

Happily disguised as Ham. Unusually quick to flee. And what was he looking at anyway?

©Yu-nagi

Shoshanna was fed up.

She'd been hiding away in this house by the sea for six months already, and the salt air was damaging her hair. Also, it made her skin feel sticky.

As always, her main job was to grind the roots of the tagi plant into a paste in a druggist's mortar. Once she had accumulated a decent amount of the sticky brown substance, she transferred it to a finer mortar where she kneaded it with face powder. Next, she emulsified it with an oil extracted from olives, which was a fairly finicky process. Too much oil and it ran off without soaking into the skin, but too little and it cracked.

Shoshanna rolled up her sleeves and observed her own brown arm. When she touched it, the skin looked normal and healthy. She moistened a cloth and rubbed at her skin, but the colored paste did not come off.

"Perfect."

Satisfied with her work, she took the knife with the rounded tip and skillfully packed the foundation into an ointment jar. Although she was still young, working with knives was her forte. After all, her other task was to cook for her lazy older brother.

He had left for work about ten days earlier. Although she'd had no word from him, she wasn't worried. He was an outstanding worker, even among their fellow countrymen. As his caretaker, she strived at the very least to not get in his way and to leave the house as little as humanly possible. When she absolutely had to go to the market, she pulled her hood low over her eyes and never forgot to bring a knife to protect herself.

She sighed. She had made up her mind to tell herself that she was fed up with the current situation. She wasn't afraid about being left alone in an unfamiliar land, nor was she lonely. She was simply bored and frustrated. That's what she told herself.

Just then, someone knocked on the front door. A light knock repeated three times. A pause, then a fourth knock. Then a hard knock and a soft one. Today was the ninth division of formest Diana, so the password was correct. Shoshanna grinned. Her brother was back.

"Salvador!"

She slid back the heavy bolt. As expected, a lanky young man was standing at the door. He had dirty-blond hair and brown skin. A white cloth was wrapped around his head, and in the basket on his back were several rolled-up carpets. He looked exactly like a snail.

"What in the world is that big bundle on your back?" she asked, her mouth falling open.

He hadn't had the bundle when he left. He narrowed his catlike eyes and laughed hollowly.

"There was something of a mix-up. Oh, I almost forgot! I have a present for you for being such a good girl and looking after the house!"

He pulled the largest carpet from the basket and threw it down on the floor. It landed with a thud. He kicked it open with one foot. From the center of the carpet appeared—a child.

"You said you wanted a pet, didn't you?"

The child had huge eyes with long lashes. The features were feminine, but the short hair made her think it was a boy. He had a muzzle over his mouth and was staring at her in terror. He looked a few years younger than Shoshanna, who would be eleven this year, and was dressed exquisitely.

Shoshanna stared back at him, wide-eyed. "I did say that, but…"

Her eyes met the bluish-purple eyes of the boy. In them she saw fear and entreaty.

She sighed. "But I wanted a bird."

"Isn't this like a bird?"

"Not at all."

To begin with, this was much bigger. The pet Shoshanna had begged her brother for at the market was a sweet little parakeet that could sit on her finger. But when she'd asked him for it, he'd only shrugged indifferently.

"Oh, it doesn't matter. Just feed it and take care of it for now."

"Why me?" She sulked. She didn't want another annoying job. Salvador shrugged and looked at her innocently.

"Better than leaving it with Krishna, isn't it?"

Remembering the sadistic man with the two black spots in his pupil, Shoshanna nodded hurriedly.

"Oh, yes."

"Then I'm leaving it to you."

Apparently, the conversation was over. He was already humming as he examined the ointment jar she'd just finished preparing. Opening the lid, he scooped some of the thick cream onto his index finger and rubbed it into his skin.

"This came out well. I'll take two or three with me. My stock is running low."

With that, he repacked his basket and stepped toward the door.

"Where are you going?!" Shoshanna couldn't help asking.

Salvador looked down at her like he'd stumbled on something unexpected. She must have looked very pitiful, because his eyes widened for a second, and he cleared his throat. But then he placed his hand on the door, and Shoshanna sank to the floor in disappointment.

Salvador was hopeless.

The door opened with a pitiless creak. The sinking sun cast a shadow into the room.

Before he vanished, her brother turned toward her.

"Where am I going, you ask?" He smiled happily. "*To work*, of course."

Lit from the back by the setting sun, his face was red as blood.

Shoshanna

Eleven. Good with her hands. Wanted a parakeet but got a human boy instead and doesn't know what to do. Rubs a brown foundation-like substance on her skin.

Salvador

Shoshanna's older brother. Basically lazy but apparently good at his job. Dirty-blond hair and catlike eyes. Rubs a brown foundation-like substance on his skin. Left for work again.

Krishna

A sadistic man mentioned by Salvador and Shoshanna. Apparently has two black spots in his eye.

The Captive Child

Eight or nine. Bluish-purple eyes. Is dressed exquisitely.

The Royal Security Force headquarters were located at the western end of Amadeus Road in the capital.

In one corner of this enormous facility, Randolph Ulster was flipping through a thick stack of documents bound with black string. On the yellowed cover was written the words *Daeg Gallus*—the Rooster at Dawn. Randolph had been working the case for years.

As he was reading, the door slid open, and an extremely grumpy, extremely handsome youth peered in. It was Kyle Hughes, deputy chief of the investigative unit Randolph commanded.

"Those asses in the Gaina Unit are bloody useless," he spit out icily, dropping a mountain of documents on Randolph's desk. The marble slab groaned beneath the unexpected load. Randolph slowly looked up.

"How could anyone be so incompetent? Is his brain full of maggots…?!"

Gaina—Jeorg Gaina, that is—had led the raid on the Earl John Doe Ball the other night. A prototypical sheltered noble's son, he'd never gotten along with Kyle, who was a strong believer in meritocracy.

"I've been on the tail of that arms dealer in Melvina, and I haven't gotten a wink in three days! That bastard crosses borders like he's playing hopscotch! I'm incessantly butting heads with the border police. Of course, the second he turned his back, I got in a few good blows! I had to slap my horse's ass all night long just to get back here in time. Infernal swine!"

With bags under his bloodshot eyes and a five-o'clock shadow, Kyle seemed to have misplaced his usual lady-killer looks somewhere on the road. He scowled demonically and scratched his head, possessed by fury.

"So here I am, tired as all hell, and right away that ass Gaina comes swaggering up to me, bragging about his marvelous achievement at the old Montrose residence! I listened because I didn't have much choice, and he says those snot-nosed slaves belong to some minority race in Soldita! I wanted to talk to one of the culprits because I thought he might be the one I've been after in another case, so I fill out a shitload of forms to get permission, only to learn he's died of poisoning in the jail…!"

"Poisoning?" Randolph echoed.

Kyle pulled out his seat violently and stared ahead of him.

"Poisoning. Whenever those scumbags from the southern gangs are arrested, the first thing they do is pop some poison and kill themselves, so it's standard practice to cuff their hands and feet and muzzle them, but that incompetent fool Gaina handled him like any old thief! I was so furious, I told—I mean reported it to Captain Bart and snatched the rights to the investigation from that bald-headed ass on the spot! So now this is our mountain."

He pointed to the towering pile of documents. Their subordinates practically broke down in tears at his words.

"What the devil's he thinking? I swear that handsome face is the only thing he's got going for him…!"

"Impossible! Absolutely impossible! We can't take on another case!"

Randolph, however, received the news calmly, reaching out for a document.

"What kind of poison was it?"

"I've asked the Alchemy Division to find out. Morie said by the looks of the corpse, it was probably a nerve agent."

"Must have been a tiny amount if it got past the pat down. Yet still enough to cause instant death… Interesting."

Even poor poisons were unlikely to be found on the market, let alone one of such high purity.

"Did he have the *sun tattoo*?"

"Of course I checked him down to his asshole, but I didn't find anything. To tell you the truth, I'm so tired, I could drop dead right here. I wish I could run straight over to Miriam at the Folkvangr and rest my poor head on her breast until I feel better. You think I could put that on the expense account? Oh, sorry, just joking. Honestly, do you have to look at me like that?"

For some reason, Kyle was covering his face with both hands, so Randolph nodded solemnly.

"In that case, he either had nothing to do with the Daeg Gallus case or else he was a sacrificial pawn who didn't know what was going on… Probably the latter."

That lot tended to favor nerve agents.

"Was there any evidence that Paradise was being used at the ball?"

"Not in the documents. Seems there weren't any signs of it, and none of the regular users were there… But then again, this is the Gaina Unit we're talking about. Can't trust 'em past the tip of your nose."

Kyle scratched his head. Jeorg Gaina was a lieutenant, but so far, he'd been put in charge of only petty crimes that could just as well be handled at the branch offices.

"What about Deborah Darkian?"

"You think that old witch would open her mouth over a trifle like this?" Kyle scowled.

Deborah Darkian. Although her name came up in association with all sorts of organized crime, she was a master scammer who never let them pin her down.

"I heard Deborah was the one who leaked the story to Gaina in the first place. Gave him names, too. Said the band that was offering a show with foreign dancers struck her as suspicious. That fool Gaina went as far as to thank her for cooperating in the investigation. Thanking Deborah, can you believe it?! I could die of embarrassment to think I work for the same organization as that delusional ninny. He's not worth wasting breath on! I feel like bashing my revolver straight into that hairless dome of his the next time I see him. I'd have been doubting her the moment she came to see us at the Security Force instead of telling her husband about her worries!"

Deborah's husband, Simon Darkian, had come from the military and currently served as comptroller of the treasury. He was widely rumored to be next in line for a promotion to secretary of the treasury. It should have been possible for him to quietly clear up the matter behind the scenes.

"But she intentionally chose a raid on the ball. Obviously, that would lead to rumors. Her reputation would be damaged. If she didn't care, that must mean—"

Randolph squinted slightly.

"—that she created an uproar on purpose."

What could her motivation have been? The incident at the old Montrose residence likely needed reexamination. Randolph turned the problem over slowly in his mind.

Kyle, whose rage seemed to have subsided slightly, looked up as if he'd just remembered something.

"By the way, that girl showed up again."

"What girl?"

"Constance Grail. First there was the little showdown at the Grand Merillian and then the affair with Teresa Jennings. She seems to be everywhere these days. I know the connection is still unclear, but don't you think we should take the initiative to question her?"

"That won't be necessary," Randolph replied curtly as he looked over some documents. He heard Kyle make a confused noise, but he didn't look up. "I've already assessed the situation."

"...You already questioned her? You? The man who treats criminal suspects mercilessly but acts the gentleman toward witnesses?"

Kyle leaned forward in his seat in confusion.

"I do believe it happened just as you were leaving for the border of Melvina...," Randolph said.

They'd given Melvina's Merchant of Death a bit of rope to hang himself on, but he'd suddenly gone into hiding, so it had hardly been the time for a personal chat.

"I'm engaged to her."

There was an awkward silence.

"What?"

Kyle Hughes may have been flippant and short-tempered, but he wasn't stupid. He had to have known the answer to his next question before he asked it.

"…To whom?!" he shouted.

Which meant what he was really saying was that he didn't want to believe what he'd just heard.

Randolph finally looked up from his work and confirmed the truth in a most matter-of-fact tone.

"To Constance Grail, of course."

※

Once again, Constance was the it girl. As she glanced over the mountain of letters that Marta had come staggering in with, her gaze paused with interest on one with a black border. Even the sealing wax was black, which meant it must be a death announcement—but…

Written on the black-edged paper in ink as black as a starless sky was this simple message:

You are summoned to the Starlight Room of the Grand Merillian for questioning.

"…What is this? A subpoena…?"

Her voice was hoarse with alarm at the intimidating note. The truth was, she had all too clear an idea of what this was about—which confused her.

"*That's the Darkian crest,*" Scarlett muttered in disgust as she glared at the seal Connie hadn't recognized. Darkian?

Connie's face must have been frozen in fear, because Scarlett let out an exasperated sigh and explained.

"*Take a good look. There's no stamp from the Ministry of Justice, is there? This thing has no legal validity. It's a prank,*" she pronounced in a decisive tone that did wonders to calm Connie's nerves. "*That sealing wax smacks of the Darkians—oh, you don't know them, do you? It's Deborah's family crest. Revolting how much time these middle-aged women have on their hands.*"

Deborah? It took Connie a second to remember who that was. She was the host of the Earl John Doe Ball—the woman with the black butterfly mask.

"*You know how ladies who are done bearing heirs suddenly start hosting salons with the literati? To be blunt, they're killing time. That's what the straitlaced ones do, at least.*"

Scarlett narrowed her eyes in displeasure.

"*The rogues, on the other hand, prefer hunting.*"

"Hunting…?"

"*Needless to say, I'm not talking about lugging a rifle around to shoot wild beasts. It's much more hideous than that. No—they amuse themselves by choosing a sacrificial victim and tormenting the lamb until their taste for lowbrow entertainment is sated. Deborah Darkian was famous for her hunts. She calls them 'investigations.' In truth, they were no more than opportunities to make an example of someone. It's disgusting to think she still hasn't grown out of that stupid pastime,*" she spit out. "*She's brought down quite a few people that way. But nobody knew what happened at her hunts. None of the participants would say a word about them. It seems they were made to take an oath of silence. Idiotic nonsense, but we had our own nickname for it.*"

The amethyst eyes glared at the black-bordered envelope so evocative of death.

"*The Silent Ladies' Tea Party, we called it.*"

※

"This is from Deborah Darkian?"

Randolph and Connie's engagement might be a sham, but they figured they ought to at least make some minor pretense of acting like fiancés.

That was why he had taken time out of his busy workday to stop by the Grail residence. She had invited him up to her room, saying she had something complicated to tell him about. Of course, she wasn't worried he'd take advantage of the situation, but for the sake of appearances, she left the door slightly open.

Randolph drew his brows together as he looked over the black-bordered envelope she'd handed him.

"Well, given that it's a prank, and this scrap of paper bears no legal weight, I see no reason for you to go out of your way to give her the time of day," he said. However, when he noticed his fiancée hunched apologetically in her corner of the room, he pressed his temples as if he had a headache and groaned.

"...You're going, aren't you?"

"Oh, no, it's only that if I reject the invitation, I'm afraid I'll seem rude... And also, I think she may know something about Scarlett..."

She couldn't help sounding like she was making excuses. Randolph sighed and looked again at the note in his hands. The furrow between his brows deepened.

"The date is the day after tomorrow. Why didn't they send this sooner?"

"...Hmm?"

"I've got a meeting with the deputy director of the commerce policy bureau that day. If I'd known about this a week ago, I could have rescheduled..."

"...Hmm?!" Connie blinked in confusion. Did he mean to say...? "Were you thinking of coming with me?"

"I wasn't just thinking of it—I was definitely going to." He sighed and set the card down on the table. "Not going isn't an option for you, is it?"

"No..."

Connie felt horribly ashamed. Her back hunched lower. She knew it was dangerous. But Deborah Darkian held enormous influence in society, didn't she? She probably had some information about the execution ten years ago.

And Connie wouldn't be alone. Scarlett would be with her.

"Deborah Darkian is a cunning woman. She does things differently from Scarlett Castiel."

Connie looked up, surprised that Randolph had read her thoughts so accurately. His cerulean eyes were aimed straight at her. Her heart thumped. She realized something. Normally, Scarlett would have a quick comeback for this sort of comment, but this time, she said nothing. Connie glanced at her. She looked unusually troubled.

Connie tensed.

Had she just made a terrible choice?

An inexpressible feeling of anxiety overcame her.

"Make sure you watch your step," Randolph admonished her.

"Yes..." She felt slightly dizzy. She wished she could lay down and rest. Maybe when she woke up, everything would have worked itself out nicely.

"The chauffeur will be here shortly. Are you ready to go?" he asked.

"...Ready to go where?"

He blinked, looking as confused as she felt.

"I thought I sent you a letter about this..."

A letter?

Connie gulped, glancing at her bureau, where mountains of envelopes towered perilously.

She had been so distracted by Deborah Darkian's invitation that she'd forgotten all about the other letters silently waiting for her.

"...Um..."

Cold sweat beaded on her forehead. It must be in there.

Somewhere in that mountain.

Randolph looked back and forth between Connie and the graveyard of unread letters, then nodded.

"When I didn't hear back, I simply assumed you were too busy to reply," he said coolly.

"I'm so sorry..."

She was clearly in the wrong here. In a flash, she bowed her head. Randolph furrowed his brow in mild consternation.

"I've made plans for us to meet some people today. An old friend of mine caught wind of the engagement and is quite curious to see my fiancée. You don't mind, do you?"

She was about to say that of course she didn't mind—but one thing concerned her. Just who was this person with the power to summon Randolph Ulster? She had a bad feeling about this.

"...Where are we going, by the way?" she asked timidly.

"Elbaite," he answered curtly.

"El...baite...?"

"Yes."

Connie was becoming tenser by the second. Randolph gave her a perplexed look.

"*Oh my,*" Scarlett piped up. Until now, she'd been sitting with chin in hand looking bored, but now she floated up. She looked over at the frozen Connie and smiled. "*You'll finally have the honor of meeting that lying schemer.*"

Elbaite—as in the Elbaite Villa. If Connie wasn't mistaken, that was the residence of the crown prince and princess she'd heard so much about.

The room where the crown prince and princess granted audiences was absurdly long and narrow, with a color theme of gold and crimson. When Connie looked up, she discovered a magnificent mural of the Moirai and an enormous chandelier in the center of the ceiling. She prostrated herself beneath its luxurious light.

The figure sitting in the glossy, crimson velvet armchair spoke quietly to her.

"Lift your head."

She obeyed. The face looking down at her was delicately drawn, almost like a beautiful woman. The prince smiled.

"So you're Constance Grail?"

This was the personage who had broken off his engagement to Scarlett Castiel and sworn eternal love to Cecilia Luze, a mere viscount's daughter. Crown Prince Enrique, idol of all young noblewomen in love with the notion of love, was looking down on Connie from the dais.

His brilliant magenta eyes wandered ever so slightly as he hesitated.

"...Yes, I see, you really are..."

"Shockingly ordinary?" Scarlett said, finishing his sentence. Connie tried with all her might to pretend she hadn't heard and keep the same expression before the crown prince.

Enrique quietly shifted his gaze away. How strange.

"I believe Cecilia will be arriving shortly—"

Abruptly changing the topic, the crown prince placed his hands on his knees. For some reason, he had refused to meet her eyes. As Connie was puzzling over this, she heard light footsteps. Someone was running toward them.

"Ah, here she is," Enrique said, sounding relieved.

"I'm sorry to be late!"

A beautiful woman came flying in, her long hair flowing like honey down her back and her eyes a smoky rose color. Her limbs were long and supple, her face almost unbelievably pretty.

"Randy!"

Crown Princess Cecilia broke into a huge smile the instant she saw Randolph, who was standing next to Connie. However, His Excellency the Grim Reaper was as cold as if she were some dangerous wild animal.

"I've been wanting to see you!"

She came straight at him with arms wide open, but he dexterously evaded her hug, still glaring at her without a word. Her status had just been lowered from wild beast to pestilent insect. Connie shivered. *Terrifying.* However, the princess didn't seem to mind. Still smiling brilliantly, she turned to Connie. Her large rose-colored eyes grew peculiarly round.

"Oh my, I didn't expect this! So plain! So adorable!"

Adorable?

Connie's own eyes widened. Maybe the princess was a wonderful person.

"*I'm going to tell you right now—that wasn't a compliment,*" Scarlett pronounced coldly, bringing Connie back to reality.

Instead of taking her place beside the crown prince, Cecilia walked over to Connie and slowly knelt. Then, with a terribly innocent expression on her face, she tilted her head. The word *sweet* must have been invented for this woman.

Still with that carefree smile on her face, she pointed at Randolph.

"Now, this man may look frightening—and in fact he is, as well as ridiculously serious and excessively strict, and he never, ever smiles— but I think at the bottom of it all, he's not so bad. So please don't lose patience with him!"

At that moment, a blizzard cold enough to freeze her solid erupted next to Connie. *Can I go home yet?*

Cecilia Adelbide was probably the most famous royal in the land. Born a lower noble, she had overcome countless obstacles to marry Crown Prince Enrique. Crowds were said to have flocked to the capital from around the kingdom just to have a glimpse of the happy couple on their wedding day.

The daughter of Viscount Luze, Cecilia had been a sickly, weak young woman who was rumored to have hardly ever left her domain before debuting in society. Her fateful meeting with Enrique took place at her very first ball in the capital. However, their meeting was also the beginning of a tragedy, because at the time, Enrique already had a fiancée: Scarlett Castiel, possessor of overwhelming beauty and bloodline.

What followed hardly bears repeating.

Cecilia was known as an affectionate princess. She was fair, selfless, and never discriminated based on rank. Not only did she actively support the orphanages and hospitals, she was known to serve at soup kitchens in person. Some people went as far as to say she was the second coming of Saint Anastasia.

"Now, Cecilia," Enrique said timidly to his wife, attempting to melt the icy mood. "That's not much of a compliment, is it?"

"Hmm? Oh, I wasn't complimenting him."

"…Ah, you weren't?"

"No, I wasn't," she said with a casual shrug before turning again to Connie. "Do you mind if I call you Connie?"

The glittering rose-colored eyes peered at Connie. She was very close. Overly close.

"O-of course not, Your Highness."

She nodded enthusiastically, stepping back just a tiny bit. "And you call me Cecil, all right?"

"What?! Oh, no, I could never be so bold—"

"Why not? I was born a viscount's daughter. Just like you, I believe."

But that was ridiculous! It was Enrique who answered Connie's silent plea with common sense.

"Don't make unreasonable demands on her, Cecilia."

Cecilia snorted.

"And don't snort, Cecilia."

"Yes, Your Highness."

She turned away from the crown prince and snorted again quietly. Connie pretended not to hear.

A smile spread again over her doll-like face.

"I've been so worried about you, Randy. I mean, there you are, finally married after all these years, and then Lily goes and does *that*. I'm so happy an adorable little creature like Connie is going to be your wife. Do let us have tea together soon. Are you free next week on the holy day?"

Connie sensed all kinds of vitriol in that little speech, but it was the invitation added so casually at the end that truly bewildered her.

"What?!"

"…Your Highness, please don't jest."

"I wasn't asking you, Randy. Was I, Connie?"

Dismissing Randolph's move to block, Cecilia squeezed Connie's hand. Despite the silk glove, her palm was so cold, Connie almost jumped backward.

"You want to come, don't you?"

The crown princess smiled brightly. That was all, but still…

"Oh, um, yes…"

But still Connie felt as if she were being coerced by an irresistible power. She nodded. It was a royal invitation. She would have had a hard enough time turning it down in writing, but in person, she was nowhere near bold enough to say no.

"I'm so glad! I'll send a messenger later!"

"Your Highness."

Randolph's voice was so low, it seemed to crawl along the floor. The crease between his eyes was like an ocean trench, and disgust was written boldly across his face. *Eek. Very scary.* Most people would burst into tears if someone looked at them like that. At least, Connie herself would. She would wail. If Randolph made the princess cry, surely even he would be charged with lèse-majesté. Worried, Cecilia glanced at her.

But Cecilia simply clapped and exclaimed, "Ooh, what a face!"

Connie drew back. She was in quite a fix, caught between these two scary characters.

"You know, Randy," the princess said, cocking her head adorably, "I really do think it was unkind of you to intentionally choose a day for this audience when I have royal duties I can't get out of. I know you were worried about your adorable little fiancée, but this treatment really has injured me. As luck had it, I was able to steal a few minutes away, but it was extremely difficult."

She kept going in that naive tone of hers.

"But I forgive you, because I had the rare fortune of seeing you look unhappy."

Her lips, as delicately tinted as pale flower petals, turned slowly up to form a half-moon. Connie froze, sensing something icy in those gently narrowed eyes.

"I…"

Connie was so flustered that for a second, she didn't know who was speaking. The calm voice paid no heed to the tense atmosphere. A moment later, she realized it belonged to the princess.

"As I told His Imperial Highness earlier, I must greet some visitors from the southern realms today. I'm very sorry, but since I've had the pleasure of meeting you, I really must be leaving. Please don't think me terribly rude. It has been an honor to meet with the two of you for even the briefest of moments. If it were my own choice, I would not leave at all. Can I trust that you understand that?"

In a complete about-face, her expression now conveyed sorrow, and her tone was tinged with sincerity and regret. She was the very picture of a chaste, graceful princess.

"Farewell, my honorable guests."

Smiling a noble smile that concealed her emotions completely, Cecilia walked out of the room.

"…Well. Please make yourselves comfortable. Randolph, feel free to be your usual self," the crown prince said, resting his arm on the armchair.

"She's as condescending as ever, I see," Randolph replied, furrowing his brow. Enrique smiled bitterly.

"You two never did get on well. I hope you'll overlook her faults for my sake."

"I don't think my overlooking them will do much to solve the problem. That personality must make her a lot of enemies."

"I suppose. But given that we don't have children, I'm grateful for it. To be frank, I don't have much interest in being king. I'll be happy if Johan's supporters keep gaining momentum."

Feeling that she shouldn't really be overhearing this conversation, Connie shrank backward.

Johan Adelbide was the king's second son—that is, Enrique's younger brother. Unlike the childless crown prince and princess, he had already been blessed with heirs.

"But enough of that. The envoy from Faris should be arriving soon."

He narrowed his magenta eyes. Randolph nodded.

"Now that you mention it, the Guards Regiment did receive a request to protect an important personage. They're coming today? I thought…"

"Yes, the original plan had them arriving last night. Now the sun is almost overhead, and they still haven't sent a word of apology. Far from it—they show no sign of hurrying and send no word of why they're late. Perhaps, since we are still a young kingdom, they consider us a territory of the great land of Faris. Mighty anachronistic of them, I'd say. They've always been an arrogant bunch."

Enrique's face twisted in irritation.

"They said this is about strengthening the alliance, but I'm sure they're here to pester us for money again. They put on a good show, but rumor is they're in financial crisis."

As soon as their audience with the crown prince ended and they left the reception room, Randolph said, "I think you probably realized this already, but Cecilia is…"

He paused and glanced down at her with his cerulean eyes.

"…a twisted person."

Connie nodded solemnly. She was indeed.

"She's incapable of telling the truth. In fact, she throws every situation off its axis. For that reason, I wanted to avoid meeting with her at this stage—but she seems to have more little birds in her service than I realized."

Connie heard him sigh quietly.

"However, she is able to act passably in public. Obviously, people don't like that she comes from a viscount's family, but she has yet to cause a major scandal. She does a good job of maintaining her public facade, I suppose. Which is why I'm convinced that she must have had a good reason for acting as she did today."

Randolph paused and gazed at Connie with a serious expression.

"I may be overthinking this, but I hope you'll bear that in mind."

"...I will."

Randolph had planned to escort Connie home, he said, but some pressing work came up, and so they went their separate ways from the Elbaite Villa.

As Connie walked through the expansive gardens with their interplay of greenery and water, she decided to ask Scarlett a question that had suddenly bubbled up inside her.

"Scarlett?"

"What?"

"Why did you hate Cecilia so much?"

True, the crown princess wasn't the saint Connie had envisioned her to be. But what had led Scarlett to treat her as an enemy? Up till now, Connie had assumed it had to do with Scarlett's passion for Enrique, but just now at the villa, Scarlett had shown no signs of jealousy.

"Hate her? Hardly. It was the opposite.."

Connie looked puzzled. "The opposite?"

"Yes. She was the one who hated me in the beginning. In which case, I was entirely within my rights to counterattack, was I not?"

So it was Cecilia who had viewed Scarlett as a rival in love? Just as Connie was thinking that made sense, Scarlett said something unexpected yet again.

"Of course, I was far from the only person she hated."

"...Huh?"

"But maybe hate is the wrong word for it."

"...Huh?!"

"Didn't you notice? She may have been laughing frivolously, but all the while she was hostile toward everyone in sight. It was the same ten years ago."

"Hostile?"

Maybe that was it. She wasn't sure. The only thing she knew was that at the very end, the depths of her rose-colored eyes had been so cold, they nearly froze Connie solid.

"Although these days she seems to be better at hiding it. It was much worse the first time I met her. I always thought it was odd that nobody noticed. I don't even know how to describe the look in those eyes of hers. If I had to choose a word for it…"

Scarlett thought for a moment, then made a satisfied sound.

"…I'd call it loathing."

"Loa…thing?"

Connie stopped walking. Maybe what Crown Princess Cecilia had won for herself by overcoming all those obstacles wasn't true love after all. Her arms crawled with unnameable terror.

Just then, someone called to her.

"Are you lost, young lady?"

She turned around to see a man she didn't recognize standing behind her. He looked a few years older than her father. He was slender, handsome, and in the prime of life. His clothes were by no means showy, yet his eyes were the same shade of magenta as Enrique's. Which must mean…

"Oh, it's His Majesty King Ernst."

"His Majesty…?!" Connie squealed idiotically. Why would the king of the land be walking out here all alone?

She scrambled to prostrate herself, but the king stopped her, saying, "You may stay as you are. I heard you were at the Elbaite Villa, so I hurried to finish up my duties."

"…You did?"

What in the world was he talking about? As she was silently puzzling over this, Ernst Adelbide turned a kindly smile on her.

"Don't you see? I've come to meet you, daughter of the House of Grail."

"…Meet me?!" she once again squealed. She immediately slapped a hand over her mouth, but Ernst appeared not to notice.

"It's simply marvelous," the king said in a tone as relaxed as if he'd been talking about the weather. "A month ago, no one even knew who you were. Today you are the talk of the town. You made a stir at the ball, became engaged to the famous Randolph Ulster, and now you've been invited to the villa."

He smiled gently at her. Still, she felt uncomfortable, as if her skin was under some sort of pressure.

"Tell me, how did you do it?"

When the magenta eyes looked down on her, she finally realized why. His eyes weren't laughing.

"Speaking of which, some have called you the second coming of Scarlett Castiel," he said, lowering his voice, as if to imply that this was what he'd actually come to say.

"Um, I…," Connie began, looking away. Her gaze fell on a carpet of tiny flowers.

"They're violets," Ernst whispered, following her gaze. "Throughout most of the continent, violets tend to be bluish purple, but ours are much redder."

Connie nodded. Because the color of the petals was so similar to the royal eye color, violets were known as the flower of Adelbide.

"Do you know why?" Ernst asked.

"N-no…"

"Well then, I'll tell you. According to an ancient legend of this land, violets are haunted by a careless, blundering spirit who got too close to the souls tormented by hellfire and was horribly burned. What do you think of that?"

It must be some sort of metaphor. Cold sweat dripped down her cheek. She felt he was ridiculing her for getting too close to Scarlett, or perhaps trying to restrain her. Or was she imagining things?

S-somebody help me…

As she stood there going paler by the second, she heard someone sigh.

"Step aside, Connie."

Something slipped inside her body. The sensation was familiar, and she did not resist. Her consciousness was pushed into a corner of her being again.

Scarlett slowly raised her face.

"Well, let me see. If it was curiosity that drew the ghost too close, then she could indeed be called a fool."

Despite the extraordinary circumstances, Scarlett was obnoxiously unflustered.

"But maybe…the spirit of those little flowers was reaching out to help the dead who suffered so terribly."

"…An interesting theory, but does it have any basis?"

"If the violet had anything to be ashamed of, it wouldn't bloom so boldly, would it?"

Ernst widened his eyes at her imposing attitude, as grand as an actress reading lines, then smiled wryly.

"Yes, you *are* like her."

"Don't tease me."

Her tone was unbelievably curt, given she was speaking to the most powerful man in the kingdom. Connie waited nervously for the scene to unfold.

"If I were Scarlett Castiel, this is what I would say," Scarlett said, smiling like a child playing a prank. "The affairs of weeds are none of my business."

Ernst stared at her dumbfounded for a moment, then brought his hand to his mouth. After a pause, he said, "Yes, that does seem like something she would have said."

After that, he said no more. The false smile of a few moments earlier was nowhere to be seen. In its place was a pained expression—perhaps of deep regret.

※

Two days later, Connie visited the palace grounds again. She was there for Deborah Darkian's suspicious tea party.

In addition to the public halls in the Grand Merillian, there were many rooms that required special permission to enter. This one, the Starlight Room, had once been used to suppress royals and nobility.

Located on the top floor of the building, the room's walls and ceiling were entirely covered in paper the color of lapis lazuli. Because there were no windows, it created a powerful illusion of nightfall. When Connie looked closely, she saw that it was evenly dotted with gold leaf meant to represent small stars glittering in the candlelight.

Toward the back was a depiction of a blindfolded goddess holding a sword in her right hand and a scale in her left.

In the center of the room sat a heavy, round mahogany table surrounded by six chairs with armrests and navy velvet upholstery. Four of the chairs were already occupied.

In the far chair sat Deborah Darkian. The corners of her blood-red lips curled upward when she noticed Connie standing stiffly by the door.

"Welcome, Constance Grail. I see that your head is still firmly in its place."

She gestured for Connie to take a seat directly across from her.

"As I'm sure you realize, you must never speak of what happens today in this room. Do you agree?"

The moment Connie sat down, she immediately felt the curious gazes of four pairs of eyes. They were not so different from the gazes of children—children who tortured insects and then stomped on them when they grew bored, unaware of committing any crime. A chill ran down her back. She wanted to look away, but she resisted the urge and kept her eyes on Deborah.

"I recognize those three. They're part of Deborah's clique. I'm fairly sure they're all at least countesses," Scarlett said, scrutinizing the faces of the noblewomen on either side of Deborah. At least countesses? That meant Connie, a mere viscount's daughter, had even less right to speak. Her heart pounded at the thought, but she nodded calmly.

"…Yes, I do."

"Do you? Then sign your oath in blood," Deborah said in a bored tone, sliding a jewel-encrusted dagger and a piece of paper with an oath written on it toward Connie. Scarlett frowned in distaste.

"An oath signed in blood? Just what era do you think you're living in, woman?"

Connie signed her name with a feather pen, then pressed the dagger's blade silently against her pointer finger. A bead of blood rose from her skin.

"Well," Deborah said, smiling with satisfaction as Connie handed her the paper with the bloody fingerprint on it. "Do you know why we've called you here today?"

Interpreting Connie's silence as a *no*, Deborah continued in a singsong voice.

"We received a letter from your friend—Pamela Francis."

"From Pamela…?"

"Does that name ring a bell? Poor thing, the platinum-blond hair she was so proud of has turned snow white. All because you forsook her so heartlessly. Didn't you, Constance Grail? Wasn't it punishment enough to chastise her as you did at the ball? That alone made it impossible for her to show her face in society. But then to brush off her hand when she reached for help—oh yes, we have her medical report right here."

"What kind of quack wrote that? It must have been the Darkians' family doctor. What a farce," Scarlett said.

Connie was silently trembling. Pamela Francis? She never thought she would hear that name after all this time.

"Nevertheless, no matter how much poor Pamela is suffering, your actions do not constitute a crime under the law. It's simply horrible, isn't it? As a daughter of the sincere Grail family, you must understand that. In which case—"

Deborah's ashen eyes flashed sadistically.

"If the law will not judge you for your crime, then we will do it ourselves."

Most likely, this was Deborah Darkian's true self.

"They say that in the old dynasty, there was a law of revenge that allowed an eye for an eye, so to speak. That is, if you injured someone, then you must be injured in the same measure. A wonderful law, don't you think?"

"—I'd add that the law she's talking about was instituted to prevent excessive acts of revenge. You had better study well before you speak or you'll end up hanging yourself, Madame Idiot."

Scarlett laughed. Needless to say, Deborah couldn't hear her, but even if she had, nothing would have changed. For Deborah Darkian, that was not the important point.

"I made a promise to poor Pamela. I told her that no matter what, I would send her the hair of Constance Grail."

"...Acts of violence are against the law."

"Violence? Dear me, did you think we were going to hold you down and forcefully chop off that dirty-colored hair of yours? The lower ranks really do have barbaric ideas," Deborah scoffed, pushing the oath back toward Connie.

"Look there. The oath you just signed in blood says you will obey all decisions of the investigative committee. That means you will submit to whatever punishment we decide on."

"Punishment...?"

"Yes. We are now going to discuss your actions, and then we will decide—the weight of your crime and a suitable punishment, that is. If you break your oath, well then, I may call in my private guards, who are waiting outside the door, and ask them to assist us. Of course, that would not be a crime, either. After all, we're following the rules."

Deborah's self-serving claims made Connie sick to her stomach. She remembered Randolph saying that she did things differently. She certainly did. Deborah and Scarlett had nothing whatsoever in common.

She tried to calm her pounding heart before she spoke.

"Am I the only one who will be judged?"

Four prickly gazes immediately turned in her direction. She tried not to flinch.

"Was I the only one who forsook Pamela at that ball? What about everyone who turned a blind eye? I'm certain many people there harmed her with cruel words. And Pamela herself committed a crime. You know that, I'm sure. If you claim to be serving justice, then you ought to call everyone who attended that ball here before you. Including Pamela Francis."

They must not have expected a mere viscount's daughter to argue back. Deborah's lackeys exchanged flustered glances. Deborah, however, continued smiling.

"Oh, that reminds me. Lord Ulster has taken over your family debt, has he not?" she said abruptly. Unsure what she was after, Connie frowned.

"But you know, someone with a little influence can increase another person's debts all they want. And they can do it without your even knowing it."

"What are you saying…?"

"What, indeed? The question is, what would you do if that happened? Ask the Ulster boy for help again? If that continued, some stupid bloke might go after him next. Would you want something like that to happen to your fiancé? Or…"

Deborah paused to smile with great amusement.

"Perhaps you wouldn't care, because he's only a fake fiancé to start with."

Connie flinched.

"Why so surprised? Anyone could figure that out if they thought for a few seconds. The part I don't understand is why. Why would Randolph Ulster want to protect a girl like you?"

Deborah narrowed her eyes, as gray as a muddy river bottom, and took Connie in.

"Will you tell me the reason?"

She curled her bloodred lips slowly into a smile. Connie shrank from that expression. Deborah felt no remorse about tormenting her this way.

"You wouldn't want to meet the same fate that Scarlett Castiel did, would you?"

Connie's eyes widened at the whispered words.

"...Or perhaps you don't remember, since you were only a child when it happened. It was simply awful. That beautiful face she was so proud of was lying on the ground covered in mud, just like a plaything. Everyone—even the lowest of commoners—was clapping and laughing at her in scorn."

Deborah was smiling as if she found this outrageously funny.

"Such a humiliating end. I myself could never have stood the disgrace."

At that moment, all expression vanished from Scarlett's beautiful face. Her fists trembled, perhaps from anger.

Hardly knowing what she was doing, Connie grabbed Scarlett's hand. She felt nothing. Still, when she squeezed, Scarlett turned slowly toward her. She looked slightly surprised. Connie gave a tiny nod. Scarlett pouted for a moment, then, as if she were layering herself on top of Connie, she slipped inside.

Connie closed her eyes. She wasn't running away. Maybe that's what she'd been doing the other times, but this was different. She hadn't taken Scarlett's hand to ask for help—she'd taken it to fight.

"...Yes, it was. Oh, this is such a boring farce, but I'll do you the favor of going along with it."

Deborah blinked in confusion at this completely different tone from Connie. Then she said, like a teacher scolding a dull child, "I'm sorry. Did you say something?"

"My, my, Deborah Darkian, your hearing seems to have gotten worse. You must be getting old."

"What did you say?"

Her smile did not vanish, but this time her tone was angry. Her lackeys were staring at Connie like they'd seen a ghost. She knew how they felt. Painfully so. In fact, crouched in a corner of her own consciousness watching the scene unfold, Connie had the same expression on her own face.

The peerlessly wicked Scarlett, however, merely snorted.

"You still didn't hear me? Then listen well. I—"

Scarlett paused and looked down at her hands. She squinted discontentedly, raised one eyebrow, and looked back at Deborah.

"No—*we* are going to pass judgment on *you*."

"…Pass judgment?"

Deborah smiled like she'd heard a bad joke. *Just you try*, her eyes seemed to say.

Connie flinched slightly, but Scarlett continued, apparently unbothered. "Yes. Speaking of which, the Earl John Doe Ball was quite a disaster, wasn't it? That must have been a heavy blow for you."

"Are you talking about that shady musical group? With all due respect, I reported them to the Security Force. To think they were engaging in human trafficking. The very idea sends chills down my back."

"Then the slave trader didn't know he himself was going to be sold? That explains some things."

"Just what are you trying to say…?"

"May the Black Butterfly flourish."

Deborah's cheek twitched slightly.

"That's what the slaver said to the people gathered round. You didn't know that, did you?"

For the first time, the composure disappeared from that twisted, scornful face.

"I thought it was strange that he was using Old Farish to conduct the auction. After all, even among the higher nobles, there aren't many who understand it."

"…You don't mean to say *you* do?"

"*Ie rua.*"

The words that flowed like music from Connie's mouth were unintelligible to her. But judging from the expression on Deborah's face, she was speaking Old Farish or whatever Scarlett had called it.

"Anyone in society would have known he was talking about you. And everyone at that tasteless gathering had some connection to the Darkians. It really is hard to disguise one's appearance, isn't it? Even with their faces covered, I could tell right away who they were. Of course, I knew that the man engaged in such lively conversation with the slaver was the Marquess of McLain—yes, your husband, Esther," she said to one of the lackeys. "Oh, you didn't know? You poor thing."

Scarlett lowered her eyebrows as if she was touched by the woman's plight.

"But things turned out well for the marquess," she continued. "After all, he wasn't thrown in prison even after what he'd done to a young child. Of course, that only holds if this was his first offense."

The blood drained from the woman's face.

"Dear me, does that strike a chord? But everything will be fine. He'll probably be charged with a lighter crime if he reveals the name of the ringleader. You know what my fiancé's job is, don't you? Depending on the evidence the marquess provides, I'm sure he can arrange things nicely."

The marchioness looked as if she was clinging desperately to this possibility. Scarlett turned a beautiful smile in her direction. *"I'll leave the rest to you, Connie,"* she said, slipping out of her body and standing beside her.

Connie clenched her fists. The Marquess of McLain knew that Deborah Darkian was involved in human trafficking. Deborah was clearly upset. If only she could somehow obtain a statement from the marquess—

"Whatever do you mean to say?"

That was why she could hardly believe her ears when Deborah suddenly spoke.

"Huh?"

In a flash, Deborah had put her masklike smile back on.

"Did you ladies hear something just now?" she asked in a horribly calm voice, looking around the table. Her gaze was enough to freeze the heart.

"Esther, was there something you wanted to say to me?"

The marchioness went white as a sheet.

"That reminds me, wasn't the Marquess of McLain *just about* to leave the kingdom?"

Esther stared at her in a daze, but eventually, she succumbed and nodded several times in a panic.

"And he won't be back for quite a while, will he?"

"No, not for a long time," came the shaky reply. Only then did Deborah smile with satisfaction. She turned to Connie and cleared her throat in evident pleasure.

"Do you understand now?"

Connie had nothing to say. She couldn't believe what had just happened.

"You tried hard. And if—yes, if Scarlett had been the one here in front of me, I might have bent my knee. After all, she was a Castiel. But you are not. You are a mere viscount's daughter. Did you honestly think you could crush a Darkian?"

She narrowed her eyes and laughed.

"Well, ladies, shall we take a vote? Is Connie the one who deserves judgment, or am I? Unfortunately, Susannah is not with us today due to an illness, but that doesn't matter. Never fear, Constance—we decide by majority vote. You just may be acquitted of this crime. It's a marvelously fair system, isn't it?"

But it isn't fair at all, Connie thought, *because I'm sure she'll use her lackeys to swing the decision.* Deborah, however, remained calm as could be.

Finally it made sense. She had misunderstood. She had thought this would be like the balls she'd been to. The venue and the guests might be different, but she'd expected a meeting of people who each had their own private schemes. That was why, despite her fears, she had decided to accept the invitation.

People had ears. They had hearts. If she addressed them seriously, they might hear what she had to say. That's what she had believed. But she had been wrong. The outcome had been decided from the start, because this—

This was no more than a mobbing.

"Go ahead and try."

A gust of bone-chilling air came from Scarlett's direction.

"If that's what you people intend to do, I'll show no mercy," she spat, sparks of static electricity flying off her.

Deborah frowned for a moment, then appeared to have decided to act as if she didn't care.

"…Then again, I don't yet know what kind of girl you are. If you're a good, simple girl who will kneel before me, then I may decide that this was all a misunderstanding on Pamela's part."

In other words, if Connie swore allegiance to Deborah, she would overlook everything.

"Do you have anything to say for yourself?"

Predictably, she looked certain that Connie would accept the offer.

It was so frustrating. Connie was angry at Deborah's cruelty, but even more so at her own powerlessness. She hated that she was incapable of finishing the fight—that all she did was drag Scarlett down. It made her angry. She hardly ever felt this strongly about anything. It was almost as if Scarlett were still in possession of her.

She had already made up her mind, although she was on the verge of shaking. Reprimanding herself for her fear, she made herself reply.

"I—I…"

"What was that? I couldn't hear you."

What will be, will be, Connie thought and took a deep breath.

"I don't think your way of doing things is right at all…!"

Deborah's smile visibly tensed, then quickly turned to a look of annoyance. She opened her mouth as if she was about to issue an order. Connie bit her lip and steeled herself for whatever might come.

If my hair is all you want, take it.

Just then, the door swung open.

"Hello, everyone, I'm here!" the newcomer chirped in an incongruously cheerful voice. "I got caught up dealing with some paperwork, and it took much longer than I expected!"

A woman with bright-yellow hair walked into the room. Deborah looked up at the intruder in surprise. For a moment, her face distorted as if she'd just swallowed a bitter pill. Very quickly, however, she restored her smile.

"How rude of you to come without an invitation," she snapped. "Are you unaware of the rules of society? I'm sorry to say we have no seat for you here. Please leave."

The woman opened her blue eyes theatrically, glanced at the table, and tilted her head in puzzlement.

"No seat? How strange. I spot an empty chair right there."

"That's—"

"Susannah Neville's chair? Well then, there's nothing to worry about. I'm here as Susannah's representative."

"…What did you just say?"

Deborah's eyebrows arched. The woman pulled a sheet of paper from her pocket.

"Here's the letter assigning me as her delegate. If you're going to insist that this is an investigation, then naturally, I have the right to sit at the table, do I not?"

The paper did indeed state that Susannah Neville was delegating her right to attend the investigation, and it ended with both her signature and her family crest.

For some reason, not only Deborah but all three of her lackeys turned pale at the sight of it.

The mood grew awkward, but the woman took no notice. She briskly picked up the dagger lying on the table and pressed a bloody fingerprint onto the oath. Then she sat down innocently in Susannah Neville's chair.

Deborah smiled cruelly. "…Useless fools. I told them not to let anyone in."

"Oh, you mean those valiant puppies guarding the door? You mustn't blame them. They could hardly have expected a member of one of the four great noble families to come striding up."

She was referring to the four powerful families, all holding the rank of duke, that had loyally supported the royal family since the founding of the kingdom.

©Yu-nagi

The Castiels, the Richelieus, the Darkians, and—

"I know most of you already, but for the sake of the newcomer, I'll introduce myself. I am Abigail. Abigail O'Brian."

The O'Brians.

Abigail looked slightly younger than Deborah but probably over thirty. She had a peculiar face that somehow reminded Connie of a frog. No one would have called her beautiful, but when she smiled, there was a certain sunny, friendly charm to her.

"Sh-shall I read the minutes?" one of Deborah's lackeys asked in a hollow, shaken voice and began to carefully lay out what had happened so far. Abigail interrupted her.

"The minutes? Oh, I'm sorry. I'm not the least bit interested in this investigation. I have only one thing to say. Esther, Janine, Caroline—if you don't want to be crushed, come with me."

Her words were concise. Concise and—for a noble, a group that in general favored convoluted speech—extremely direct. All three of the women she had just mentioned gulped.

"It shouldn't be a difficult decision. Just imagine for a moment. Who will be better off, those who ingratiate themselves to the O'Brians, or those who stay with the Darkians? If you come with me now, I will protect you in the future. I believe you know what kind of person I am. But if you go against me, I will show no mercy. Of course, you know that as well. Oh, you still can't decide? Then I'll put it in simpler terms."

Her eyes, as blue as a cloudless summer sky, turned to each of the pale noblewomen in turn.

"Whichever side you choose, the Darkians will not protect you."

Silence descended.

"…How unpleasant, Abigail," Deborah said, stone-faced now and making no effort to disguise the raw loathing in her eyes. "You're threatening them. If you continue to terrorize my dear friends, I'm going to have to take this up with the law."

"That will never do, *Debbie*," Abigail said, as kindly as if she was soothing a child in a fit of anger. "What happens here must never be spoken about, isn't that right? You made that rule yourself, so please abide by it."

She brought her pointer finger—the one with the fresh cut on it—to her mouth and smiled playfully.

In the end, the investigation concluded without a vote. Deborah said she wasn't feeling well and left early. As she did, she threw Connie a glance so frigid, it made her shiver.

The other three women awkwardly made their exits as well. That left only Connie and Abigail O'Brian in the Starlight Room.

"You shouldn't do such dangerous things so thoughtlessly. If you're going to do something, you must prepare well. This isn't the kind of crowd you can beat with a hit-or-miss approach," Abigail advised, sounding very much like an elder.

"Yes, ma'am," Connie answered. She was right. Constance Grail was careless, short-tempered, and indiscreet. She slumped, disappointed in herself.

"I used to make all sorts of mistakes myself when I was young," Abigail said comfortingly. Connie looked up. The playful blue eyes met her own.

"…Thank you."

Connie didn't know what her intentions were, but there was little question Abigail had come to save her. Abigail gave her a meaningful look.

"If you're going to thank anyone, you should thank Randolph Ulster."

"…His Excellency?" she echoed, thrown off by the unexpected words. Abigail held back a laugh.

"Yes, *His Excellency*. Just the other day, he came to my home saying his fiancée had gone and stuck her hand in a hornet's nest, and would I help her? He was also the one who looked into the members and persuaded the most vulnerable one, Susannah Neville, to write out a letter delegating her power to me."

"His Excellency did that?"

She knew he'd been worried about her. But this? How could she put it? It was—extremely embarrassing.

"I was born into a branch of the Richelieu family. When Randolph was a boy, he was as pretty as an angel. He was always following me around saying Abby this, Abby that, and I treated him like a little brother. But now he's grown so big, and there's not a shred of that angelic boy left. Although it was rather sweet what he did this time."

She giggled again.

"I like sweet little things. So, Constance Grail, if you'd like, you may call me Miss Abby."

Scarlett let out an exasperated sigh.

"Shameless woman, does she think she's still a teenager?"

Abigail said she had some business to see to at the exhibition in the gallery of the Grand Merillian, so she and Connie parted ways outside the Starlight Room. Just before she disappeared, she turned back toward Connie.

"Don't hesitate to call if you're ever in trouble!" she called out, smiling her extraordinary smile.

"Constance Grail?"

As Connie was walking through the courtyard toward the front gate, someone grabbed her arm. Turning around in surprise, she met the slanted, dark-green gaze of a redheaded woman. She looked to be in her early twenties, and her pale skin was spotted with freckles.

"I knew it was you! Do you mind if I talk to you for a minute? It's about what happened the other day at the Grand Merillian…"

Connie didn't know how to react to this sudden encounter.

"Oh, um, but who are you…?" she asked in surprise. The redheaded woman's eyes flashed, and she smiled derisively.

"Amelia Hobbes. I'm a reporter at the *Mayflower*. As you can see, I'm a commoner— Did I offend? Shall I give you my card, Lady?"

"No, it's just—"

"Oh, you don't need to change your attitude just because you know I'm a reporter. Whether you flatter me or talk down to me, it won't change what I write in the least. So do as you please."

She was obviously making fun of Connie. Connie tensed. It was bad enough when Deborah or Cecilia did it, but she didn't even know this woman.

"Anyway, when did you start idolizing Scarlett Castiel?"

"...Huh?"

"Was it a reaction to the pressure of being a member of the sincere Grail family and all that? Did the good little girl get tired out? Then again, I've heard that your ancestor did some nasty things in the Ten Years' War. What's your comment on that issue?"

"...Huh?"

"But what I really wanted to ask you is whether to your family, being sincere simply means not giving ground when it comes to your own desires. To me, that sounds less like sincerity and more like plain old stubborn selfishness. Quite a bold claim, if I do say so. Oh, by the way, Teresa Jennings died. Care to comment? Were you happy? Or was it frustrating to see all the news focused on her?"

Connie stared at her in disbelief.

"Yes, that must have been frustrating for a pushy person like you. I can't really understand that line of thought, but I'm sure that's how you would have reacted. Very interesting. Also, about your engagement to Randolph Ulster—have you slept with him yet?"

"What?!" she shouted at this bombshell of a question.

"Girls like you always do surprise me with their lack of chastity. Am I wrong? Although your last fiancé did run off on you. I did want to find out what His Excellency the Grim Reaper is like in bed. He seems so uptight. Well, all in due course. Speaking of the Richelieu Ulsters, there always have been dark, cruel rumors circulating about them, all the way back to our kingdom's founding."

What in the world was this woman saying?

Connie's mind was a complete blank. She felt she was being washed away in a sea of words.

"Amelia, I think that's enough."

Suddenly, the noise stopped.

A tall man in glasses had walked up to Amelia. Just how long had he been standing there?

"We're here today to do a story on the exhibit. The organizers are waiting for us. Let's go."

"But we can do that any old time…"

Amelia hung her head. The man frowned.

"Listen to me, Amelia. Marcella told me to inform her right away if you made any more trouble. If that happens, she'll transfer you to a department as dead as a graveyard. Please don't make me sell out my own coworker."

Amelia pursed her lips, then shot the man a frustrated glare.

"I understand. I'll talk to you more later, Constance Grail. Of course, I'm sure you'll respond in a *sincere* manner when I do."

She walked off, her heels clicking.

Left behind, the man in glasses turned to Connie. "I'm sorry my colleague was rude to you. Amelia has a bad habit of losing sight of her surroundings when it comes to work."

"Oh, no, it's…"

The man had a kind, timid face. He must have been in his late twenties, but his unkempt hair, slightly hunched back—and also, if she was honest, his threadbare suit—all gave him a pitiful air. Connie could easily imagine that he spent his days scrambling after Amelia.

"I'm Aldous. Aldous Clayton, with the Mayflower Company. Please get in touch with me if Amelia bothers you again."

He pulled a card from his breast pocket, handed it to Connie, and then hurried off after Amelia.

"What just happened…?"

Connie was overwhelmed. As she stood there in a daze, Scarlett shrugged carelessly.

"Just some cats scratching at you."

©Yu-nagi

Constance Grail

Sixteen, so much drama lately she feels like she might get an ulcer. Is seriously going to need antacids soon.

Scarlett Castiel

Will make Deborah cry later.

Randolph Ulster

Thinks Deborah Darkian may be involved in the incident at the Earl John Doe Ball. Twenty-six, sort of feels like the wild antics of his (fake) fiancée have been interfering with his life lately. Has been pursuing the criminal organization Daeg Gallus for a long time.

Kyle Hughes

Randolph's right-hand man at the Royal Security Force. Looks like a dandy but is maniacal about work. Had his sights set on an arms dealer in Melvina, but the guy gave him the slip, and everything went to hell. Going to kill Gaina. Needs to make up his mind whether he's an ass guy or a tits guy.

Enrique Adelbide

The crown prince. Magenta eyes, handsome, but seems unhappy. Says juvenile things out of the blue, such as "I… really don't feel like being king at all…"

Cecilia Adelbide

The crown princess. A twisted beauty with rose-colored eyes. Ten years ago, acted like she wanted to kill everyone she saw like some kind of bad girl from the countryside. Her eyes never smile.

Ernst Adelbide

The king. Magenta eyes, ultimate power, but for some reason prefers strolling around by himself. Goes on and on about violets but fails to make a strong impression on Connie. Still seems to care about Scarlett, with whom he was once close.

Deborah Darkian

Called the Black Butterfly, a picture-perfect evil woman. Pissed off because she was all excited to play with her new toy, but someone got in the way. Hates Abigail.

Abigail O'Brian

A duchess. Blond hair, blue eyes, a distant relative of Randolph. Not beautiful but charming. Much like someone else we know, tends to act on knee-jerk impulse. Also much like someone else, was careless when young.

Amelia Hobbes

Reporter at the *Mayflower* #1. Curly red hair and gray-green eyes. Immediately tries to one-up Connie.

Aldous Clayton

Reporter at the *Mayflower* #2. Dowdy glasses, scruffy hair, stooped back. Timid, constantly chasing after his colleague Amelia.

Several days after Connie's showdown with Deborah Darkian, an unusual visitor appeared at the Grail residence.

"It's been a long time, Connie!"

The gossip-loving viscount's daughter Mylene was waiting for her in the drawing room with a broad smile on her face. Connie hadn't seen Mylene since the night of the Grand Merillian ball. Although she was a little insensitive, she wasn't mean, so Connie considered her a friend.

Her quick greeting finished, Mylene literally leaped at Connie.

"When did you meet Amelia Hobbes?!"

"Meet her? She's the last person I want to meet. Why?"

Connie couldn't help frowning. It was an unpleasant memory. Mylene pulled a rolled-up pamphlet from her purse.

"She wrote an article about it! The viscount's daughter, Miss C—that's you, isn't it? How unfriendly of you not to tell me! I'm a huge fan of Amelia's!"

Connie digested her friend's words, then gave her a puzzled look.

"...An article?"

This was what it said.

According to some, the viscount's daughter Miss C was pressured from a young age to meet her parents' ideals, and she did try to live up to the expectations, but in the end, she rebelled by devoting herself to evil.

In particular, she became a fervent admirer of the great criminal Scarlett Castiel and began to model her own life on Scarlett's, according to some. One night at a certain ball, she copied Scarlett's behavior. She succeeded with flying colors in drawing attention to herself. Having her powerful desire for approval fulfilled in this way led Miss C to pile one wicked act upon the next. Ultimately, she became engaged to young Count R.

However, behind the scenes, she was driving innocent third parties to suicide, engaging in human trafficking, using illegal hallucinogenic drugs, and partaking in frequent orgies...according to some.

Who was this person?

Connie slapped her forehead and moaned.

"It's complete nonsense...! Terrifying nonsense...!"

"Yes, I suppose so," Mylene admitted. "This wasn't published by the Mayflower Company, and the writer was Anthony Hardy, not Amelia Hobbes, so I was suspicious. That's the pen name Amelia uses when she can't write about something openly. Conspiracy theories and the like. Plus, it's about you. But I'm still disappointed. I was a fan of Amelia Hobbes. She's a star among working women. I thought of her as a role model."

"A role model?"

Connie gave Mylene a puzzled look. Mylene blinked as if she were combing over her memories.

"Didn't I tell you? I don't intend to get married; I want to be a journalist. Of course, my top choice would be the Mayflower Company."

"Really...?"

"Yes. My father's business has been in the red for several years. The problem is, there are still four unmarried daughters in my family, including me. If all of us marry, our dowries will bankrupt the family. My parents said that one of us would have to become a maid for a high-noble family or else go to a nunnery," she explained. "Well, if those are my options, I'd rather make my own living doing something I like. Thanks to Lady Lily, young noblewomen can work outside the home now without as much criticism— Hey, what's the matter?"

Connie was staring at Mylene with her mouth hanging open.

"…I'm just in shock that you would say something so sensible…," she mumbled. Mylene burst out laughing.

"You said it yourself, Constance Grail! If I like gossip so much, why don't I become a reporter?"

"But I wasn't serious!"

She *had* said that. She definitely had. She remembered saying it. She'd been teasing her friend for liking gossip more than dresses or dessert. But it had obviously been a silly joke!

As she sat there dumbfounded, Mylene started laughing again.

"I know that. But back then, everyone else gave me the cold shoulder. They wouldn't even say something like that as a joke. It made me happy to know you accepted me."

Mylene Reese smiled a very grown-up kind of smile.

Several days had passed since the initial shock of the report on "Miss C."

Connie was preparing to go to the Elbaite Villa for tea with Crown Princess Cecilia. She had just changed into a crisp lime-green dress and climbed the staircase to her room when she stumbled on Marta acting very strangely.

The head maid was standing in front of Connie's door, hand frozen, on the verge of knocking. She was looking down at a white envelope in her hand. After a moment, seeming to have made up her mind, she clenched her fist—but then, still unsure, she slowly lowered it. Then she stared at the envelope again.

"…What are you doing?" Connie asked. If she left her alone, Marta would probably continue the same cycle for the rest of the day. Marta flinched and turned to Connie with a harried expression.

"Oh, nothing, it's just…!"

"A letter of protest?"

Snatching the envelope from Marta's hand, Connie read out the alarm-red letters on the front. It was from…

"The Violet Association…?"

The crease between her brows grew deeper with each word. She'd never heard of this association before. Confronted with Connie's suspicion, Marta gave a resigned sigh and explained as politely as she could. The Violet Association, it seemed, was a not-for-profit citizens' group.

"It's been around since I was a girl, and the members claim to be humanitarians, but…"

Marta didn't know exactly what they did, so she'd been unsure about giving the letter to Connie.

Connie considered this. "But why would they send us a letter of protest? Has Father gone and done something again?"

"No, this time it's not the master of the house they're after; it's you, Miss Constance…"

"Me?!" she squealed in surprise. She honestly had no idea what was going on. Could rumor have gotten around that the infamous Miss C was actually Constance Grail?

"The Violet Association was the group responsible for getting public executions banned ten years ago, arguing they were barbaric and inhumane. Of course, it all started with the beheading of Scarlett Castiel. And then there was the gossip column about you the other day. The article touched a bit on Scarlett Castiel, so perhaps—"

"You found out?!" Connie screamed, mentally running through the fraudulent article fabricated by the red-haired reporter.

Like when she reported on orgies, orgies, and more orgies…

"Marta, it's not true! All of that was made up!" she shouted, stepping closer to Marta in desperation. Marta stared at her in shock. Then, slowly, her expression returned to the one Connie had known since childhood.

"Well of course it was! Is that the reason you've been looking so out of sorts the last few days?"

Connie blinked at her.

"I took the liberty of writing to that third-rate press to express my anger," she said, her stout body swelling with indignation. She pounded her chest several times as if to reassure Connie.

"You did?"

"But what I'm really worried about is this Violet Association, because I hear they take quite drastic measures. If they happen to approach you on the street, please pretend you don't know anything," Marta warned her.

"I promise I'll be careful," Connie answered, nodding meekly.

The perfect early-summer sun poured down on the street, casting shadows through the leaves of the trees. Connie felt her neck burning and wished she'd brought her parasol.

"Allow me to introduce myself. I'm Kimberly Smith," the slightly pudgy, middle-aged woman standing in front of her said in a nasal voice. She was wearing a voluminous peach dress of the sort that new debutantes favored and carrying a frilly pink parasol. Her face was covered with a thick layer of foundation. "I am the president of the Ladies' Committee of the Violet Association."

Connie rubbed her temples.

Why is this happening to me?

The woman showed up about an hour before the coach Cecilia had sent from the palace to pick Connie up was scheduled to arrive.

Connie had finished getting ready and was tottering around in the high heels she'd dragged out from the back of her closet. It was all Scarlett's fault for insisting she simply must wear these open-back shoes with her perfectly in-season lime-green dress. The problem was, they were more unruly than a wild horse. Connie had no choice but to try to get used to wearing them before her carriage arrived.

Of course, she hadn't intended to leave the grounds. If she went outside, it would only be to walk from the garden to the front gate—no more.

Unfortunately, just as Connie tottered like a newborn fawn toward the gate, her eyes had met those of the woman peering in at the Grail residence.

"Have you by chance had the time to read our letter? You *are* the young lady who looks up to Scarlett Castiel, are you not?" the woman shrieked from the other side of the gate. Connie wearily stepped outside the gate and stood facing Kimberly Smith.

"You must have mistaken me for someone else," she said, rejecting the woman's assumptions.

"Pardon me for saying so, but Scarlett committed countless acts of inhumanity. Only after she was purged was society righted again. And now, thanks to your childish behavior, all our struggles have come to nothing. Do you understand what I am saying?"

Yes, I suppose.

Connie's mind wandered.

She felt like she'd just been through this.

Whether it was Amelia Hobbes or Kimberly Smith, everyone Connie interacted with lately seemed to be uniformly hard of hearing. Was it the change in the seasons?

"And the very notion of using hallucinogens...," Kimberly accused, narrowing her eyes as if Connie were a filthy animal. "Don't tell me you've been using *Jackal's Paradise*?"

Jackal's Paradise?

"Don't play the fool with me!"

Connie frowned. "I've never even seen a hallucinogenic drug, let alone used one. It's unfortunate that you don't believe me."

"Unfortunate? Down to the last lord and lady, your people discriminate against us commoners, and you think—"

This sounded like it was going to continue for quite some time. Connie was gripping her head once again when a familiar voice interrupted the woman.

"—Then are my parents discriminatory as well?"

Turning around in relief, Connie glimpsed the fluffy chestnut hair and eyes of her good friend Kate, the master baker.

Gone was her usual amused smile, in its place a blank face.

"My father is a baron, but my mother was a kitchen maid. Do you still make that claim?"

Kimberly drew her brows together in embarrassment under Kate's direct gaze.

"…You're Kate Lorraine, aren't you? I've heard the rumors about your family. Yes, they do seem different. They're—yes, they're quite wonderful."

"*Wonderful?* Why? Because my mother was a commoner? Because my father chose to marry her? That's the sort of thinking that's discriminatory."

Her voice was horribly quiet.

"For my whole life, nobles have looked down on me because I have common blood in my veins, and when I go out in town, commoners have avoided me because I'm a noble. Noble or commoner, they were all the same when it came to ostracizing me because I was *different* from them."

Kate wasn't blaming the woman or deploring her own misfortune—she was simply stating her truth.

"But this girl standing in front of you, Constance Grail? She's never once treated me like that. She's always treated me like plain old Kate. Do you know how hard that is to find? Can you imagine what a saving grace it was for me? I don't think you can. Because you—" Here Kate paused to take in Kimberly. "You've never been discriminated against by a *commoner*. If you're going to accuse Connie of things just because she's a noble, then you're the one who's stuck in your own head and can only see what you want to see. You're as discriminatory as the worst of them."

Kimberly flinched. Kate wasn't speaking loudly, but she wasn't being overly quiet, either. It was still midday, and the street was crowded. Perhaps noticing the curious eyes turned her way, Kimberly gave Connie a conciliatory smile.

"I believe we've misunderstood each other," she said, a slightly frustrated glint in her eye. "I'll be on my way—for now."

Kate watched her peach-colored form vanish quickly into the stream of passersby.

"There's something wrong with anyone who would believe a two-bit article like that," Kate muttered, then turned slowly toward Connie. She still wasn't smiling.

"Is it true you're engaged to the Earl of Ulster?"

Connie gulped. Seeing her reaction, Kate's face took on an injured expression.

"...So it is true. You don't tell me anything. I know I said I'd wait for you to talk when you were ready, and I haven't changed my mind—but it still hurts."

Connie couldn't find anything to say, not even an excuse. After all, what was there to say?

Anything she said might get her friend tangled up in this mess.

As she stood there in a daze, Kate smiled a little self-mockingly.

"I knew it."

"Kate—"

"Never mind," Kate interrupted, then spun on her heel and returned the way she'd come.

Not long after, the carriage arrived from the Elbaite Villa.

Connie hunched in a corner of the luxurious coach, her arms wrapped around her knees. When she thought about Kate, the amount of hatred she had for herself was starting to make her feel crazy. She could hear Scarlett going on about something as she sat with her hands pressed against her temples and her head down. She tried to brush her off, but she wouldn't stop saying her name.

"*Connie?*"

"What now?"

"*Is Jackal's Paradise illegal now?*"

"I don't even know what Jackal's Paradise is."

"*It's a hallucinogen that was popular ten years ago. It was supposed to take you straight to paradise without many side effects, so people loved it.*"

Connie blinked and raised her face. "The use of any kind of hallucinogen is illegal now. You absolutely can't use that stuff," she said to the bad girl who only looked refined. Scarlett pursed her moist lips.

"*How boring.*"

"Scarlett...!"

"*But in my day, it was legal! I think everyone was using it. Unfortunately for me, it didn't suit my constitution. I hated that saccharine smell, like they'd boiled down flower nectar. Oh yes, speaking of Jackal's Paradise...*"

The carriage clanged to a halt, interrupting Scarlett. The horse whinnied. A moment later, the coachman's loud voice announced that they had arrived at the palace.

"Miss Grail."

Connie had just filled out the requisite paperwork at the main gate to Moldavite Palace and was heading toward the villa when a young man in a black military uniform called out to her. Needless to say, it was Randolph Ulster. He had received a note reading, "I'd love to see you as well, Randy"—an invitation so light, it could have floated away on a spring breeze. Yet, once again, he'd slipped away from work to accompany Connie to the royal tea.

She felt an odd strength fill her when she saw him.

"Oh, um, I wanted to tell you...thank you for the other day!" she said awkwardly.

Randolph looked at her quizzically. "For what?"

How many times had they repeated this exact conversation? Connie gaped for a minute, then smiled. The tension drained from her.

"Deborah Darkian's investigation. Duchess O'Brian told me Your Excellency asked her to come."

"Oh, you mean Abigail? Deborah Darkian is the type who will tell you that white is black with a smile on her face, so you have to fight back with equal force. Abigail may look harmless, but she's got a faction behind her that is equal to Deborah's. She takes good care of her people, too." He paused to glance at Connie. "And she reminds me a little of you."

His face was as expressionless as ever, but she thought she caught a shade of teasing in his cerulean eyes—maybe.

"Do I...?"

There was no way she could ever face down Deborah Darkian like Abigail had. What in the world did he think they had in common? As she was puzzling over this, Scarlett interrupted indifferently.

"I think he's talking about your unremarkable face."

Unbelievable.

As Connie was walking with Randolph toward the Elbaite Villa, passing through the symmetrical, mazelike gardens arranged on either side of a central fountain, she heard someone shouting.

Looking around in surprise, she saw a not-quite-elderly man agitatedly cross-examining several younger men who could have been his sons. She couldn't hear exactly what he was saying, but she could see that the men receiving the scolding were so pale, she felt sorry for them.

"...That's Kendall Levine, a high-ranking diplomat," Randolph whispered. Connie looked up. "He's a special envoy from Faris. Those other men must be his subordinates. I've seen them before."

Connie nodded. This must be the envoy whose tardiness Enrique had been complaining about just the other day at Elbaite. He appeared to have made it safely to the palace.

She was just thinking that she probably ought to greet him even though he looked busy when he noticed their presence. He had light-russet eyes and thinning gray hair, which had receded unfortunately far from his forehead.

He lowered his voice abruptly. Gesturing at his subordinates with his chin, he slipped out of sight behind a fence that had been erected on the lawn.

What in the world?

"How insulting!" Scarlett huffed. *"To hide like that so blatantly! Whatever could they be talking about? Wait here—I'll go and see."*

"What?! Please don't, Scarlett...!"

Of course, she ignored Connie completely and floated behind the fence, out of sight. Connie gripped her face.

"What's wrong?" Randolph asked suspiciously.

"Nothing, Scarlett just—" she began, then stopped. She'd told His Excellency the Grim Reaper about Scarlett, but...

But...did he believe her?

What would she do if those cerulean eyes were filled with scorn or suspicion? She looked timidly up at him. His eyes were as unclouded by emotion as ever.

"Well, what did she do?"

Connie blinked. "Um...she said she was going to eavesdrop on Mr. Levine and his subordinates."

Randolph nodded.

"She would do something like that," he said as if the whole situation were normal, gazing off in the direction of the special envoy. "Miss Grail?"

"Oh, sorry..."

She must have had an idiotic expression on her face. Randolph peered at her curiously. For some reason, she felt terribly agitated.

"It seems one of their party has disappeared," Scarlett reported when she returned. This must not have been what she had expected to hear, because she seemed lost in thought.

"They called him Ulysses, I think. They seem quite upset over it. I don't know who he is, but he sounds like a pain in the rear end."

She shrugged as if she'd lost interest.

"Did she find anything out?"

Randolph must have guessed from Connie's expression that Scarlett was back.

"It seems they can't find one of the people who came with them, someone named Ulysses," Connie relayed.

Randolph's eyebrows shot up. "Ulysses?"

"Do you know him?"

"I didn't know he had come to Adelbide—" The cerulean eyes grew distant, their owner deep in thought. "If that crafty man is so furious over the mere fact that this Ulysses has disappeared, then he could only be talking about one person."

Randolph cast a penetrating look at the spot where the group had been talking a few minutes earlier.

"Ulysses Faris—the Seventh Prince of Faris."

According to the history books, after the downfall of the Faris Empire, all members of the imperial family except Cornelia Faris had been executed.

However, Faris had always been a land obsessed with bloodlines. That was why the flag bearer for the coup d'état was the young son of a duke and an imperial princess. When the empire was dissolved, this boy with the blood of the bygone royal family in his veins became king. Thus was born the new royal family of Faris.

The noble bloodline had continued unbroken through the present day.

"Prince…Ulysses?"

"Yes. Age nine, I believe," Randolph said, frowning. Connie couldn't help drawing her brows together, too.

Scarlett was the only one who didn't seem to care much. She was perched on top of the fence, which was about as high as Connie's shoulders.

"Then he's still a child? He must have wandered off and gotten lost, I suppose."

The Royal Castle of Adelbide was quite large. The grounds had room for both villas and then some. A nine-year-old boy had to be aching to go play. Scarlett's hypothesis did seem plausible.

"But when did he disappear...?"

"Yesterday."

"...Hmm?"

"According to the fellow with the ebbing locks, he was already gone by last night."

"...Hmm?!"

"What's wrong?"

"Then he can't just be lost! Something definitely happened to him!"

Connie relayed the information to Randolph in a panic. His frown deepened.

"Yesterday? Then why hasn't the envoy said anything about it? We didn't even know the Seventh Prince was along on this trip. It was the Fifth Prince, Jerome, who was supposed to come. I heard he fell ill just before the trip and had to recuperate, and that was what delayed their arrival..."

Randolph narrowed his eyes and glanced over his shoulder, still frowning.

"I'm sorry, Miss Grail, but I must—"

"Return to your office?"

Randolph looked at her in surprise.

"...Am I wrong?" she asked, confused by his reaction.

"No, it's just..."

"Then you must go quickly!"

They had no time to waste. This was a nine-year-old child they were talking about. She didn't know what had happened to him, but she was certain he must be terrified. If they could find him and help, she wanted to do it as soon as possible.

"...Yes. Be careful, Miss Grail. Of Cecilia."

"I will." Connie nodded. "I'll watch closely to make sure I don't miss anything, and I'll try not to let her trip me up. But that might be impossible, so if I find myself in trouble, I'll borrow a bit of Abigail's swagger, and if that still doesn't work, I'll use your name, Your Excellency. But even with all of that, I might be no match for her..."

By this point, her initial conviction had withered into a pitiful moan. Suddenly, she heard someone laughing.

Huh?

Jerking her face up, she saw only Randolph with his usual blank face. However, the lines around his eyes seemed a little softer than usual.

"Very nice," he said.

With that, Randolph headed back to his office and Connie continued walking toward the castle, talking furtively with Scarlett.

"*To sum up their conversation...,*" Scarlett said, of course still referring to Levine, "*the boy was definitely in the palace until yesterday. Yesterday was the ninth. Incidentally, there were no official visitors listed for that day in the register at the front gate.*"

"Wait, how do you know that?!"

"*What do you mean? We just saw it! You wrote your name down in there yourself! The records from yesterday were listed on the same page. I simply looked over your shoulder.*"

"Oh..."

Once again, she was reminded of Scarlett's superhuman power of memory.

"Does that mean someone snuck into the palace?" she asked.

"*Do you think you could sneak past the eyes of those guards? I noticed it the other day, too—this place is guarded a lot more closely than it was ten years ago. Are there always so many guards around, or is it because the special envoy is here from Faris? But even so...*"

Connie shrugged. She had no idea, since she almost never came to the castle. She'd noticed there were a lot of guards, but she'd thought that was normal.

"...So much changes in ten years," Scarlett muttered, lost in her memories. When Connie glanced at her, she covered it up with a perfect smile. "Anyway, there are plenty of ways to go about it without taking the risk of sneaking in. After all, you don't have to come in through the front gate."

"But how else do you get in?" Connie asked. Scarlett smiled condescendingly back at her.

"Those mountains of food and dresses and the like don't just fall into the castle from the sky, now, do they? Plus, if someone inside wants to summon a person for private reasons, it would be annoying to bring them through the front gate. There's got to be a passageway for tradespeople."

"A gift?"

Connie was talking to the man at the reception desk at the back gate of the palace, which was quite a bit less sumptuous than the front gate.

"Yes," she answered, a troubled look on her face. "I was invited for tea by Crown Princess Cecilia, so I selected the very finest gift for her. Since it was quite large, I ordered it sent to the palace in advance..."

"I'm sorry, but I believe that sort of item would go through the front gate."

The man at the desk wore glasses and seemed very serious. His answer was exactly as predicted—by Scarlett, not Connie. She was therefore able to continue speaking unruffled.

"But the lady there already told me she hadn't received anything. She... um, Miss Janet, I think it was...said that maybe it had been sent back here by mistake."

That much was true. Connie had intentionally gone back to the front gate to ask about the imaginary package. The moment the woman told her it hadn't arrived, she had dropped to her knees and wailed as if the world were ending. Unable to witness such misery—or more likely, wanting to get rid of Connie as quickly as possible—the receptionist had suggested this possibility.

"Janet said that?" the man in the glasses asked, looking up in surprise at this mention of his coworker's name. "In that case, I'll look into it. I haven't heard anything, so it's unlikely, but when was it sent?"

"On the ninth."

The man pulled his register out of a drawer. Scarlett floated over him and, with a satisfied smile, rested her chin in her hand.

"The ninth... Let me see... Oh yes, here it is. As I thought, there is no record of a package from the Grail house. I'm very sorry, but there is nothing more I can do. Please check again with the dealer you purchased it from."

Connie arrived at the Elbaite Villa precisely on time. She was led toward Crown Princess Cecilia's rooms by one of her ladies-in-waiting.

"Well, did you find anything out?" she whispered to Scarlett in the long hallway.

"*There was a butcher, a tailor, a jeweler...all sorts of people, but the one who stood out was Vado, a trader from the Republic of Soldita,*" she whispered into Connie's ear with a voluptuous sigh. "*How about we start with him? After all, it's* perfect."

Scarlett tilted her head gracefully as she peered down at Scarlett.

"We have arrived," the young lady-in-waiting announced softly. From inside, Connie could hear an exceedingly cheerful voice invite them in.

The door opened.

"*The man was going to the Elbaite Villa,*" Scarlett said. "*He came to see Cecilia.*"

She smiled as stunningly as a rose in full bloom.

"Welcome!" Crown Princess Cecilia exclaimed, a broad smile on her face. When she noticed that Connie was alone, she tilted her head sweetly.

"Randy said he was coming with you. Did he change his mind?" she asked. When Connie told her that something unexpected had come up at work, her smile vanished. Very quickly, however, she replaced it with a calmer smile. "He works so hard," she added, gesturing elegantly for Connie to come inside.

"Sit down, sit down! It's been ages since I had a guest in this room!"

Connie did as she was told, sitting in the guest chair.

The room, though furnished with items of the best quality, was extremely odd. Several lanterns decorated with colorful, exotic geometric patterns hung from the ceiling. On the walls were strange wooden masks and a tapestry with a millefleur pattern. Connie couldn't help staring at all the unfamiliar objects scattered through the space.

"Unusual, aren't they?" Cecilia asked in a vaguely proud tone. "I collected them from all across the continent. Of course, I wasn't the one who did the work; it was my traders."

She smiled. The word *traders* put Connie on edge.

"…They must be very good at their job," she said.

"You know, the people from Soldita are just so merry. They've got such quick tongues, I can't help buying things I don't need."

"Do they come often?"

Silence. Cecilia looked at her and calmly turned her mouth up.

"…Yes, they do. One came just yesterday, in fact. He had a big wicker trunk on his back full of carpets from Rafina to show me. But why do you ask?"

Her innocent expression was as placid as a still pond—which was terrifying in its own way. Connie found herself unable to speak. After a moment, Cecilia said in an even more cheerful voice than before, "Dear me, the tea is getting cold!"

Two steaming teapots were sitting on the glass-topped table, the four corners of which were beautifully etched. Cecilia pulled one of the pots toward her.

"This one is just for me," she said with a smile. "I'm sure you've heard that I was very frail as a child. I have this special herbal tea to thank for my eventually growing strong again. I apologize if it seems rude, but this is all I ever drink. It's a kind of medicine, so for you I've ordered regular black tea."

"…Medicinal tea?"

"Yes. It's from the Far East. I've put Vado to quite a bit of trouble to get me a regular supply. Oh, Vado is a trader I'm very close with," she answered, pouring herself a cup of tea with a practiced hand.

"…I apologize, Your Highness. I was wrong about you."

"Wrong? In what way?" Cecilia asked, blinking her rose-colored eyes.

"Yes. With the story about you having been poisoned being so famous, I assumed you were just being very careful, even in your daily life."

A peculiar smell drifted from the porcelain cup of brilliant red liquid. It wasn't at all sweet but more of a green smell, like newly sprouted leaves.

"Are you talking about Scarlett Castiel?" Cecilia asked in a terribly flat voice. "You must have been only a child at the time, but you talk as if you are quite familiar with the incident."

She smiled, showing no sign of distress. However, her pale eyes bored coldly into Connie.

"Oh, no, I've only heard rumors that the great criminal Scarlett Castiel tried to poison you."

"Then I'll tell you what happened. On *that* day, Scarlett marched into my house. No warning at all. You see, Enrique had canceled his plans to see a play with her and instead was by my side. I was in bed with a fever, and he had come to check on me. She was angry and insulted."

Connie glanced at Scarlett, but she was looking down blankly at Cecilia.

"It wasn't until that night that I realized she'd poisoned one of the water jars at my estate. Ridiculously enough, it wasn't me but my pet fish that died. The maid had chanced to change the water, and that was what saved me. Scarlett's earring had fallen by the jug, and a half-used bottle of poison was found in her room. You know what happened after that. She was executed for her crime."

She related that much of the story calmly, but now she cast down her eyes in regret.

"But my own crime was falling in love with Enrique even though I knew he was engaged. I'm certain I am paying for that crime now. It's my fault we haven't been blessed with a child. It's a calamity for Enrique, too.

For my sake, he has turned down all talk of procuring a mistress. He says that his younger brother, His Highness Johan, can take over. After all, they have a little prince as well as a princess. That's far better than making the child of a viscount's daughter heir to the throne—don't you agree?"

"Oh, no, not at all…"

"But that's how the world works, Connie. You see, Enrique plans to one day find some excuse for giving up his right to succession. He's felt that way for a long time. He talks about being granted a little domain somewhere and living there peacefully."

Noticing Connie's expression, Cecilia paused to smile wryly.

"Oh, he's said all of this in public. Of course, some people aren't very happy about it."

"She's still good at changing the subject, I see," Scarlett interjected in a bored tone. *"Always so elusive. She truly is thick-skinned. Although it seems someone must have it out for her."*

Scarlett smiled. Not catching her meaning, Connie shot her a questioning look.

"I mean, that tea smells horrid. My guess is it contains some kind of poison to prevent pregnancy."

Poison?

"I'm certain of it. It smells just like the tea the seductresses used to drink before they played with fire. A cup here and there is one thing, but drinking it every day must wreak havoc on her insides and make her prone to blood clots in her lower body as well. That tea turns your body cold as ice and swells you up, and I even heard of women whose hearts eventually stopped beating because their circulation had grown so weak."

Shocked by this frightening speech, Connie watched as Cecilia's lips approached the rim of the white cup decorated with blue flower petals.

"No!" she blurted out, bringing Cecilia's hand to a sudden halt.

"…Whatever is the matter?"

Connie clapped her hand over her unruly mouth, but of course that wasn't enough to calm Cecilia's suspicion.

"Is there something wrong with my tea?"

"…Um…" Connie's eyes darted around the room, while Scarlett sighed. "It's just that, well, that tea, I think it has a lot of medicinal herbs in it…"

"Yes, and?"

"W-well, maybe, I thought there might be something in it that's making you unwell… Because I noticed the other day when I met Your Highness that your hands were very cold—"

"Dear me, Connie," Cecilia interrupted. "The truth is, I know what's in this tea, and I have great faith in it. You're such an open book. I don't think you realized that based on how the tea looks. If you had, you would have acted this way from the start. But you haven't drunk any, so you can't know how it tastes. Which leaves…the smell?"

A direct and fatal strike.

"Ummmmmm, somebody told me about it once! Th-the smell, too! I have a f-friend who knows a lot about those things…!"

"What erudite friends you have. Is this a person whom you trust?"

Connie paused for only a moment before turning back toward Cecilia. "Yes."

"And you say this is bad?"

Connie nodded meekly.

"If you're lying to me, you'll pay the price. But now that I think of it, I never took the trouble to look into it, since it was the same thing I used before," she said with interest, glancing over her shoulder.

"You heard what she said, didn't you?" She turned quietly to several ladies-in-waiting who had been sitting at a distance. "Please call someone right away who knows about medicinal herbs."

The herbalist who presently arrived said it would take several days to determine the contents of the tea, and Connie left the villa shortly after.

"*Idiot.*" Scarlett sighed in irritation as soon as they were alone. "*You shouldn't have said anything. Now she has her eye on you.*"

"But I couldn't very well let someone go on drinking poison and not say anything."

"*What if I was saying nonsense?*"

"That's true—you are a liar," Connie said, frowning. "But I usually know if you're lying or not."

"*…You certainly are getting cheeky lately.*" Scarlett widened her eyes before puffing out her cheeks. "*I think that scheming woman just might be one I need to get revenge on! And here you go giving my enemy a helping hand!*"

"But you don't know that! There's no evidence yet. And if the crown princess dies, you'll never find out!"

For once, Scarlett didn't have a comeback. She sighed, apparently having given up, and changed the subject.

"*This trader of hers, she said he was carrying a wicker basket on his back, didn't she? You could hide a small child in there. And if you knocked out the child ahead of time, you wouldn't have to worry about them thrashing about.*" She snorted. "*Yes, yes, I know—we don't have enough information to say yet if the schemer is involved or not. After all, she's stupid enough to drink poison that kills off unborn babies without even knowing it. They might simply be using her. Let's investigate a bit more.*"

Connie was very much in favor of that, but unfortunately, she had no brilliant ideas how to do it. Scarlett took one look at her troubled face and continued talking as if the solution was obvious.

"*As they say, if you want to know about seamstresses, ask a tailor, and if you want to know about singers, ask a theater manager. Since we want to know about a trader, don't you think asking someone in the business is our best strategy?*"

Connie looked up suspiciously at Scarlett, wondering who she could be thinking of, but Scarlett went on as if it was obvious.

"*You still haven't figured it out? Neil Bronson, of course!*"

Connie stood outside the Bronson Company headquarters on Anastasia Street. A flag hanging from the eaves bore the family crest along with a laurel branch, the symbol of the Castle-Town Revitalization Association.

Neil was still under partial house arrest, but Connie had heard he was working again. Although she hadn't sent word ahead that she was coming, when she told the woman who answered the door that she wanted to meet with Neil, she disappeared for a moment, then showed Connie into the back office. The store was bustling, and the faces of the staff were untroubled. Apparently, the boycott had ended.

"It's good to see you, Constance," Neil said in greeting. Since their last meeting, the stylish trader's son seemed to have converted to an earnest youngster. He was wearing an undyed cotton shirt without a trace of embroidery over extremely simple gray pants. His formerly long, loose locks were now trimmed short. Connie must have let her surprise show, because Neil smiled wryly.

"This look doesn't suit me?"

"I'm s-sorry. It's not that—it's just…a surprise. Is that the style ladies prefer these days?"

"No, I've had enough of ladies for a while…," Neil said, seeming to drift away for a moment.

"Sounds like she had her way with him," Scarlett noted.

Connie looked away from Neil. Lady Custine was very scary.

They chatted a bit, and then Connie said she wanted to ask him about a trader from Soldita, though she couldn't tell him the reason.

"I'm sorry," he said contritely. "We don't have any connections to the Republic of Soldita."

"Useless good-for-nothing!" Scarlett scoffed. Connie, too, blinked in disappointment. Neil must have been expecting her reaction, because he went on unperturbed.

"…So I'll write you an introduction to meet with *someone*."

"…Someone?" Connie asked.

"Yes. He's an upstart, but his power is universally acknowledged. I doubt all the traders in the capital could outdo him even if we joined forces," he said, running his feather pen over a sheet of paper. When he was done, he dropped red wax onto the envelope and sealed it with the Bronson Company stamp.

"Walter Robinson, king of the shipping business. You've heard of him, haven't you?"

※

"Well, this is a surprise."

Walter Robinson appeared to be in his late thirties, with deeply tanned skin and a large frame. He looked as brutal as a pirate in a picture book. But after the conventional greetings, this man whose face would no doubt induce instant tears in any child who saw it broke into a smile. He looked remarkably friendly and open—*just like a little boy*, Connie thought.

Walter Robinson was a self-made man, having risen from poverty to wealth in the span of his own relatively short career. His primary battlefield was the sea, where he had opened trading routes with several countries previously unconnected to Adelbide. This had earned him a knighthood.

"I never expected to see the day when a well-established firm like the Bronson Company would come slinking in with head bowed. No doubt that was the decision of the son, not the father."

He grinned again. The Walter Robinson Company had branches in foreign countries and was a purveyor to high-noble families so well-known that even Connie, with her scant connections in society, had heard of it. Although she was a noble herself, she had feared that he wouldn't deign to speak with a mere viscount's daughter, and so she secretly let out a sigh of relief.

"I'm, um, very grateful that you've taken the time to see me today," she said.

"What are you saying? I'm the one who should be thanking you. The Bronson Company is small, but they've been baronets for three generations. That kind of history is the one thing I can never come close to. If they could rent that out to me, I'd be eternally grateful... Also, I wanted to take a look at you for myself."

His brown eyes twinkled.

"Actually, my top customer is the O'Brian household. The duchess was talking about you just the other day. She said you were like a little sister to her and asked me to look out for you if anything came up."

Connie blinked in surprise.

"She's a lady who looks out for her people. Sometimes so much so that I worry about her. Anyhow, this here letter says you have something you'd like to ask me. Go ahead, ask me anything. If I can tell Lady O'Brian I helped you out, I don't doubt she'll buy a teardrop pearl necklace or a moonlight silk dress from me out of sheer happiness," he said with a playful wink.

It seemed that despite his brawny pirate's physique, Walter Robinson was a highly amiable man.

"...A trader named Vado from the Republic of Soldita? I've never heard of him."

Walter Robinson frowned, racking his brain, before continuing.

"But if you're talking about a member of Soldita's minority tribes, he's most likely from the Caniellia Autonomous District in the south. They're a secretive lot, so it wouldn't be odd if I'd never heard of him—but you said carpets from Rafina? We trade in those as well, and the weavers are real artisans. They only sell their goods wholesale to people approved by the cooperative, so a limited number of traders deal them. Since those blokes are my competitors, I generally have an idea of what country they're from and what trading house they're with. I'm fairly sure none is from the Autonomous District."

Walter rested a finger on his chin.

"It's mighty strange that I've never heard of this trader who can come and go as he pleases at the palace. Let me look into it. I'll send a messenger if I find anything out."

He gave a few instructions to his secretary, who had been waiting off to the side of the room.

As Connie was getting ready to leave, she suddenly thought of something else she wanted to ask him.

"Um," she began timidly. "I also wanted to ask you about herbs for inducing menstruation..."

"Inducing menstruation?" Walter gave Connie a suspicious look, then darted a glance down at her belly.

"Oh, it's n-not for me!" she cried, going pale. Walter burst out laughing.

"I was only joking! I'm sorry. I can see why Lady Abigail likes you. Are you asking about herbs for aborting a child? There's always demand for those, and I don't doubt they can be bought anywhere. What exactly are you looking for?"

"Well, it's something you can drink as a tea, and it smells like the forest."

"The one most people use is made by steaming the roots of the amyura plant. It smells like ripe fruit, and it's horribly bitter, so I doubt that's the one you're talking about. If it smells like trees, it's probably from the oreia plant. Nobles use that one a lot. Compared to amyura, the flavor and smell isn't so strong, and it's far more effective. But it's scarce and expensive, and you can only get it through special outlets."

"Special outlets?"

Walter nodded. "That's right. Faris has a patent on it."

By the time Connie left Walter's office, the sun was already low in the sky. The tactful trader had kindly ordered a carriage for her, so she thanked him and climbed inside. The carriage was painted black, with wooden shutters inside that she could raise to watch the streets roll past.

"I could never have done that," Scarlett murmured, settling into the covered seat across from Connie.

"Done what?"

"Neil Bronson went out of his way to write an introduction for you because you came to his rescue before. You should be proud of yourself."

"Scarlett...," she said, feeling a bit emotional. When she looked up at her, the most beautiful face in the world was smiling gently down at her.

"I'm happy for you, Connie. I do believe you've won yourself a servant to order around for the rest of your life."

"You got it all wrong…!"

That had sounded so promising at first! As she was shouting at Scarlett, the carriage suddenly stopped. Connie peered around in confusion.

"Pardon me," the coachman said apologetically from the other side of the screen. "There seems to be something wrong with the back wheel. I'm going to have a look."

"Oh, all right."

Rays of sunlight seeped in from the west between the cracks in the shutter. The carriage had stopped on what looked like a side street on the outskirts of the city. The street was abandoned, so the stopped carriage wouldn't bother anyone. Connie was gazing at the setting sun when Scarlett interrupted her reverie with an irritated complaint.

"…That man is taking forever. Whatever could he be doing out there?"

"Maybe we got stuck in a mud puddle."

"If that were the case, you'd think we'd hear some grunting and huffing. I'm going to look—"

"…I'm sorry to have kept you waiting. The rear wheel was nearly off. We'll be back on the road in a moment," the coachman called with quite perfect timing.

"See, everything is all right!" Connie said, turning to Scarlett—but her face was blank. "…Scarlett?"

"It's different."

"What is?"

"His voice is different than the man before. Can't you tell?"

The moment the meaning of Scarlett's words sank in, a chill ran down Connie's back. She knew the quality of Scarlett's memory too well to say she was imagining things. Her mouth went dry, and her heart pounded.

"But I could be wrong, since I never saw what the first coachman looked like. What should we do?"

Connie had no idea. Should she wait for the man to climb onto his seat and start the carriage? Or—

"*Kiriki kirikuku,*" Scarlett said, looking up suddenly.

"What?"

"*It's Lily's spell. I'm sure this is the kind of situation it's meant for.*"

The conversation at the Maurice Orphanage flashed across Connie's memory. Scarlett was right—that was the "spell" the redheaded boy, Tony, had said he learned from Lily Orlamunde.

It's supposed to show you who the bad guys are.

The man was still outside the carriage. Connie steeled her will and slowly lifted the shutter—then gasped. A middle-aged man was peering at her, his face pressed up to the other side of the window.

"Is something the matter?"

The man tilted his head, grinning. Scarlett nodded solemnly.

Connie desperately tried to calm her pounding heart.

"Kiriki kirikuku," she said.

The man's eyes widened. His smile vanished, and he placed a hand on the carriage door. Scarlett clicked her tongue. A flash ran through the steel latch. The man jerked his hand back, grimaced, and retreated a step. This brought only a moment of relief, however, because he quickly pulled something from inside his jacket. It glinted dark gray—a gun.

"*Get in the back!*" Scarlett shouted.

Connie commanded her trembling body to hunch down and crawl toward the back of the carriage. She managed to squeeze herself into a corner but could go no farther. Curled there weakly, she pressed both hands over her face. An instant later, a gunshot rang out. Once, then twice. Connie pressed her eyes shut. There was a third shot. She could hear her own heart pounding.

Finally, silence.

She didn't hear anyone trying to enter the carriage. Still, she remained frozen in terror.

"*It's all right now,*" Scarlett announced quietly. Connie slowly opened her eyes. Blood was splattered across the window, streaming down in countless rivulets like rain. Connie clapped her hand over her mouth.

"What in the world…?"

Just then, the window was pulled open from the outside. Connie screamed silently.

A tall man appeared. He had a long, straight nose and cold eyes. His hand held a smoking pistol. Connie tried not to think about the lumpy form lying at his feet.

The man stared silently at Connie and then, for some reason, backed away. Connie was still frozen in shock.

Scarlett let out a surprised gasp.

"At first I didn't recognize him—but I think that man is Aldous Clayton."

Aldous Clayton?

Connie didn't know who she was talking about.

"You know, the reporter from the Mayflower Company."

That timid man with the kindly face, unkempt hair, and hunched back? The one who had been bossed around by his redheaded colleague and had looked so miserable?

That was the *Mayflower* reporter Connie remembered.

"Mr. Clayton? Really?" Connie asked in surprise. Scarlett nodded.

"I'm sure of it. I never forget a face. But I didn't realize he was so manly."

Connie glanced at the man again. She'd thought he was leaving, but now he was standing still as a statue. He turned slowly toward Connie—and stared straight at her. His expression was sharp enough to cut, nothing like the timid man she'd met the other day.

A tense silence descended.

Aldous was the first to speak.

"Damn it! I could have left you if you hadn't realized."

His face distorted in annoyance. Connie pressed her hand over her mouth. She was always so careless about what she said. She wished she could sew her lips shut.

A searching look came into his cold eyes. This man was capable of killing someone in cold blood. Still sitting on the floor of the carriage, Connie scooted backward. Her head bumped into the wall with a loud bang. She saw stars. For all sorts of reasons, she was on the verge of tears.

She glanced at Aldous Clayton. He was looking at her as if he'd just discovered a drowning sea turtle.

"…There's no two ways about it. You look like an idiot."

He scratched his head with one hand and with the other pointed the barrel of the gun at her. Connie looked up at the ceiling.

He was right—she was the biggest idiot in the world.

When a gun was pointed at you, you couldn't exactly say no.

Connie was loaded into another carriage and taken to Rosenkreuz Street, known as the finest pleasure quarter in the capital. The sun had long since set, but the places of business spilled soft light onto the people crowding the street. The colorful lanterns floating in the darkness reminded Connie of an otherworldly night festival.

As ordered, she timidly stepped down from the carriage.

She was standing in front of a milk-white gate decorated with golden carvings. Beyond it stood a symmetrical white palace.

There was no doubt about it. She was at the legendary high-class house of prostitution, Folkvangr.

The instant this fact dawned on her, Connie sank to her knees in shock.

"Am I being s-sold?!"

The woman in the lavish room with the plush crimson rug was laughing uncontrollably.

"So she figured out who you were, and you were so surprised, you brought her back here with you? Well, I must admit that your disguise isn't very good. Cocksure, as usual—oh, my stomach hurts from laughing so hard. Sometimes you do the funniest things, Rudy…!"

The woman finally stopped laughing and dabbed her eyes. Aldous looked at her crossly. Connie was staring at them both with her mouth agape.

The woman's hair was loosely braided and pinned up on her head, yellow as the sun.

Her eyes were as blue and clear as a summer day.

She was not beautiful, but her smile was magnetic.

"What's the matter, Connie? You look like a dove who got shot by a pellet gun."

The woman staring at Connie with a hint of playfulness in her eyes was none other than Abigail O'Brian.

"I don't talk about it much in public."

They were sitting at an ornate golden table set attractively with fresh fruit and bite-size cakes and tarts. The two women waiting on them were likely prostitutes. One had a gentle disposition and soft eyes in her pretty face, while the other was a slender vixen who struck Connie as competitive. Both their perfect appearances and their movements oozed sexiness.

The beauty with the soft eyes poured a thick amber liquid into Connie's glass from a ceramic pitcher. Her plunging neckline revealed a lushly curved chest so pillowy, it looked ready to spill right out of her dress.

"The whole of the Rosenkreuz area used to belong to the O'Brians. But ownership changed over time, and now we have only this small piece of land," Abigail explained.

"Abby is the mistress of this establishment, isn't that right, Rebekah?" the woman with the soft eyes interjected, having finished pouring the drinks.

She looked over at the other beauty—Rebekah, apparently—who had narrow eyes and a gentle smile and was dividing up some fruit. She snorted scornfully.

"Miriam, you're such a fool. She's called the 'owner.'"

"Really?" Miriam answered curiously, then gave Connie a long stare. "Abby is our benefactress."

She smiled proudly. "You see, until a few years ago, Rebekah and I worked at the lowest-class brothel there is, and we were treated like slaves. Not here in the capital. Farther north, in the country. It was like a prison. They didn't feed us properly, so we were constantly starving. And if we left the brothel without permission, they beat us."

Despite her cheerful tone, her words were heavy as lead.

"But because of our contracts, which we can't even remember signing, we couldn't run away or press charges. We were literally being kept alive to die. None of the prostitutes there could even read."

"I could," Rebekah corrected.

"Then, all of a sudden, business started going downhill. Just as the good-for-nothing owner was planning to skip town, a woman showed up saying she ran a brothel in the capital. She said that if he was going to shut down his establishment, she was willing to buy us all on the spot. That was Abby. Of course, our owner was overjoyed and sold us all for dirt cheap…though later we heard that Abby had a hand in the sudden downturn in business that led to the sale in the first place."

Miriam giggled.

"Everyone who works here was rescued by Abby. Of course, some people resent her for it and try to go after her. When that happens, Aldous always comes to the rescue."

Miriam glanced quickly at Aldous and flushed. Rebekah smirked.

"Plus, Abby's the one who owns the *Mayflower*, where Aldous works."

Although it was established only recently, the Mayflower Company was one of the kingdom's few publishing houses, dealing in everything from newspapers to popular fiction. Connie looked at Abigail in surprise, but she smiled and shook her head.

"Properly speaking, I'm just an investor. And since some people don't like to see women in public roles, I do that under my husband's name."

Rebekah sneered at Miriam as if to say, *See, I told you so.*

"I still stand by that you're a fool," she said.

Giving the two women a sidelong glance, Abigail suddenly clapped as if she'd remembered something.

©Yu-nagi

"Oh yes, I'm sorry about this cur over here," she said, turning to Connie. "It must have been terrifying to be brought here against your will."

Aldous scowled at this apologetic statement. Abigail, however, seemed not to care in the least.

"The truth is, some young people have been spreading bad drugs around the neighborhood lately. They're very secretive about it, too. Don't you think it's rude for newcomers not to introduce themselves? I asked Rudy to look into it, and he said he was on the brink of figuring it out—but now he's gone and killed someone?"

Aldous made a sour face. "The bloke looked like he wouldn't give a damn if I shot his foot off. That wasn't a dealer; he was a trained soldier. I'll tell you something—if I hadn't shot him, this Constance Grail would be in one hell of a hornet's nest right now...!"

"Oh, I'm very grateful to you, Rudy. I knew I could count on my hound. You really oughtn't sulk like that."

Aldous swallowed back his words.

"But how interesting," Abigail said, bringing her hand to her cheek and elegantly tilting her head. "That doesn't seem to be the whole story."

Connie, who was completely lost in this conversation, took a moment to think over what had happened.

From what she could make out, Aldous Clayton had been tailing a mysterious drug dealer when he chanced to witness the man preparing to attack Connie.

Her first reaction was confusion.

"...But why?"

Why would a drug dealer from Rosenkreuz Street try to attack her? Even stranger, why would he know Lily Orlamunde's spell? She had no idea what it all meant.

As she was trying to figure it out, there was a commotion in the hallway. It sounded like an argument over whether someone could enter the room.

"You can't!" a voice cried out, but the door slammed open anyway. Connie stared in disbelief at the figure who strode confidently into the room. "Oh my!" Abigail gasped.

He had black hair, a muscular build, and was wearing a black military uniform. His eyes, the only spot of color, were as blue as two strokes of melted lapis lazuli. Although his face was as expressionless as ever, Connie thought he looked weary. He gazed around with terrible sternness, but when he saw that the girl with hazelnut hair was alive and well, the tension in his face seemed to fade a tiny bit.

Connie blinked in surprise.

She hadn't seen Randolph Ulster since earlier that day. Everyone was looking curiously at him, but he simply shrugged and said in a not-at-all-diffident tone, "Pardon me. I heard my Constance Grail was taking up your time."

※

Several hours earlier, Randolph Ulster walked into his office, having come straight from his unexpected encounter with the special envoy from Faris, Kendall Levine, and his party.

"Ulysses, the Seventh Prince?" Kyle Hughes asked.

He had been drawing up a report on his recent encounter with the arms dealer, looking about as energetic as a dead fish, when Randolph arrived. He looked up at him suspiciously. Randolph nodded.

"Yes, it seems he was among the delegation from Faris. He hasn't been seen since yesterday, and I was wondering if you'd heard anything."

"Not a word… But what the hell is going on?"

Kyle turned around with a cranky frown and yelled at a subordinate looking at a map spread over the marble desk in the center of the room.

"Hey, Talbott! Didn't you have a copy of the list of important persons from Faris that was going around the Guards Regiment? Let me see it!"

No sooner had Kyle glanced at the list of names the man handed him than he clicked his tongue vulgarly.

"Oh shit, one of the envoys listed his own brat as a member of the party. That's probably Ulysses. Our officials approved this two weeks ago—so it seems they did this deliberately. What the hell could their motive be? I highly doubt they brought him along to see the sights."

"I can't say for sure, but I have an idea," Randolph said.

Kyle shot him a questioning look.

"There's a dispute over succession going on in Faris right now, I believe."

"Oh, that?" Kyle muttered.

Six months earlier, the current king of Faris, Hendrick, had fallen ill. His heart had nearly stopped beating. Although he had passed the immediate crisis, he was aged and his condition was unpredictable, so naturally talk of abdication had arisen.

"The proper thing would have been for the First Prince, Fabian, to become king, but just before Hendrick fell ill, Fabian died unexpectedly in an accident."

Apparently, he'd been fox hunting when his horse suddenly threw him, breaking his neck. The king was so heartbroken over the loss of his beloved son that some said he fell ill as a result.

"The trouble is, the Second Prince, Roderick, was born to a mother of low rank, and he has little support at the palace. He should have moved quickly to win allies, but before he had a chance, it seems the king's condition worsened, rendering him unable to choose a successor. Ever since his younger children learned they had a chance at the throne, they've been fighting among themselves."

King Hendrick had seven children with a right to succession, and Ulysses was the youngest.

"I heard that on their visit, the envoys brought up the possibility of the Fifth Prince, Jerome. The pretext for the visit was strengthening the alliance. I thought that if he was here as an official representative of his country, then he must be a powerful candidate for king, but—"

"I heard he fell ill. I don't think he died, but it looks like he was pushed out in this game of musical chairs."

"The same thing happened to the Sixth Prince, and he's already given up his right to the throne and absconded to another country. No doubt Jerome will end up having to do the same. If he survives, that is," Randolph said.

"That would leave four princes and princesses alive and with the right to succession, including Ulysses."

Randolph shook his head.

"There are rumors that the third-oldest among the royal children, Princess Alexandra, has already been locked up by the henchmen of the Fourth Prince, Theophilis."

"The princess? Oh yes, I do remember hearing that sons and daughters have equal standing in that family."

Ironically for a country so concerned with bloodlines, Faris had lost much of its royal blood during the breakup of the empire. No doubt the policy allowing both men and women born into the royal family to take the throne was a measure of last resort intended to protect royal bloodlines.

"They've never actually had a woman on the throne, though. No doubt Alexandra's popularity among the commoners was what led to her downfall," Randolph said.

Princess Alexandra was said to be a prudent and fair woman.

"Given the current situation, the Fourth Prince, Theophilis, seems to be the strongest contender. I heard his older brother Roderick was so overwhelmed by all the fighting and scheming that he shut himself up in the villa. Theophilis is the son of a high-noble woman, so no doubt he's got all kinds of tricks up his sleeve… I wonder which side Kendall is on. You think someone told him to get Theophilis's little brother Ulysses out of the way so Theophilis can hurry up and become king? Or maybe he's going for the long shot with Ulysses?"

"I can't get a good read on Levine, but he used to be Ulysses's tutor.

Judging by how upset he was, he may have simply been trying to protect him. The prince's mother is supposedly a noble from Soldita, so I doubt she has many pawns at her disposal in Faris. She may have thought Adelbide was a safer place for her son than his own kingdom."

She had been wrong, it seemed. But Randolph still didn't know why the diplomat would intentionally hide the fact that Ulysses had been kidnapped. The Security Force's assistance would be indispensable in searching for the boy. Anyhow, the whole thing stemmed from a failure of security at the palace. To put it bluntly, Levine could have used that as a bargaining chip to gain an advantage in his negotiations. No matter how upset he was, a man appointed for his bargaining ability could hardly have overlooked an opportunity of that nature.

Could some other motivation be at play?

Whatever the answer was, Randolph needed more information. Most likely, he'd have to ask the party from Faris what was going on. Which meant he needed to engineer an opportunity to talk with Kendall Levine.

As Randolph was heading out of the office to make various arrangements, someone called to him.

"Lieutenant Commander Ulster!"

It was an administrator from the reception desk, sounding panicked. When Randolph asked what the matter was, the man told him a post horse had just arrived from the House of Grail.

"...From the Grails? What was the message?"

"A-a-actually..."

When he heard the news, Randolph frowned.

Constance Grail, it seemed, had gone to the Elbaite Villa and never come back.

※

Abigail saw Connie off from the brothel, giggling as the younger woman climbed into a carriage with Randolph.

An awkward silence descended.

"A messenger from your house came to the office saying you'd never returned from the palace," Randolph said. "When I looked into it, I learned you had gone to the Walter Robinson Company—but when I asked him about you, he said you'd already left. By carriage, moreover. Considering the time, I knew you should have made it home by then. I traced your route and discovered your carriage abandoned by the side of the road outside the city, with a body lying next to it, dead of a gunshot wound. That did send a chill down my back."

Connie covered her face with both hands. She had to admit it was a terrible scene.

"Although I soon learned you'd been taken to Abby's Folkvangr," he added.

"...Um... I'm so sorry..."

"There's no need to apologize. I don't think you could have avoided the situation. But from now on," he said, turning to Connie with a serious expression, "when you do something, it would be helpful if you could let me know in advance."

"I understand."

This was awkward. Very awkward.

"Fortunately, the original coachman was only knocked unconscious. Once he's been patched up, I can ask him what happened—although I doubt he knows anything."

It seemed that Connie truly had been in danger. She was grateful for Scarlett's quick wits. Where would she be now if she hadn't realized the second coachman was an impersonator?

Suddenly, Connie realized something.

"...Scarlett?"

There had been no sign of her for quite some time. Now that Connie thought about it, she realized she'd been very quiet at Folkvangr, too.

She looked around and saw Scarlett standing a slight distance away. She looked listless and kept nodding off.

"What's the matter? Are you all right?" Connie asked, walking over to her. Scarlett turned sluggishly toward her.

"*...I'm...fine. Just sleepy. I've felt like this before. After...I chased off that brutish...military policeman...at Deborah's ball. I think...when I use that power, I get like this. But for some reason...today I feel...more tired—*"

Suddenly, she vanished. Connie gasped. But she quickly reassured herself that everything would be fine. The same thing happened when Scarlett rested. Everything was fine. At least, she hoped it was.

For some reason, even though she had no good reason to worry, her heart was pounding.

The carriage arrived at the Grail residence. All was dark outside the house. A lamp had been lit, but it cast only a faint, flickering light. Randolph stepped down first and took Connie's hand to help her.

"Randolph," someone said unexpectedly from behind them. Connie flinched. When she turned around, she could make out a man standing in the darkness. His face was in shadow, but his voice sounded young.

"Is that you, Kyle? ...Sorry, Connie, it's a colleague of mine."

The young man he'd called Kyle scratched his head.

"Sorry for ambushing you here, but I've got an urgent message. The man you asked me to look into—the one who was shot dead? Well, he had a sun tattoo at the nape of his neck. Daeg Gallus, no doubt about it."

A sun tattoo?

"I see. I'll return immediately. Miss Grail?"

Connie was lost in thought, her hand on her forehead.

"What's the matter?" Randolph asked.

"Oh, it's nothing, only that when you mentioned the sun tattoo, it reminded me of something..."

"Have you seen one?" Randolph shot her a piercing look.

She felt like she had, but she couldn't remember where. It was so irritating. If only Scarlett were here, she'd have known right away.

She could imagine her pursing her lips and calling Connie an idiot as she told her the answer.

Just then, a memory flickered across her mind.

"…That's who it was."

The young woman in the bloodied rose-colored dress.

"At the masked ball, there was a woman who collapsed. She had a tattoo of a sun on her chest. I'm not sure if it's the same one you were just talking about, but…"

"Wait a second. Was this it?"

Kyle pulled a wrinkled piece of paper from his breast pocket. Dexterously lighting a match with his other hand, he held the light up to the paper, illuminating a drawing. When she saw it, Connie nodded.

"…Yes, that's it."

"I see. Blasted Gaina. I'm gonna shoot that bastard next time I see him," Kyle spit out before adding, "I need to check something in the case file. I'm going back to the office."

With that, he turned on his heel and left like a passing storm.

"Oh!" Connie exclaimed after he was gone. She'd forgotten to tell him something. "I think that woman was an acquaintance of Scarlett's."

Randolph hesitated for a moment before shaking his head.

"I don't think that could be. They have nothing in common."

"But Scarlett knew who she was. She said her name—Jane. And she said it was nostalgic to see her."

"How nostalgic. It's Jane." She was sure that's what Scarlett had said when she saw the woman.

Randolph's face went white.

"Is that true?" he asked, his sharp gaze boring into her. She stepped backward.

"Y-yes…"

"Is Scarlett with you now?"

Connie shook her head. "Is something wrong?"

"Did the woman who collapsed smell sweet?"

"What?"

Unable to answer right away, she retraced the memory. It was the night of the Earl John Doe Ball. She'd been nibbling on the buffet against the wall of the large room. She hadn't noticed Jane at first. Then why had she made such a lasting impression? She finally remembered.

It was the smell.

She remembered her because of the smell. That saccharine, flowery smell.

When Connie told Randolph that yes, she had smelled sweet, he narrowed his eyes.

"Jackal's Paradise," he said, his icy words ripping through the still night. "You haven't heard of it? It's an outlawed hallucinogen. People call it 'J.' And some call it 'Jane.'"

※

"Jane? Oh, I was going to tell you about that on the way to the Elbaite Villa. Remember? Kimberly Smith, the woman dressed all in pink, brought up Jackal's Paradise just before we left. I didn't know it had been banned. I wanted to tell you about it, but we got to the palace before I had a chance."

By the following day, Scarlett had bounced back remarkably well. When Connie told her she'd been so worried about her sudden disappearance that she'd hardly slept that night, Scarlett brushed it off.

"And by the way, I've never seen that woman in the rose-colored dress before," she added.

"Oh...," Connie said dejectedly, her shoulders slumping.

Just then, Marta came in announcing an unexpected guest. Connie's eyes widened. Marta must have thought she hadn't heard, because she repeated the name.

"Kate Lorraine is here, miss."

Connie had thought Kate was out of patience for her, and indeed, her expression when they met was vaguely strained. That was enough to tell her Kate wasn't here to make up.

"…A messenger came from the Grail house last night. He said you hadn't returned yet and wanted to know if I had any information."

The servants must have gone to her as well as Randolph, knowing how close they were.

There was no way Connie could tell her the truth. When she failed to explain herself, just like the last time, Kate went on, seeming to have made up her mind.

"Connie, what in the world are you doing? Is it something dangerous? If it is, I wish you'd stop…!"

She sounded on the verge of tears. Connie was moved.

"Why won't you tell me anything…?!"

Nevertheless, she could not tell her the truth. If she did, Kate would try to help. Of that, she was sure.

"…I'm sorry, Kate."

"Why?" she shouted. The sorrow in her voice pierced Connie's heart.

"I'm sorry."

But still she pushed her away. Kate looked like she couldn't believe what she was seeing. Connie pressed her lips together.

"If that's all you came to say, I would like you to leave."

That evening, Marta came to Connie's room with a strained look on her face.

"Miss, a messenger has just come from the Lorraine house. He said that Miss Kate has not returned home."

"What…?"

The sun was already setting. Kate had left the Grail house before noon. Marta was the one who had seen her off, so she knew well how much time had passed. No wonder she was acting so anxious.

What in the world could have happened? Desperate to do something, anything, Connie ran outside. She raced through the courtyard to the front gate. She was about to run out into the street when her feet came to an abrupt halt.

Just inside the gate was a small parcel wrapped in string. It was lying there haphazardly, as if someone had tossed it over from the outside. The package was about the size of both her hands and bore neither a stamp nor a name.

"*I wonder what it is?*" Scarlett whispered. Connie had a very bad feeling about this.

She returned silently to her room and untied the string with trembling hands.

The second she unwrapped the parcel, her heart skipped a beat.

Inside was a chestnut-brown lock of hair.

That soft brown hair that Connie loved so much—

The blood drained from her head. Her heart pounded.

On top of the lock of hair was an intricately decorated invitation. She read it over and over, but the words wouldn't process in her blank mind.

"*...Tomorrow at noon, come alone to the banks of Lake Bernadia.*"

The sound of Scarlett's voice finally brought the meaning of the words home to her. The invitation slipped from her trembling hands. As she watched it flutter to the floor, she noticed a message written on the back.

The letters looked as if they'd been scrawled hastily. *Don't tell anyone about this*, they read.

If she did—

Next time, it's her finger you'll get.

Constance Grail

Sixteen, has just made a striking debut in a gossip rag. Unpardonable redhead! Feels like her brain is going to explode from everything going on. Recently recognized by her (fake) fiancé as "my Constance." ←**new!**

 Scarlett Castiel

Eternal sixteen-year-old, doesn't know how to handle her anger over the fact that more than two hundred pages have been written and we're getting nowhere. Tries directing her fury at the suspicious character who's after Connie, only to find herself laid out from the exertion. Honestly, who's even heard of that happening?

 Randolph Ulster

Twenty-six, somehow has accepted the existence of a ghost. Probably because his (fake) fiancée, who is turning out to be a simpler person than he expected, keeps talking to the air and acting surprised about nothing. Finally starting to realize that his (fake) fiancée may actually be an extremely reckless person.

Kyle Hughes

Was looking as energetic as a dead fish while struggling to complete the arms-dealer incident report, but revives upon hearing about a new case. Workaholic. For now, would like to kill chief blunderer of all blunderers Jeorg Gaina for not noticing the sun tattoo on the injured woman at the Earl John Doe Ball.

 Cecilia Adelbide

Told the story of her attempted murder ten years ago, but it's unclear how much was true. Says she's unable to have children, but in reality is being fed poison that prevents pregnancy.

Kimberly Smith

In her mid-forties. President of the Ladies' Committee of the Violet Association. Was slamming Connie with criticisms until Kate came to the rescue and shoved her out of the ring. Likely the only person other than Pe and Pako Hayashiya who can strut around shamelessly wearing all pink.

 Neil Bronson

For some inexplicable reason, has changed his look from stylish city boy to unworldly virgin. May be a sign of his yearning for chastity, but probably best not to delve too deeply into this. Recently recognized by Scarlett as Connie's servant to order around for the rest of her life. ←**new!**

Walter Robinson

In his late thirties. Large man with a scary face like a pirate's. Founder of the Walter Robinson Company and king of the shipping industry, he excels in international trade. Playful, pulled himself up by his bootstraps. The House of O'Brian is his best customer; seems to be friendly with Abigail.

 Abigail O'Brian

Seems like a good-natured big sister, actually empress of the underworld. Constantly diving into dangerous situations and getting barked at for it by her pet hound.

 Aldous Clayton

Seems like a weak, miserable young man, actually a faithful and shrewd hound. Likely handsome. His owner has a habit of diving into dangerous situations, which fills his life with worries.

Miriam

Prostitute at Folkvangr #1. Beautiful, gentle woman with soft eyes. Breasts.

Rebekah

Prostitute at Folkvangr #2. Beautiful, competitive, slender. Small breasts.

Kate Lorraine

Thanks to the abundant use of foreshadowing, appears to be the equivalent of a nameless victim killed midway through an after-noon detective drama. ←**new!**

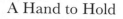

It happened one day when Abigail O'Brian visited Elizabeth Emanuel, her friend of ten years, at Elizabeth's home. By the time she realized that the "tea party" was only a pretense—that she herself was the only guest—it was already too late.

"I just adore interesting things," Elizabeth announced.

Instead of saying *I know*, Abigail gazed intently at the woman in front of her. It wouldn't be quite accurate to say they were bosom buddies, but ever since they were innocent girls—and even after Elizabeth became Lady Emanuel—they'd seen a fair amount of each other. Abigail knew very well that Elizabeth was unequaled in her fondness for *interesting* things. She also knew she was quite cunning.

"And that's why I'm at such a loss right now," Elizabeth continued with a faint but unconvincing smile. Abigail urged her on with narrowed eyes. "You see, our favorite little princess has been invited to the Earl John Doe Ball."

"You mean Scarlett Castiel?"

The duke's daughter had formally debuted only very recently, but her stunning beauty and fiery temper had instantly made her the talk of society.

"Precisely. But can you believe it? The hostess of the ball is none other than Deborah."

Deborah Darkian. The mere mention of that name brought Abigail's hand to her forehead to ward off a sudden headache. That woman was a walking disaster.

Deborah hadn't always been like that. It was frustrating. At one time, Abigail had considered Deborah a friend. But that was long ago, when they were around ten.

Whether or not Elizabeth knew how complicated Abigail's feelings were, she gave a suggestive, theatrical sigh.

"You know how tiresome Deborah is about everything. I can stomach the first bite, but a whole night of it gives me heartburn," she said as casually as if she were complaining about the menu at a fancy dinner. Abigail pressed the pounding spot between her brows, Elizabeth's lack of appreciation for the seriousness of the situation making her headache suddenly worse.

"…If you don't like it, why don't you do something about it?" she moaned.

"Me? I love interesting things, but you know I abhor annoying ones!"

"I've had enough of annoying things myself!"

Elizabeth had known Abigail long enough to not bat an eyelash when she raised her voice.

"Fine, but I know you're too kind to ignore this one."

If Deborah was the spark that ignited wildfires, Scarlett was the raging flames. There was no way the two of them could spend a peaceful evening together. After all, both were queens incapable of backing down. If someone wasn't there to stop them, the ball would unquestionably end in a disaster too hideous to watch.

"…Beth, you really are terrible."

"You just realized that?"

Instead of saying, *Of course not*, Abigail glared intently at the woman in front of her.

※

"Oh, is that what's going on?"

The girl nodded, sounding very grown-up for her age.

Lily Orlamunde, with her perfectly straight platinum-blond hair, her aqua-blue eyes, and her doll-like features, was one of Scarlett Castiel's few friends. She, too, had debuted only recently, but her kind, fair personality had already won her quite a few passionate supporters.

Now, talking to her for the first time, Abigail realized something else— Lily had a quick mind.

"If I get involved in an obvious way, Deborah will probably dig in even further. I was hoping that you'd be able to help—can I ask that of you?"

"For you, Duchess? I'd be delighted."

Lily hadn't planned to attend the masked ball, but she readily agreed after hearing Abigail's explanation.

"Thank you—it's a huge help. I'll make it worth your time, of course."

"Oh, there's no need for that."

"No?" Abigail blinked at her flat rejection.

"After all, it isn't often that Abigail O'Brian becomes indebted to a person."

That was an odd thing to say. Abigail tilted her head, but Lily just gazed back at her innocently. She must have imagined it.

Lily looked the confused Abigail in the eye and smiled affectionately.

"That's why I'd rather you *stay* indebted to me."

Abigail's cheek twitched.

※

The day of the Earl John Doe Ball arrived.

In addition to Lily, Abigail had also called on a young man to whom she was related by marriage, a little brother almost, to serve as backup in case anything happened.

"I'm sorry to put you to so much trouble," she said.

"I've got the day off, so it's really no problem," he answered, nodding with his standard lack of emotion.

Randolph Ulster had just taken a job with the Royal Security Force. Abigail smiled at his poker face.

"Thank you. And to make it worth your while—"

"To make what worth my while?" Randolph interrupted her.

"What?"

"That won't be necessary."

"…Why not?"

Abigail stiffened with an odd sense of déjà vu. She thought back to Lily's splendid response the other day.

"I've been in your debt for years," Randolph said.

In this case, however, it was simply that while Randolph looked a bit stern these days, inside he was still the same angelic boy.

An exhausting week had passed since Elizabeth Emanuel had tricked Abigail into getting involved. Her eyes grew hot at this unexpected kindness.

"Ronny…!"

Without meaning to, she used his boyhood nickname. And just like she used to when he was a boy, she rushed toward him with arms open to hug him.

"I wish you wouldn't call me that," he said, casually dodging her hug even as he delivered this mild rebuke. That hurt.

However, she did her utmost to pretend not to care and instead asked him to keep watch at the entrance to the old Montrose residence. Of course, she knew about the hidden passages in the estate, but the presence of a young man in military attire should serve as a restraint.

As he was leaving, Randolph turned back toward her.

"Abby?"

"Yes?"

"Do you really think Deborah Darkian will try to do something?"

She wasn't able to answer, but it wasn't because she didn't know. It was because she knew *all too well*.

She simply tilted her head slightly and, in lieu of an answer, smiled.

The party was at the peak of excitement.

The theme was apparently historical, and the ballroom was decked out with art from the Darkian collection.

Deborah herself was dressed as Saint Anastasia. With her immaculate white dress, she wore a decadent black butterfly mask. It was a strange combination, but no one at the party was straitlaced enough to care.

Just then, a buzz ran through the already boisterous crowd.

A beautiful woman wearing a half mask made of jet had appeared. Her youthful form was encased in a suggestive red dress. People stepped aside to open a path for her as she walked. Beside her was a platinum-blond girl wearing a white mask edged in gold thread.

Deborah watched them for a while, looking bored, and slowly parted her lips as they drew near. It was the duty of the host to introduce new guests.

Even if everyone already knew who was beneath the masks.

"I do believe these faces are new. May I ask your names?"

"...Our names?" Scarlett asked suspiciously. Lily whispered something into her ear. "Oh, that's how they do it? In that case..."

Scarlett curled her lips into a smile.

"Eris. For tonight alone, I shall permit you to call me by that name."

It was enough to determine who would play the leading role that night. Abigail was filled with admiration.

Following this unilateral announcement, which could hardly be called an introduction, a wall of people surrounded Scarlett. Some were rumored to be unsavory characters, but Lily casually weeded them out. It seemed she was going to earn Abigail's indebtedness after all. The line of people was still endless, however. They were like ants swarming to honey.

Deborah, of course, was not pleased about this.

Suddenly, there was a shrill scream.

It's begun, Abigail thought, scanning the room with narrowed eyes.

"Somebody!"

People gathered round the source of the desperate cry. Abigail, too, hurried in that direction. Pushing through the crowd, she spotted a masked man and woman embracing in the center of the room. No—they weren't embracing.

The woman was *stabbing a knife into the man's stomach.*

Blood frothed from the man's mouth as he slowly sank to the floor.

The uproar turned instantly to silence. Everyone was struck dumb by this abrupt tragedy.

As blood dripped from the knife in her hand, the woman slowly raised her head as if to find her next victim.

Someone gasped. Terror spread, contagious. Everyone in the room was watching the woman's movements, hearts in their throats. If anyone moved, panic would no doubt erupt. Abigail held her breath as she imagined the worst possible scenario. What could she do to keep the crowd calm? She tried and failed to come up with a strategy.

But that was not the case, it seemed, for *her.*

"How ridiculous," Scarlett scoffed, stepping in without hesitation.

"Scarlett!" Lily cried in shock.

"It's fine," Scarlett shot back with a shrug. "After all, it doesn't smell like blood."

The woman holding the knife froze. Striding past the clearly shaken woman, Scarlett gazed down at the bloodied man on the floor like he was a worm.

"How long do you plan to keep up your shoddy act?" she asked him.

Under the searing gaze of those amethyst eyes, the man—who should have been on the brink of death—squirmed uncomfortably.

He really was a horrible actor.

Scarlett snorted. "Whoever came up with this plot must be a moron."

Her mocking gaze was directed at the woman in the butterfly mask. Deborah's bloodred lips curled dangerously at this bald challenge. Snapping back to reality, Abigail took a step forward, the crowd at her back.

She was not what the world considered a beautiful woman, but she had learned a little about how to draw people's attention.

The room was quiet enough to hear a pin drop. The sound of her heels clicking as she walked forward was enough to naturally attract every eye.

When she stopped in front of Scarlett, the latter gave her a look that said, *What are* you *doing here?* She'd expected that. Ignoring the sharp gaze, Abigail began to clap slowly.

"Thank you for bringing such an interesting twist to our party," she said.

Scarlett arched her brows skeptically.

"Welcome to this incognito gathering. We're pleased to have you," she continued with a bright smile. Scarlett pouted but seemed to resign herself to giving up the fight. She watched as the bloodied man and woman scurried off, then turned silently on her heel and walked straight toward the spiral staircase.

The tension in the room melted.

A few minutes later, the party was once again rollicking along.

Scarlett and Lily seemed to be resting in the lounge upstairs. Scarlett was leaning against a window frame, cocktail in hand, with Lily beside her. When Lily noticed Abigail had joined them, she slipped tactfully away. *Yes*, thought Abigail, *she really is a quick-witted girl.* Which made Abigail all the more nervous about what sort of interest she would demand for the service she had done that night.

"Scarlett."

She must have noticed Abigail as well, because she did not look surprised when she turned languidly toward her.

"How inelegant to call me by that name," she said indifferently, then smiled as if she'd just remembered something. "Deborah Darkian must be angry."

"Yes, she is. Thanks to a certain someone."

"I wonder who? Could it be the impudent individual who chose to remain in the wings but then, at the very last minute, barged onstage and disgraced the hostess?"

Abigail's cheek twitched, but she quickly sighed in resignation.

"When did you realize that?"

Scarlett instantly traded her languid distance for a playful smile. "Lily isn't the type to go out of her way to accompany me to a ball from pure kindness, now is she?" She cast a meaningful look at Abigail. "But it's a different story if she can win the gratitude of one of the four great noble families."

In other words, she'd known from the *start*.

"Abigail O'Brian, do you think I ought to thank you?"

Her eyes were like jewels, and her skin glistened with a faint sheen, perhaps from the heat of the crowd. Even the lock of hair falling against her lightly flushed cheek looked as perfect as a statue. As the owner of Folkvangr, Abigail was used to seeing beautiful women. But Scarlett's beauty transfixed her.

"Thank you for your unwanted help, that is?"

Abigail realized something then.

Scarlett Castiel would never cling to anyone's hand.

True, Lily was not a complete stranger to her. But Lily herself had told Abigail quite clearly—this was an arrangement of favors given and taken. Neither fully let their guard down with the other.

Scarlett was pure fire. She did not easily allow other people near, and she was even prepared to reject a hand extended to save her. Even if Scarlett was hurt, Abigail doubted she would ever ask for help.

What an arrogant, difficult—but also fierce girl she was.

If only she had someone, Abigail couldn't help thinking. She seemed so terribly isolated.

Even one person would be enough. Someone who wasn't afraid of the fire—someone who would leap in and grab the hand of this incredibly difficult and yet incredibly magnetic young woman.

If only such a recklessly good-natured person existed somewhere in the world.

Someday, may that person take the hand of this girl.

This was Abigail's small prayer—but as it turned out, the goddesses did not answer it.

Scarlett Castiel was executed only a year later.

※

"How frightening!"

Constance Grail was sitting in a corner of her room, shivering.

It was the day after her showdown with Deborah in the Starlight Room. When Scarlett heard her praising Abigail O'Brian like a heroine for rescuing her from a tight spot, she informed her that Abigail was quite the imposter and told her the story of the Earl John Doe Ball around ten years ago.

"I can't believe you tried to pick a fight with Deborah…! You can't do things like that! You'll get hurt one of these days!" she said.

"That may be, but it's no business of yours," Scarlett snapped back.

But Constance was focused on something else. Scarlett had coldly pushed away her unusually emotional outburst. After all, even if she was stabbed, Scarlett's body was already six feet under.

"Of course it's my business!" she said.

"Why's that?"

"Because I don't want anything bad to happen to you…!"

Scarlett—who as usual was perched on the dresser—blinked and looked down at the girl with the unremarkable face, who appeared quite worked up. She seemed to have forgotten entirely that Scarlett was already dead.

As she stared at those clear green eyes, fury suddenly overwhelmed her.

She glared at Constance with all her might, but Constance—who was brazen in the oddest ways—showed no sign of noticing.

In the end, it was Scarlett who gave in.

"…Is that so?" she asked, turning away aloofly.

Her next words were full of chagrin.

"I didn't know Constance Grail could be so saucy."

AFTERWORD

Constance Grail, the heroine of this tale, is not blessed with particularly good looks, brains, or athletic ability. She's the kind of girl who tends to end up a wallflower.

Quite unexpectedly, Scarlett Castiel—a wicked woman who was executed ten years earlier—rescues Constance from a tight spot and, in exchange, demands that Constance help her exact revenge on the outrageous villains who drove her to the executioner's block.

Half against her will, Constance becomes Scarlett's accomplice, and so our story begins. Of course, two young women so completely different both inside and out can't be expected to get along from the start. Is this constantly quarreling party of two getting closer to the truth or further from it? Will they be able to safely win revenge for Scarlett? I hope you'll stick around to find out.

This novel began as a story on the user-generated fiction website Let's Become a Novelist (*Shosetsuka ni Narou*). I never dreamed back then that it would be published as a book, and in fact, when I was first approached about that possibility, I thought I was the victim of some new kind of scam. Of course, I soon realized that wasn't the case, but I'm a chicken to the core. When they asked to meet me to talk about the details, I chose a place in a completely different neighborhood from where I lived,

I didn't use my real name, and my e-mails were so curt, they sounded like spy memos. Now I realize I must have come off as an insanely shady character. But I was nevertheless able to have the fabulous experience of publishing this book, for which I am deeply grateful.

I benefited from the help of many people during the publishing process. I wish I could cry out a thank-you in the center of the world, but since I suppose that won't be possible, I'll settle for expressing my gratitude in this afterword.

First, I'd like to thank the person who gave me every opportunity I've had, Fujino Omori. Readers, you don't need me to tell you how wonderful the *Is It Wrong to Pick Up Girls in a Dungeon?* series is, so I'll just say I was shocked the first time I met him to learn that human beings really can have halos. I understood then how such a lovable person could create a story that captured the hearts of men and women, young and old alike. Thank you so much.

To Yu-nagi, who breathed life into the characters in this book, thank you for creating such mesmerizing illustrations. Every time I looked at them, I realized I wasn't alone in this undertaking, and though it's awfully bold of me, I'll admit I think of you as my war buddy. I have you to thank for bringing so much vividness to the world that Connie inhabits.

To my editor, aka my shadow strategist, thank you for fitting out a first timer who didn't know the rules or the routes of this game so well. I never would have reached the finish line if you weren't there running alongside me with lantern in hand, making sure I didn't get lost at every turn.

The truth is, I still don't feel like this is my own achievement. It would have been completely impossible for me to send a book out into the world by myself. This is *our* book.

And if the readers who have just finished reading it could think of it as their book, too—as a story that belongs to all of us—well, nothing in the world could make me happier.

Until we meet again,

Kujira Tokiwa